A Good Stock
Richard Roux

GREENHORN MOUNTAIN BOOKS

Published by Greenhorn Mountain Books

Bakersfield, CA

greenhornmountainbooks@gmail.com

Copyright © 2018 by Richard Roux

All Rights Reserved

ISBN-13: 978-0-578-40360-1

Full Page Map: Samuel Augustus Mitchell, California, Oregon, Washington, Utah, New Mexico, 1854 (edited to focus just on California). David Rumsey Map Collection, David Rumsey Map Center, Stanford Libraries.

Contents

Also By Richard Roux

———◆———

NON-FICTION

Bootleggers, Booze, and Busts: Prohibition in Kern County, 1919-1933
Bootlegger Tales: More Drips, Drops, and Drams

THE GOLDEN EMPIRE SERIES

A Branch Too Weak
A Good Stock
Love & Loss on the Razor's Edge

OTHER WORKS

The Cave of Treasure (With Jeff R. Smith)

Dedication

──•·•◆•·•──

To my grandmother, Zelma Roux. The consummate storyteller, my grandmother had a memory that rivaled the best. There wasn't much she didn't remember from her almost eighty-five years on earth, and she could weave a story to make you feel as if you were there, in that moment, too. She loved life, her family, and just being herself.

Not one to let a story end, she also avoided saying goodbye when she was done with a visit because goodbyes are forever.

So, it isn't goodbye, grandma. Your love is eternal. I'll see you later.

Zelma Elayne Roux
October 28, 1932 – October 21, 2017

Mark Twain Quote

———◆———

T here is more real pleasure to be gotten out of a malicious act, where your heart is in it, than out of thirty acts of a nobler sort.

Mark Twain in Eruption

Acknowledgments

———————◆◆◆————————

E very writer brings with them a set of life experiences and influences that are incorporated, consciously or subconsciously, into the world they create on paper. I'm no different.

Many of the places mentioned in this book are places that I have actually been, seen, and experienced firsthand. There is something to be said about feeling the dirt between your fingers, the chilly, clear water of the Kern River, and the glaring hot sun in the summer, as well as the frigid cold snow, in the meadows, peaks, and hollows of the Greenhorn Mountains and the Kern River Valley. To me, it brings a sense of realism to the story. One that I hope isn't just in my own mind's eye.

And it would be errant on my part to not mention other writers who have influenced my interest in blending local history, telling a story, and fiction. Once again, the works of Bob Powers and William Harland Boyd. Their books, as well as the work of Ardis M. Walker, helped me flesh out some of the locations in this book. All three of them were great storytellers, and I have yet to read anything they have written that wasn't informative and entertaining.

Chapter 1
A Brewing Storm

————————————◆————————————

Juglans Nigra, otherwise known as the Eastern Black Walnut, grows wild along riparian zones in eastern North America. Often reaching heights over one hundred feet tall with an elongated, straight trunk when allowed room to grow, this versatile tree can be found as far north as Ontario, Canada, west to South Dakota, all the way down to Florida, and to the southwest into Texas. It's a species that provides much to many—the soil, animals, and humans.

A hearty tree, its roots take to the earth quickly and stake a claim on life, allowing for an increased survival rate of seedlings and the extension of their lifespan for as long as one hundred and thirty years.

Within four to six years this variety of tree is mature enough to produce fruit that ripens in autumn; a tasty nut, encased in a hard shell, shrouded by a brownish-green soft husk. A walnut—the seed that is eaten when broken free of its casing; the same seed that begins the life cycle of new trees.

The Eastern Black Walnut, like other lifeforms, competes for survival. Precious resources, such as minerals, water, and sunlight are sought out as necessities. For many species of flora and fauna, survival is a matter of luck and timing. Did a seed sprout amidst a congested forest? Was there a drought? Did wildlife happen to choose the growing, young stem or roots as a meal? Were insects sweeping through the region? Did all of the perfect conditions exist at exactly the right time for the sapling to mature into a mighty walnut tree? Most plant life has no control over the situation.

There are some species, however, that have the ability to gain an advantage over the competition. The walnut tree is one of these. It is allelopathic, with the ability to release chemicals from its roots that harm and inhibit the growth of other plant forms to give it an edge in the game of survival. An adaptive tactic, it isn't unlike what humans are capable of to give themselves an advantage over others. People like the Roberts Boys, who steal, rob, intimidate, and kill to get what they want. Caustic parasites, the Roberts Boys don't give their unfortunate victims a chance, for they prey on the weak and unsuspecting, and a fair fight isn't in their vocabulary. Victims, like Danny Vance and his friend, Sam, are subject to the nonexistent mercy of the Roberts Boys.

Outwardly, a walnut tree is attractive, the grayish-black bark arranged in a diamond pattern from the trunk to its heavy branches; individual diamonds like scale armor, separate entities united as one living organism. To the trained and untrained noses alike, these trees emanate a spicy or bitter odor, not entirely unpleasant nor appealing, but distinct all the same. That fragrant, decorated bark covers and protects a straight-grained wood that is deep brown in color, and desired for its durability and strength, yet ease to work. In the hands of a skilled craftsman, the wood from a walnut tree can be transformed into beautiful cabinets, tables, and other useful and attractive types of furniture that display the pattern of the grain. Used in flooring, the maintained planks are capable of outlasting the people who laid it down and walked upon it daily.

This type of wood is also desirable in the construction of coffins, the final home of the human shell that embodied the newly departed spirit. A number of the victims of the Roberts Boys weren't given the pleasure of being lowered into the ground in a fancy coffin. Their soulless bodies withered away off well-traveled paths, victims first of the brutality of the Roberts Boys, and second of the elements.

In the hands of a skilled craftsman, a block of walnut can be turned into a work of art. Cut to the correct length and width, a craftsman begins to shave and shape the wood, eventually to the point where a smoothing plane is used to create a piece of wood free of burrs and pits. It is now a piece of polished wood with a purpose; with angles and curves, maybe even a grove, designed to provide support and absorb shock.

Affixed to this handsome piece of wood is a tube of iron that was first heated and rolled around a chemise in one-foot sections, welded into three-foot lengths, reheated and worked, and then eventually hollowed out to a uniform circumference with a boring bit. It was now a part of a tool, an instrument capable of bringing death and destruction in the hands of skilled and unskilled alike. One shot at a time. The shotgun is a dependable and devastating weapon at close to medium range. A man doesn't have to be a marksman to carry out his intentions with this weapon. Aimed in a general direction, and with the squeeze of a trigger, a controlled explosion propels multiple amounts of lead down the barrel out toward the intended target. The impact of the shot is largely dependent on the distance and size of the lead pellets, but it ranges from the creation of a hole large enough to fit a man's fist into, to a wide pattern of entrance wounds sprinkled across a surface.

A shotgun, like any firearm, is an inanimate tool. By itself, it was just wood and iron, absent of motive and action. However, in the hands of a man intent on destruction, it is a tool very capable of the job. Like a hammer designed to drive a nail, a shotgun's purpose is clear and effective. But they both require human hands to carry out their designed purpose.

At that moment, this product of skilled craftsmanship—shaped wood from a walnut tree and rolled, welded, and bored iron tubing—was being wiped down and oiled. As the man removed the dirt and bits of debris, as well as the beginnings of rust on the barrel, he admired the sleek curves and coolness of the metal. The grain of the wood was especially attractive. It was one of the things he and his brother fawned over the most when they originally received the firearm as a gift from their grandfather. He appreciated the time and effort that was taken in its creation, the skill of the craftsman evident in every part of the weapon. Creation was not what this man intended. Justice was what he was after. Violence was largely his intent. The hands caressing and cleaning this implement of wood and iron belonged to Danny Vance, and vengeance weighed heavily on his mind.

***

Ten miles away, camped amidst a cluster of trees on the top of a ridge were the Roberts Boys. Their number had grown from three to five. Men with little to no integrity who were fully content to prey upon the helpless and unsuspecting.

Eli Roberts, leader of this growing troop of thieves and murderers, attracted others with similar temperaments. His confidence and charisma, amplified by his taste for cruelty, had a way of drawing the dregs of society into his circle. The thirst to be led was strong with both the benevolent and malevolent alike.

The five men sat around a campfire, eating food and drinking whiskey earned through the hard work of others; the spoils of a war only one side was knowingly participating in. A jovial time was had by all in attendance. They recounted the seemingly endless crimes they'd participated in over the years—robberies, beatings, rapes, ambushes, and murders; the joy they received through the misery and pain of others was beyond the scope of believability, but it was their reality.

For the five men congregated there on the forest floor, their laughter was contagious. But the laughter revealed their comfort in the perception that they were the center of the universe and that satisfying their whims and tastes were first and foremost in importance. They relaxed in the belief that they were kings of their domain, no matter where they were. It didn't matter to them if they were on the Overland Trail to California, on the streets of Sacramento, or in their present location, the Greenhorn Mountains. They forced their seemingly unstoppable will over all who crossed their path. The terror and chaos they brought to their kingdom provided what is best called a sense of security and tranquility to Eli Roberts and his band of ruffians. However, it was a short-lived peace, for they were opportunists. There was always a desire to have more, and if the odds were in their favor and the conditions were right, they wouldn't hesitate to add another victim to their growing list.

No man can control everything that happens around them, regardless of how strong of a will they have or their willingness to bend and break others. Each man has a beginning and an end, and what happens between the two points is largely determined by the decisions made by the participants. Eli Roberts led men who abbreviated, or otherwise greatly altered, the endpoints and the chapters within the lives of others. And they felt no shame or remorse if they felt anything at all. They cared not for their salvation or their future much farther than their immediate present. Their vision was constrained by the decisions they made and their lust for more.

With souls darkened by time and deeds, they were resistant to compassion and love, and the ability to feel sympathy and empathy for others. And they were blind, not only to the wants, desires, and dreams of others but to the coming storm. A tempest was brewing beyond the control of the Roberts Boys. Their decisions and actions had created it, but there was no stopping it now. Ten miles distant, that violent storm was contained within Danny Vance. He was determined to bring these men to justice. Danny had the will to make them pay for their crimes; to make them suffer for murdering his friend and nearly ending his own life. To the Roberts Boys, he'd be a dead man walking, and he was intent on bringing them Hell.

Chapter 2
The Bearded Angel

———◆———

Francis Rutherford was a pragmatist; a practical man who had no thirst for an extravagant life, nor an abundance of material things. But he was willing to change under the right circumstances. That's why he, along with what seemed like half the world, had taken the chance on California. However, his path was a bit different than most in the Golden Empire. Along the way, he'd worn many hats not typical of most treasure seekers. In his youth, he farmed with his family but left home before the age of twenty to become a man in the West. At times, he was a market hunter, an Indian fighter, and a scout. He'd gained experience in the wilderness working for John Jacob Astor's American Fur Company, and he'd traveled with many great trailbreakers, including Kit Carson, Alexis Godey, and John C. Fremont. It was with Fremont that he'd entered the Kern River Valley, explored the region, and then mustered out of his group to build a new home in the Greenhorn Mountains. How long he'd remain hadn't been determined, but for the time being, there were animals to hunt, creeks to explore for gold, and multiple diversions to occupy his time. In the two years he'd been in the Greenhorn Mountains he was yet to be bored or enticed to move on.

It was on one of his forays around the mountains that he noticed something peculiar in the distance. Through the trees and brush a slight movement caught his eye. It wasn't bright in color or fast in its motion. The only thing that even attracted Francis' attention was that it looked out of place. It reminded him of a tactic he and many other trappers used when placing a marten set. After the trap was placed in the desired location with a hunk of meat secured to the contraption, several feathers were tied above the set. Martins are curious creatures. Not only would they be attracted to the trap by the smell that the rotting hunk of bait emitted, but the feathers gently twitching in the breeze stimulated their desire to investigate. In many cases, that curiosity killed the martin.

Francis couldn't place what it was, and he was half wondering if it was a ruse highwaymen might use to snare unsuspecting travelers. But old Francis was smarter than that. Instead of leading his mule directly to the object, he worked his way ever closer using the brush and trees as cover. Sneaking toward the distraction via a wide arc increased the distance traveled and the time it took to get there, but it mattered not to Francis. Better safe than sorry had kept him alive more times than he could remember. The closer he got, the more he sensed that something was not right, and the more guarded he became.

He had a .54 caliber percussion cap Mississippi rifle in a cloth scabbard on Mick, his mule. That'd do the trick going up against a known enemy. However, since Francis was entering the situation unaware of the number and location of potential enemies, he decided to increase his odds a bit. From a cross-draw leather holster on his left side, Francis drew one of the two .36 caliber 1851 Colt Navy Revolvers he had. Having six shots available, he felt more secure in the situation.

Senses heightened, Francis edged his way ever closer to where he saw movement. He could no longer see what originally attracted his attention, but he was heading in the right direction. From the angle of his approach, he didn't spot the movement again until he was one hundred yards away, and it wasn't until he was within fifty yards that he was finally able to see that the movement he'd spotted was a dead man hanging from a large oak tree. The light breeze caused the body to sway and turn slightly, and it was that motion that looked so out of place in the woods that Francis knew so well.

"Oh, Frankie…what are you getting into?" he thought to himself as he scanned left to right, and right to left, prepared for any threat that might materialize. This was none of his business. But then again, this dead man suspended from a tree was practically in his backyard. Someone made it his business.

Satisfied that nobody was lying in wait, Francis quietly and deliberately walked through the yellowed grass toward the man hanging in the tree. The Chinese man with greyish-colored skin, who was obviously dead, captivated Francis. He couldn't imagine how this lone man ended up, practically in the middle of nowhere, hanging from a tree. Trying to find clues, Francis examined the ground as he approached the oak. He saw several sets of horse tracks, indicating that there were two to four horses. He also noticed multiple sets of mule tracks with their distinct rounded front and straight lines back toward the heel. It was difficult to tell how many mules were in the group, but it looked to be a sizeable bunch. Francis also believed that he could see at least six distinct sets of boot tracks, but it was just a guess.

All of this created more questions than answers. Was the Chinese man a part of the group and then had a falling out? Was he bushwhacked? Could it be that the men with the horses and mules came upon the dead man and wanted no part of the situation, so they moved on? Were the tracks coincidental, already there before the man was lynched? There appeared to be only one person who truly knew the answers, and he was hanging from the tree.

With his attention focused on the dead man and the enormity of the oak, Francis didn't even notice the large limb in his path until he stumbled over it and landed on the ground next to a man whose legs were pinned under the branch. Startled, Francis quickly rolled away from the body, rising to one knee, and aimed his cocked Colt revolver at the body. It was more a reflex born out of survival, and less out of fear. But Francis realized the man was hardly a threat. He may be dead, too. The poor wretch looked like he'd had a Hell of a time. It appeared that he'd been lying there a while, perhaps an hour or two. His face was partially swollen around the eyes, and dried blood matted his hair and was caked to the side of his face. Those injuries alone looked to be enough to kill a man, but he'd suffered even more. Around his neck was a snug-fitting noose that was now loosely draped around the broken branch that was on top of the man's legs. The man on the ground was a sorry sight.

Francis believed the creature before him was dead until he noticed the slight rise and fall of the man's chest. Not trusting his eyes, Francis leaned toward the prostrate man, placing his ear near the man's mouth. Surprised, he heard a shallow, raspy breath. The man—Danny Vance—wasn't dead, or at least not yet.

Up until that moment, Francis could walk away. He'd seen dead bodies before, and he'd walked away. That is what he'd probably do with the Chinese man. He felt no obligation to give the hanging man a Christian burial, or any type of burial for that matter. This was a stranger. The man on the ground, the man who was still alive, changed the parameters of how Francis would react. What type of human would he be if he left the man there to die? That wasn't within his character. Francis Rutherford was many things, but completely heartless wasn't one of them.

Working quickly, Francis lifted the branch off of Danny's legs and tossed it aside. He then loosened the noose and slipped it over his head. There was a nasty-looking rope burn around the man's neck, but the skin wasn't broken. Francis did what he could to revive the man—talking to him; shaking him; rubbing his sternum.

Within a few minutes, Francis was able to get a response from the man. It was a momentary return from unconsciousness. He successfully gave the man some water, even if he coughed most of it up. Consciousness was but a temporary condition, though, and Danny slipped back to sleep. Francis felt confident that the man had a good chance at survival, but it couldn't be done right here, right on the ground in the shade of this oak tree and underneath the hanging dead man. He'd have to transport the injured man back to his cabin.

Francis had learned a great deal over the years. Here and there from various people, he picked up little tricks that made life easier and had got him out of a rough patch more than once. The immediate problem he faced was how to get the injured man back to his cabin. It was at least two miles away, a distance too great for him to carry the man. It was also too far for the man to ride on the back of Mick without the real threat that he'd fall off and injure himself even more.

So, Francis improvised and utilized what he learned while living amongst the Lakota on the Great Plains. A travois, constructed out of two poles and a blanket, would work to transport the injured man. He located two small trees that would work, took a hatchet that he carried, and cut them down. Trimmed and cut to size, the poles and blanket became a makeshift bed. Francis gently lifted Danny and placed him on the blanket, securing his body the best he could for the ride to his cabin.

Once again, the man briefly awakened.

"Wha?...what's going on?" Danny managed to weakly say.

"Hey, there boy...I'm taking you somewhere safe. Just hang on and try not to move around. What's your name?

Danny's eyes rolled around a bit as he took it all in. He was slipping into unconsciousness again, but before he did, he was able to mutter, "Danny...Danny Vance." And then he was out.

With Danny in place, Francis grabbed Mick's lead to begin the walk home. He looked back to check on the travois and Danny's position, and, of course, his eyes were immediately drawn to the Chinese man hanging from the tree.

"Dammit...dammit it all!" Francis thought as he assessed the situation. It just felt wrong to leave him there. Chances are, he thought, this man named Danny knew the dead man. Francis cut the rope that was tied off to the oak, sending the once-suspended body to the ground with a thud.

"Sorry friend," Francis spoke to the dead man, realizing that a response would never be uttered. He dragged the dead man toward Mick, picked up the body that seemed heavier than it actually was, and then draped it over his mule's back. Francis fastened the body's hands and feet together with some of the rope used for the lynching, cinched it down tight, and then set out for home.

"Frankie...what did you get yourself into?" That was all he could think as he headed home with Mick, the injured Danny Vance, and the dead Chinese man.

An hour and a half later, Francis arrived at his cabin. It was a cozy little home constructed out of logs, rock, and chinking consisting of grass and mud. In addition to his cabin, Francis had a lean-to style storage shed with an attached root cellar in his yard, a small corral, and a privy out back of his place. They were the basics; nothing extravagant, but completely pragmatic. His home; and now a place of refuge for the man strapped to the travois.

With Mick stopped near the front door to the cabin, Francis untied the ropes that secured Danny to the travois. He slipped his arms underneath Danny's armpits and lifted him off the mobile bed. Even though Danny weighed no more than 180 pounds, Francis felt every ounce of that weight. Straining for leverage, he half-carried and half-dragged Danny from the travois and into the cabin, dropping him as gently as he could onto his bed.

He made Danny as comfortable as he could and considered what he needed to do for the man. At the very least, the injured man named Danny needed to be cleaned up. Removal of the dried blood would allow Francis to see the wounds and treat them as best he could. Moving from the bed, Francis went to the stone hearth to start a fire that he'd need to warm some water. Once the fire was lit, Francis grabbed a bucket stowed by the door to fetch some water from the spring box that was thirty yards from his cabin.

"Aw, Hell's bells!" Francis uttered as he exited the door only to find that the dead Chinese man was the first thing to enter his sight. He sat the bucket on the ground, grabbed Mick's lead, and led the mule toward his storage shed. Without much fanfare, Francis cut the rope that kept the man from falling off of the mule, slid the body to the ground, and then pulled it into the shed and down into the root cellar. He had no idea at all what he planned to do with the dead man, but at least he could keep the body cool until he could deal with it properly.

The body securely stored, Francis removed the travois, turned Mick out to feed, and then, once more, grabbed the bucket to fetch some water.

It took twenty or so minutes for the cold spring water to heat up in a Dutch oven placed over the glowing coals Francis raked to the side of the burning logs. Using a ladle, Francis transferred water to a porcelain wash basin and then used a clean rag to wash the dried blood from Danny's face.

Little by little, as the blood was removed, Francis could tell that the source was a nasty little gash high on Danny's forehead. It was in a good position, and it would heal, but Danny would have to deal with a mean-spirited headache that could last for an extended amount of time. Not only that but there was a chance that he'd experience bouts of vertigo and have sensitivity to light. Only time could reveal the extent of the complications.

And then there was that rope burn on Danny's neck. Francis gingerly dabbed at the burn and then spread a thin layer of honey on the wound. Honey, known for its ability to work against bacteria and keep a wound moist, was the best treatment Francis had on hand. He'd also use honey on Danny's head wound. As far as any other injuries, Francis would have to wait until Danny regained consciousness to assess the situation.

With a mug of coffee in hand, and a pot of stew slowly cooking near the fire, Francis sat in a chair and waited for Danny to come around.

***

Eli Roberts and his men, with their loot in tow, rode away from the big oak tree and what they believed to be two dead men. There was no time to delay in hanging Danny again after the branch broke. Besides, even if Danny didn't break his neck or choke to death, there was a chance he'd bleed to death. Eli wasn't worried. The fact that someone might come along and discover them in the act had a greater probability than Danny living...or so he thought. He thought it better to not stick around and find out.

Up the Greenhorn Trail they rode, tracing the route Danny had walked less than an hour ago. When they reached a bubbling spring a mile or so up the path, they briefly stopped to fill their canteens and water the horses and mules.

"I still can't believe that branch broke...never seen nothin' like that before!" exclaimed George to Harry.

"Damnedest thing I've ever seen," Harry responded.

"You boys need to shut up about that," Eli scolded his men. "There'll be time to talk, but we need to put some miles between us and those bodies. Let's go!"

Remounted, the men continued up the Trail toward the pass that'd drop them down into the Kern River Canyon. Eli Roberts didn't have a master plan. He worked better without a script, preferring to act and react according to the circumstances at hand. As an opportunist, that was what worked best for him. When they encountered the two unarmed Chinese men with the mules it was a pleasant surprise. Sure, one of the men was able to slip away into the brush, and when that boy Danny came down the Trail, Eli and his men had to think on their feet. But everything worked out in the end. They had more supplies than they needed, plus several mules they could sell. It was a good day and a good take. However, those plans would need to wait until the morning. It was best to get back to their camp high on a ridge about three miles from their current position.

Nearing the point where the Trail flattens and then runs along a few miles to the small settlement of Petersburg before it begins a descent towards Keyesville, the men turned to the northeast to continue their ride up a series of ridges to reach their camp. As they made the turn, a man sitting under a large Ponderosa Pine about fifty yards in the distance hailed them. He waved at the Roberts Boys and stood up near where his horse was tied to a branch.

"Hey there! Hello! I'm Parker's man, Reynolds," the man said as he walked toward the approaching men.

"I see you made it with all of the supplies. Splendid! I already have a tent set up down along the river. Those goods are in great..."

Before he could finish his statement, Eli pulled out a revolver and shot Reynolds twice in the chest. With a shocked look on his face, Reynolds grasped his chest and fell to his knees. He was dead. Gravity took over and he fell forward onto his face. A small cloud of dust rose from the ground when the man's body came to rest.

Eli watched through the black powder smoke as the man fell. "Get his horse and check his body for anything important," Eli ordered George and Harry.

They quickly did as they were told. A horse and saddle, some tobacco, a pen knife, and a few five-dollar gold pieces were all that was left to sum up the life of a man called Reynolds. His past, his dreams, his family...none of that mattered to Eli Roberts. He was but a distraction, and an impediment to their progress. And there he would lie; without a marker, without recognition, and without a legacy. Reynolds' life was taken without a second thought by a man who seemingly had no moral fabric.

Two hours later, Eli and his men were back in their camp. Keeping with the nature of their work, the camp was maximized for mobility. They lived in tents—structures that could be quickly torn down, packed, and transported away to make a new home. Everything else they had could be stowed into saddlebags or packs. Creature comforts made life more enjoyable. If they wanted these leisure items, they'd take a trip to a town and stay a few days. But that isn't what suited them at the moment. Wherever they were, they were in their element. The pickings were slimmer here amidst the Greenhorn Mountains, especially compared to the towns of Sacramento and Stockton. However, the anonymity was refreshing.

Dismounted, Eli looked over the mules and sole horse that they'd acquired that day. They were nice animals and would bring a top price. And the supplies packed onto the mules would feed them for weeks...maybe even a couple of months.

"Take care of the animals, and place those supplies in a tent. That's our bread and butter, boys!" Eli spoke to Harry and George.

Stretching his arms into the air and yawning, Eli walked around the camp at the top of the mountain—his mountain. From his vantage point, he could see the surrounding peaks and ridges, as well as the slopes running down into the Kern River Canyon. He could also look down into more than a dozen little valleys and meadows in the distance. At the edge of one of those little valleys, about a mile and a half away, Eli could just make out a small cabin. He hadn't noticed it before, but a thin wisp of smoke from the chimney drew his attention.

"We best settle in, eat, and get some rest while we can. It's been a busy day...I have a few things I want us to do tomorrow."

Eli's voice trailed off as he zeroed his gaze in on that cabin.

Chapter 3
A Sheltered Standoff

———◆———

"**G**ood morning, sonny!" Francis excitedly said to Danny. "Glad to see you've joined the living!"

Confused, Danny blinked hard and then turned his head toward Francis, causing him to wince in pain. Danny had no idea where he was or who this man in front of him could be. He reached his right hand up to his throbbing forehead, touched his tender wound, and brought his sticky fingers away. With his other hand he felt his neck, and, as with his forehead, found his fingers sticky. Danny brought his fingers to his nose to further investigate the tacky residue.

"Honey," said Francis. "It's honey to help with the healing. Harvested it myself a few months back...little devils stung the dickens out of me. Good honey, though."

Danny was still disoriented, but things were becoming clearer. Obviously, he was injured. He was in a bed, in a structure where this man had taken him. And images of Sam hanging from a tree, and himself looking in the faces of three men...the Roberts Boys...and then not much more. It was all a bit fuzzy, but that was to be expected.

"Wha...What's your name?" Danny managed to say in a raspy voice.

"I'm Francis Rutherford. You can call me Francis or Frank if you'd like, but you might try to take it easy on the talking for a while."

Francis stood up and walked to a shelf. He grabbed a jug and two tin cups and then set them down on his small table. Danny watched the man as he pulled the cork out of the jug, thinking that the little popping sound it made when it was pulled sounded louder than it was. Francis poured a deep, dark purple liquid into the cups, placed the jug on the table, and then handed a cup to Danny. Moving his chair close to the bed, Francis sat down and took a sip from his cup.

Sniffing the liquid in the cup, Danny tried to identify what it was. It had a heavy smell of fruit, but it also had a somewhat sour aroma. This man, Francis, had taken care of him thus far, Danny thought as he brought the cup to his lips and took a sip.

"Good God! What is that?" Danny inquired in a husky voice after he swallowed the liquid down.

"Elderberry wine...made it myself," Francis proudly said.

"No kidding...it's horrid," Danny said in a rather uncharacteristically straightforward manner.

Francis laughed and took another sip. "I know, but believe it or not, this is the best batch I ever made! It'll grow on ya...the second cup is much better than the first. Besides, there's something about that berry juice that cures a lot of ailments...aches and pains, sore throats and headaches. Of course, it could just be coincidental, too."

Amused, Danny took another sip. The liquid felt thick as it passed down his throat.

"I've got all of those and not too much to lose at this point."

"That a boy! You've been through a lot, Danny. That's your name, isn't it? You were able to tell me that much when I found you."

Danny confirmed that it was, indeed, his name, and then asked Francis to tell him what happened. Reaching for the jug, Francis poured some more wine into each of their cups. As they sipped the wine, which did become more tolerable with each swallow, Francis relayed to Danny what he knew.

He told him how he'd been out hunting for bear and was on his way back to his cabin when something caught his eye in the distance. How he'd snuck up to the location because he thought it was a trap, that he discovered a Chinese man hanging from the tree, and then literally stumbled onto Danny. Francis also explained how he constructed a travois to haul Danny back to his cabin, and that, almost as an afterthought, he also brought the Chinese man back to his cabin and stowed him away in the root cellar.

Things were now coming back to Danny. It was the Roberts Boys. Of course, he had no idea that they were in this part of the country, but he explained to Francis about the run-ins he'd had with the bunch—outside of St. Joseph; on the Overland Trail; in Sacramento. And now here.

Danny wasn't sure how he ended up on the ground, but he remembered a man kicking him; every time he moved in the bed the result of those kicks became more evident. A few ribs were either broken or badly bruised. And he recalled sitting on one of the mules and then swinging in the air. Slipping from consciousness...and then that sickening, sharp cracking sound of what was the breaking of the branch he was hanging from. It was a lucky break that led to his salvation.

Danny also told Francis about Sam, the dead man in his root cellar. Sam was his employee and his friend. He was grateful that Francis had cut Sam down and brought him back to his cabin. He explained that Sam had some family back in Sacramento and that the right thing to do was take his body back to them. It didn't seem like many white men in California had much respect for the Chinese. Francis was too embarrassed to admit that if he hadn't found Danny, then he would've just left Sam swinging in the breeze.

And as if an oil lamp was suddenly lit and revealed what was hidden in the darkness, Danny suddenly thought of Ah Joe. Francis only found one man dead. Maybe Ah Joe was able to hide or run away. Or maybe he was dead, his body lying somewhere in the brush.

"Did you see another Chinese fellow there?

Thinking about all of the footprints that he'd seen around the tree, Francis had no way to discern which tracks belonged to whom.

"No...just you and your friend. I'm sorry, Danny. I can go back there and take a look around if you'd like."

"I'd appreciate that, Francis...and I cannot thank you enough for all you've done. But if you go...I need to go with you."

"Well...you ain't going nowhere today, Danny. It's best you take it easy. How 'bout we try to wander over there tomorrow?"

Danny truly disliked the notion of waiting, but he realized it was best. If Ah Joe was dead, there wasn't anything he could do for him. And if he was alive, then Ah Joe could take care of himself. Danny was too banged up to be much help to anyone, dead or alive.

Over the next few hours, Danny and Francis ate stew and drank another cup or two of wine that had somehow become quite good. Even though Danny was a prisoner of his condition, trapped in the cabin by his inability to move without a great deal of pain, he enjoyed the company of Francis. He was a kind man with a great deal of experience. Danny could see himself, under other circumstances, meeting Francis and befriending him. He was a pretty good judge of character, and, despite interacting with Francis for only a portion of one day, it was enough for Danny to get a good read on his new friend. Francis didn't have to go out of his way to help Danny. It was Danny's good fortune that he did.

Unfortunately for Danny, there was a need to visit the privy. He wasn't looking forward to shifting his upper body and putting tension on his ribs. He was also hesitant to test his legs. They were sore and didn't appear to be fractured, but they, too, ached when he moved in the bed.

Francis helped Danny sit up and swing his legs over the side of the bed. With his feet planted firmly on the floor, and with aid from Francis, Danny struggled to his feet. He tried to remain quiet, but the pain from his ribs was too much, and he let out a curse. It was a sharp, intense pain that reverberated from his ribs, through the cartilage, and out through the muscles and connecting tissue. A pain that reminded him that he was alive, but made him question whether or not that was the preferable choice. At least his legs stayed under him when he stood, and the pain in his ribs wasn't as great in that position. His head...that was another story. The wound throbbed and he was dizzy. All of this was to be expected, and with time, all would be better.

With Francis' help, Danny limped out to the privy and conducted his business. When he was finished, Francis helped him over to the root cellar to see the body of his friend, Sam.

The beauty of a root cellar, especially one that is well insulated, is that the temperature inside is an average of forty degrees cooler than the outside air during the warmer months. This was the case with the cellar that Francis built into the side of an embankment. Danny noted the change in temperature as he stepped down and into the structure.

It was dark inside, except for the light spilling in through the open door. A deer quarter, cured and smoked, was hanging in the corner, and a supply of homegrown potatoes, onions, and corn was secured on makeshift shelves. Lying on the floor was Sam's body. Danny looked at his friend and just shook his head. Tears welled in his eyes. They weren't that close as friends, but the thought that Sam was needlessly killed by the Roberts Boys and that he nearly shared the same fate, was emotionally overwhelming. Danny would figure out how to get Sam back to his family in the next day or two.

He had seen enough and was ready to lie back down. They walked back to the cabin and prepared for the painful descent to the bed. Although it wouldn't help much, Francis helped Danny remove his shirt and then wrapped some fabric tightly around his torso. It restricted his breathing to a point, but it also seemed to lessen the pain. Danny lowered himself into the bed and tried to get comfortable.

Perhaps it was fatigue, maybe it was the wine, but Danny became extremely tired. As he and Francis talked with each other, Danny's eyes became heavier, and he soon fell asleep. Seeing an opportunity to get some rest, too, Francis prepared his own nest. He fluffed up the bedding on the ground that he slept on the night before. It didn't take too long for him to fall asleep for a short catnap.

***

The two men, hidden amidst some small boulders at the tree line, watched the cabin. For the twenty minutes they'd been sequestered in the rocks, they had yet to see any movement, nor did they hear any sounds to indicate that anyone was home. But there was a stream of grey smoke puffing from the chimney; somebody must be nearby. They patiently waited, one equipped with a .52 caliber 1853 slant-breech Sharps carbine rifle, and the other armed with a light hatchet.

Their morning began early when they approached the big oak tree just off the Greenhorn Trail. They expected to find the lynched Chinese man and the other man lying dead in the grass. That wasn't the case. They were surprised, for dead men typically don't up and walk away.

But a cursory investigation revealed what happened. Someone had taken the bodies away. Where and why, were yet to be determined. What was clear was that there were a set of drag marks, approximately three feet apart, etched into the ground leading away from the tree. They could also see a set of mule tracks and the prints of a single man. Finding whoever took the bodies would be as easy as following the marks in the ground. It was too easy.

Slowly following the grooves, always mindful of their surroundings and the availability of cover, they traversed at least two miles of hills, draws, forests, and ridges to the little meadow that cradled the cabin they were now watching.

They couldn't lie in wait all day, so a course of action was needed. It required a cautious approach, and then quick action to prosper from the element of surprise. And they were willing to commit great bodily harm, and even kill if the situation called for it.

"You work your way down to the cabin and I'll cover you from here. Any problems, and I'll drop 'em dead on the spot," the man said to his partner who nodded in the affirmative.

With a hatchet in his hand, the man sprinted from tree to tree and then moved in a fast crouch toward the side of the cabin. Scanning from left to right as he moved, the man could spot no danger. The only creature about was a mule in a small corral. All was quiet, and when the man reached the side of the cabin he motioned to the man in the boulders to come on down.

Running from the rocks, the man quickly joined his partner at the cabin. Then slowly and silently they moved down the side of the cabin toward the front door, carefully placing their steps to avoid making any noise that might reveal their presence.

The element of surprise was in their favor. That is until the mule began to make a commotion, braying and balling, and generally breaking the silence and ruining any advantage the men initially had.

***

Francis was generally a light sleeper, especially if he was just taking a nap. To some it was a curse, preventing them from getting a restful sleep, but for Francis, it was just another layer of protection that made living on his own in the wilderness a survivable situation. It didn't hurt that Mick had a knack for sending up an alarm when potential trouble was near—bears, mountain lions, or two-legged threats.

So, when Mick began braying and stomping his legs, Francis immediately awoke and sat straight up. Another factor that contributed to his ability to survive was the fact that one of his Navy Colts was always within reach.

Almost as soon as he sat up his hand reached for and grasped his revolver. He rolled to his hands and knees, and then quickly crawled to the wall with his only window. Seeing no other real option, Francis chanced a peek out the window. There was nothing to see or at least nothing that was in his line of sight. He'd have to exit his cabin to further investigate.

The two men hugging the side of the log cabin were in quite a predicament. They were no longer in a position to slip up to the front door, and if they attempted to run back to the boulders or tree line, they'd be vulnerable targets. It was now fight or flight, and fighting seemed to be the better option of two unappealing alternatives.

"Let's move around to that door," the leader whispered to his partner. "Maybe nobody's there...or maybe they don't know we're here."

His partner nodded his agreement, and they began to edge down the outer wall to the corner of the cabin.

They weren't worried about being shot through the log walls. Chances are whoever was inside didn't have enough firepower to penetrate solid logs. The real danger was when they neared the door. Were there multiple men waiting inside? Were they outgunned? That last thought wasn't incomprehensible since they only had a rifle and a hatchet between them. There was truly only one way to find out.

Francis could hear something, or someone, rubbing against the log walls. The periodic sound indicated to that the movement was nearing the front corner of the cabin. This wasn't a good situation, but Francis was in a much better position than whatever was outside. He was barricaded in a building with only two openings—the door and a window.

With an efficiency of motion, Francis reached over and latched the door, which made a slight wood-upon-wood scraping sound. Then he closed the solid wooden shutter for the window and placed a rough-hewn wooden board over two opposing brackets, effectively barring the window.

Outside, the two men heard a sound from the front door, and then, nearly at the same time, they heard another noise that came from somewhere on the front side of the cabin. The question of whether somebody was in the cabin was now solved. But how many were in there? And how were they going to approach this situation now? They had no qualms about catching their prey off-guard. There was little chance of that now.

With Francis' movements around the room, Danny also woke up. Noticing Danny, Francis held his index finger on his left hand to his lips and motioned with the revolver in his right hand toward the front door. Danny understood that there was some sort of threat. Realizing that two men, even if one of them was damaged, was better than one, Francis grabbed his other Navy Colt from its secreted location under Francis' bedding on the floor and gave it to Danny. With a painful effort, Danny swung his legs over the side of the bed and watched Francis for what was next.

Two groups of men, both on the defense, and both ready to attack. But both waiting; waiting for the other to make a move; waiting for the right opportunity; and waiting to see how to act and react. Francis was the first to blink.

"I don't know who you are, or why you're here, but you ain't got no business with me!" Francis yelled.

The men outside were startled to hear the voice from inside the cabin. They looked at each other as if to decide what to do. The man with the hatchet poked his finger in the direction of the man in the lead, urging him to say something.

"We just want our friends," the man with the rifle shouted, the slight Spanish accent more pronounced with the increased volume of his voice.

Thinking of his response, Francis shouted back, "It's just me in here...I know nothing of your friends."

"We followed the drag marks from the big oak tree," the man outside responded. "One's a Chinaman...the other's a white man."

Francis was wary. This could easily be a trap by the same men who killed Sam and tried to kill Danny. He looked to Danny, who whispered that he thought those were his friends. Francis, however, wasn't satisfied.

"These friends of yours...what's their names?"

"The Chinaman's name is Sam. The man's name is Danny...Danny Vance."

Francis again looked to Danny, who dropped the revolver on the bed and let all of the tension out of his shoulders. A slight smile spread on his face as he bowed his head.

"Those are my partners," Danny said in a raspy and strained voice. "I'm sure of it! I'll be damned if I'm wrong!"

"You'll be dead if you're wrong!" He said to Danny and then continued questioning the men outside.

"Ok...what're your names?"

Without hesitation, the man outside answered, "I'm Gonzales, and the man with me is Ah Joe."

"Open the door, Francis...it's ok. I'm certain of it. Those men are okay," Danny said as he awkwardly pushed himself off the bed into a standing position.

Still not fully convinced, and with great caution, Francis unlatched the door and slowly opened it. The leather hinges made a noise like fiber being stretched.

"Well...come on, then," Francis loudly, but less aggressively, shouted. He stepped away from the door and stood at an angle where the approaching men couldn't see him, just in case.

Mustering as much volume as he could, and with a voice that wasn't recognizably his own, Danny managed to say, "Gonzales...Ah Joe...It's Danny. I'm in here!"

It took Gonzales and Ah Joe a moment to decide whether to approach the door. They, too, were afraid that this was a trap, but they were sure their friends were there. Whether they were dead or alive remained to be seen. That voice didn't exactly reassure them that it was, in fact, Danny, but they had reached the point of no return.

"We're putting our weapons down and coming in," Gonzales exclaimed in a calm, loud voice.

He leaned his rifle against the outside cabin wall, and Ah Joe tossed his hatchet to the ground. Unarmed, they walked to the door where they saw Danny leaning against the door jam. Relieved, and now disarmed in more than one way, Gonzales raised his arms in the air to indicate his confusion.

"Danny...you look like Hell!"

***

Ten miles away from the cabin, the Roberts Boys—Eli, George, and Harry—rode down into Petersburg and then Keyesville to scout out potential buyers for the string of mules and some of the supplies they'd taken the previous day. They did not need the mules, but miners would. The animals would fetch a good price, and so would the supplies Eli decided they didn't need. Then again, any price was a profit to thieves and murderers. For them, it was business as usual.

Chapter 4
Murder of Crows

————◆————

Although Danny was only separated from Gonzales and Ah Joe for a little over twenty-four hours, they reveled in their reunion as if they had been apart for years. The death of one friend, as well as the uncertainty of another friend's status, had a way of intensifying their endearment for each other.

They spent the rest of the afternoon and the evening looking over their dead friend's body and then discussing the events that had transpired. Ah Joe, using the best English he could manage, explained what happened after Danny had ventured up the Greenhorn Trail to find the pass and scout for probable locations for the men and mules to rest.

About twenty minutes after Danny left, three men quickly rode down to where Sam and Ah Joe were waiting with the mules. Ah Joe had never seen them before, but he knew their type and he suspected what their intentions were. With guns drawn, the men shouted orders, cursed at Ah Joe and Sam, and began to rough them up.

The Chinese men were conflicted. On the one hand, their loyalty to the J. Kinney Freighting Company compelled them to do what they could to protect the freight and the animals. But on the other, the desire to ensure their safety soon became their paramount concern.

As the demeanor of the three men degraded, Ah Joe and Sam became desperate to escape. They looked for an opportunity, any opportunity, to slip away. The diversion they sought happened when the mules, unfamiliar with the three men and unnerved by the shouting, began to struggle against their leads. This drew the attention of the men, at which point Ah Joe and Sam made their move to escape.

As Ah Joe hit the edge of the brush, he looked back to see a plume of dust as Sam stumbled and fell. Sam regained his feet and began to run once again, but one of the men grabbed Sam by his braid. He was pulled back, and the men began to beat him to the ground. Unarmed, there wasn't much Sam could do. The disheartening reality was that there wasn't much Ah Joe could do, either.

With self-preservation in mind, Ah Joe ran, and at times crawled, through the brush. His goal was to stay alive and put as much distance between himself and those bad men, as quickly as he could. And that meant navigating the side of a mountain and negotiating an unpleasant amount of choked vegetation down to the bottom where there was a little trickle of a creek. It was not the path of least resistance, but it was the only chance he had, and it was a good choice at that. The bad men who had focused their attention on Sam had no desire to waste their time chasing down prey that went where horses couldn't follow. Besides, what they wanted—the freight on the mules—was on the top of the ridge, not crawling through the brush.

Exhausted, bruised, and bloodied, Ah Joe made it to the bottom of the mountain alive. There were several moments where he felt like giving up due to the lack of energy and the grief of leaving his friend behind. However, it made no sense for him to stop or pine over the fact that he didn't subject himself to the same fate as Sam. It crossed his mind that maybe Sam's best chance for survival was for Ah Joe to reach Gonzales. That became his goal.

Over the next few hours, Ah Joe took his bearings and continued in the direction he believed Gonzales was camped. As the sun ended its journey in the western sky, Ah Joe's desperation increased. He had no desire to be lost in the wilderness at night, without a lantern, without friends, and seemingly without hope. When he spotted the team's wagon, the oxen, and then Gonzales, tears of relief streamed down his face.

He stumbled into camp and fell at the feet of an exceedingly confused Gonzales. It didn't take long for Gonzales to be brought up to speed about what happened—how Ah Joe and Sam were ambushed, how Sam became a victim, and how Danny was still up on that mountain. With darkness now upon the two men, it was evident that making their way up the Greenhorn Trail by lantern light would be an exercise in futility. The light would announce their presence to anyone within line of sight. And with the way the Trail ran up the meandering ridge of a mountain between brush, trees, and small meadows, they could walk past the very men they were hoping to save. They reluctantly decided that it was in their best interest to wait until the morning.

At the first light of day, they secured the oxen in a makeshift corral, gathered some supplies and the only weapons they had, and then headed out. It took them nearly half the day to hike up the Trail and reach the spot where Ah Joe and Sam were ambushed. They then spent another few hours following the drag marks the travois made. And now they sat in Francis' cabin, the light from a candle lantern and the flames burning in the fireplace juxtaposed against the darkness outside.

"No...no, you and Ah Joe have to take Sam home," Danny said as he shook his head.

Gonzales paced back and forth, indicating his growing agitation as he spoke.

"But Danny, those dogs need to pay for what they've done!"

Danny nodded in agreement, "They do...and they will...but Sam needs to be sent home. Ah Joe can't do it by himself!"

Gonzales stopped pacing and then knelt to be at eye level with Danny. It was an attempt to appeal to Danny's sensibilities.

"Then you come with us...we'll take Sam back and then hunt those men down."

"Look at me, Gonzales…just look at me! There ain't no way I can make that trip!"

Gonzales stared at Danny and his damaged body. He knew Danny was right, but he didn't like the proposition. However, he understood and agreed with what needed to be done. He wanted to punish the Roberts Boys, almost as much as Danny. Gonzales had an intense sense of loyalty and a strength of character that bound him to duty.

"Ok, Danny. Ah Joe and I will take Sam home. I don't like it…not one bit, but I understand."

With the dwindling hours of the day, they made their final arrangements. In the morning, Ah Joe and Gonzales, along with Francis, would wrap Sam in a blanket and then load him onto the back of Mick, the mule. The three men would make the precarious trip back down the Greenhorn Trail, down to where the freight wagon and oxen were waiting for their return. From there, Ah Joe and Gonzales would transport Sam back to his family in Sacramento, and Francis would return, with Mick, to his cabin to look after Danny.

It was a plan nobody truly liked. Gonzales would rather stay with Danny to seek out revenge. Ah Joe didn't relish the thought of traveling with his dead friend, presenting his body to Sam's family, or confronting the immense amount of guilt he had for being alive. Francis wasn't overjoyed about walking down and then back up the Greenhorn Trail. And Danny? He felt responsible for this whole, sad mess. If he'd been with Ah Joe and Sam, then maybe, just maybe, the Roberts Boys would have avoided ambushing the trio. Or at the very least, Danny and the Chinese men could have offered more resistance due to their increased numbers. It was a regret he had to bear. A regret that would drive the fury inside to bring the Roberts Boys to justice.

As the conversation died down, each man was left with his thoughts. After the candles were extinguished, the only light left in the room was the glow of the burning log in the fireplace. The dancing flames cast flickering shadows on the walls of the cabin. Soon, the only sounds present were the crackling and popping of the fire, and the men sleeping.

***

Eli Roberts, a man most interested in advancing the cause of Eli Roberts, was awake early, drinking coffee, and sitting by the ring of stones that contained the burning logs in his camp. He was a restless man, always ready to chase the next score, take advantage of a situation, or drop anything and everything to escape and avoid capture.

His favorite time of the day was the early morning. While his men slept, he spent time thinking about his next move. One thing was for sure, he needed to get rid of those mules. He and his men had a few options. They could take the pack train down to Linn's Valley or Visalia, but that was a risky move. Chances are, that train passed through both of those locations. Someone might recognize the mules, and at the very least, refuse to purchase the animals. Petersburg was also an option, but the number of potential buyers there was limited. Besides, the settlement was a bit too close to the site of the ambush for comfort.

No, the most practical, and safe, option was to ride down into Keyesville to trade or sell the mules. Their reconnoiter into and around the mining camps along the Kern River the previous day confirmed his belief that there was a demand for his ill-gotten goods and that it was the safest, and surest, option.

With his mind made up, Eli roused his men and had them cook break-fast. There was no sense in him doing it for himself when he had others who could do the work for him. It was one of the perks of being in charge. Why waste his energy on mundane tasks? He was the brains of the outfit;

he was the leader. And if needed, he could be a physical force to be reckoned with.

Breakfast was a grand affair, considering what they had feasted on when pickings were slim. Happening across that pack train was a real stroke of luck. They had fresh coffee, bacon, biscuits, canned sardines, and beans. More food than they'd had in one sitting in quite a while. With full bellies and cold hearts, they were now ready to begin their work for the day.

After George and Harry loaded the stolen supplies Eli wanted to sell, they arranged the mules into a string. Then they saddled the horses and gathered their necessaries for the day—canteens, pistols, and two rifles. Eli watched them work for a few minutes but was drawn to the view from their perch in the sky. He relished the smell of the pine and fir trees that cradled his camp, and he appreciated the abundant shade provided by the cluster of black oaks that hovered above the tents.

From his ridge, with a gentle breeze blowing into his face, Eli looked out across the land below. Blue sky met a wooded horizon. It was a sight to behold. The sounds of jays, woodpeckers, and ravens added a chorus to God's creation. It was enough to truly fill the heart with joy...even the heart of a man who had but little room for such things. Eli allowed himself to feel that happiness that can only come from beauty for a moment. Without difficulty, he tamped it down.

As his men finished their preparations, Eli was once again fixated on a small plume of smoke in the distance that arose from what he surmised was a chimney. The small cabin looked miniscule from this distance, but he knew it was there. The Roberts Boys hadn't ventured down into that little valley. Not yet.

With the last horse saddled and the mules readied, the Roberts Boys were ready for their ride down into Keyesville.

"Let's ride," Eli stated as he placed his left foot into the stirrup and climbed into the saddle. George and Harry followed suit. They had a long day ahead of them. Earning blood money often took a bit of effort.

***

"Gonzales, you tell Kinney to take Parker's loss out of my account and make sure that Sam's family gets a little something from the company. I can't help but feel like his life was lost because of me," Danny said as he leaned against the doorway to Francis' cabin.

"Don't beat yourself up about things, Danny...it could've happened to any of us," Gonzales replied as he, Ah Joe, and Francis prepared to make the trek over to the Greenhorn Trail and then down to where he had made their camp on Poso Flats.

Danny sighed. It was a painful sigh, both physically and emotionally. "Please...just do it for me."

"Will do," Gonzales relented. "But you do me a favor...don't you go getting yourself killed!"

Gonzales was sincere in his request. He knew Danny, and he knew that deep inside, Danny wanted to make right what he felt was wrong. Danny wanted the Roberts Boys to pay for what they'd done. Their pound of flesh was Danny's underlying desire, but his body was in no shape to gain satisfaction.

The men shook hands—Danny, Gonzales, and Ah Joe. It'd be a long journey home to Sacramento, and even a longer journey for Sam's body if it was sent back to his village in China to reside with his ancestors.

"Now...you keep that hand cannon close to you while I'm away," Francis advised Danny. "Mick and I'll be back this evening sometime. Feel free to take a nip or two of that elderberry wine, and eat whatever you'd like."

Danny nodded and thanked Francis for his hospitality. He watched as Francis led the trio away from the cabin. It was a strange sight, what with Sam's body tied across the back of Mick, the mule, Francis leading the way, and Gonzales and Ah Joe trailing behind. The image reminded Danny of an impromptu funeral procession. Danny said a little prayer to himself as the delicate wisps of dust kicked up from the men and settled to the ground. He watched as they disappeared into the trees at the edge of the little meadow.

Alone, Danny was left with his thoughts. He shuffled from the doorway to a stump in Francis' yard. Danny's legs were sore, but he was able to lower himself into a sitting position where he could spend some time with the sun on his face.

Life is filled with "what ifs" and "I should haves," and this particular moment was no different. What if he'd stayed in Sacramento? What if he'd never left Ah Joe and Sam? What if he'd refused to leave Julia with an abusive husband? He sat there and could feel a cloud of remorse and depression battling to the forefront of his consciousness. It was a battle against himself; no matter the outcome he was in it, win or lose.

From Danny's perspective, the only solution to this situation was to hunt down the Roberts Boys. What happened from there was unknown. It wasn't like there was a marshal or constable in the immediate vicinity. Danny realized that there were only a few possible outcomes to this endeavor, two of which would result in either the death of the Roberts Boys, himself or a combination of the two. Or he might never find a trace of the men. Regardless, Danny committed himself to the task. But he couldn't do anything until his body healed, which could take weeks. He wasn't in the mood to be patient, but he admitted to himself that patience was what his broken body and spirit needed.

As the cool morning air enveloped his body, he felt the warming balance of the sun. It was a fitting sensation that exemplified how he felt; a contrast of coolness to warmth, and anger, sadness, and guilt to the appreciation of being alive.

He felt the heft of the Colt Navy Revolver, and he spent some time examining the weapon. At a little over two and a half pounds and thirteen inches in length, the revolver was well-balanced and comfortable in his hands. Danny brushed his fingers from the one-piece walnut stock, down the dull metal of the octagon barrel. It felt cool to the touch. It felt powerful. Oddly enough, it reminded him of the walnut stock of his shotgun. Until that moment, he forgot that he had discarded his weapon in his panicked attempt to help Sam. Maybe he and Francis could go back and look for it in a few days? It was an unrealistic musing.

As Danny moved the instrument from side to side, he noticed how the sun reflected off the silver-plated grip strap, the trigger guard, and the brass front sight which was shaped like a cone. It was mesmerizing, as was the engraving on the cylinder of the revolver. Etched into the cylinder was a scene depicting the May 16, 1843 victory of the Second Texas Navy at the Battle of Campeche during one of the several conflicts between the independent Republic of Texas and the government of Mexico. The Navy Colt was truly a work of art, but also a deadly tool capable of propelling the .36 caliber eighty-grain lead ball out of the barrel up to one thousand feet per second.

Francis gave a hasty tutorial on how to load the weapon. Each chamber in the cylinder was loaded individually with a measurement of gunpowder from a tin powder flask. A round lead ball was placed into the top of each cylinder, and then the ball was compressed down against the powder with the charging rod. Fulminate percussion caps are placed onto the nipples at the rear of each chamber.

It was handsome, efficient, and accurate, and the only thing keeping Danny company on that lonely mountain. That, and the occasional thought of Julia working away at her kitchen on the American River.

***

After delivering Sam's body to the buckboard, Francis wished his new friends safe travels and then began the return trip back up the Greenhorn Trail to his cabin in the clearing. The trip back up the mountain was easier than the descent, largely because he wasn't trying to balance Sam's body on the back of Mick as they bounced and skidded down the trail. The fact that he rode Mick up the steepest portions of the path probably made the ascent more pleasant than the walk down. At least for Francis.

It was an uneventful trip up to where the Trail reached a plateau. But it was there that Francis noticed a group of crows—technically, a murder of crows—in the distance. He faintly heard their cacophony of calls and observed the birds dipping and diving through the sky, sitting in the trees, and generally making a big fuss about something. From experience, Francis knew that crows and ravens broadcast all matters of news in the forest. Whether it was danger or a food source, the birds made it a habit of notifying every creature in the vicinity by their actions. They weren't too far out of his way, so Francis thought it was worth his effort to investigate the disturbance. Meeting danger before it became an actual threat was another rule that had served Francis well and kept him alive.

Going fifteen minutes out of his way, Francis found the source of the crows' agitation, and it wasn't exactly what he expected. There, near a large pine tree, were two men, sweaty and tired, who were taking a break from digging what appeared to be a grave. They leaned on shovels and took turns taking swigs of whiskey from a shared bottle. With Mick trailing behind, Francis walked to the men, unafraid of the two. Hostile killers typically don't bury their victims.

"Howdy boys," Francis greeted the party.

Wincing at the burning liquid sliding down his throat, one of the strangers responded, "Hello there, old-timer. Care for a nip?"

Francis licked his lips, reminding himself that his throat was dry and that he tended to follow a rule of thumb to not pass up a drink...especially a free drink.

"I don't mind if I do," Francis happily stated as he reached for the bottle. "Much obliged!"

He took a drink of John Barleycorn and joined the men in the warming sensation that comes from consuming that corn elixir.

"Who's the unfortunate fellow?" Francis inquired as he pointed to the man splayed upon the ground.

"That used to be a man named Reynolds," one of the friendly strangers chimed. "We met him several times down on the Kern...said he was waiting for a pack train with stock for a store he planned to open."

He shook his head, seemingly out of disappointment. "Nice fellow...we found him here, bushwhacked and deader than dead...shot in the chest and picked clean—no money, no horse...nothing."

The other man joined the conversation adding, "The least we could do was give 'em a proper burial."

Francis started putting two and two together, and the bigger picture emerged.

"Reynolds, you say...I believe I have the leader of that pack train back at my cabin. He's been damaged, as well...though, not to the extent of that poor fellow there," Francis said as he received the bottle making another round. "I wouldn't be surprised if it weren't the same cowards."

The men nodded in agreement, figuring that it made sense. Francis offered to help the men finish their work, but they declined, explaining that the hard work was mostly done. After one more sip, Francis, and gave them directions to his place in the meadow and an invitation to stop over for a visit soon. He bid the men farewell and went on his way.

Just as he was about out of sight of the two men, Francis looked back in time to see them drag Reynold's dead body into the hole they'd dug. Francis thought to himself that it was a shame. Reynolds, just like Danny and his Chinese friend, were just men trying to make an honest day's pay with an honest day's work. All it took was a group of men who thought otherwise to interrupt, and ultimately end, that endeavor. Francis would tell Danny about Reynolds when he got home.

Chapter 5
Finding a Way

————◆————

O ver the next four weeks, Danny slowly convalesced. He continued to apply honey to the rope burn on his neck and the gash on his forehead, and he tried to keep movement involving his ribs to a minimum, although that was nearly impossible. But he endured. And he tried to pull his weight around Francis' place the best that he could. Cooking, keeping the fire stoked, and mending some clothing. Danny did what he could.

Francis appreciated Danny's help, but more than anything, he just enjoyed his company. Living the life that Francis did could be lonely, but not altogether unpleasant. He had occasional visitors, like the two men he met burying Reynolds—Albert Johns and James Stanton.

Albert and James were nice fellows. About a week after Francis met them under those unfortunate circumstances, they came a calling, sharing a meal and a bottle with Francis and Danny. And just like Francis, Danny found the two men to be jovial, easy to talk to, and fast friends. During their visit, they all shared stories of their time in California, and more importantly, Albert and James relayed news and rumors from the Kern River diggings.

"I've heard that there's damn near 5,000 men plying the Kern River country," said Albert as he fussed with the whiskers in his beard. "All types of men, and a few women, too!"

Puffing on a pipe, much like the one Danny's father used, James added, "And they're all having about as much success as they did up north. Oh course, I'm including Albert and I in the mix...it's very hit and miss, but ya can survive."

Danny wasn't sad to be out of the mining game. There was the thrill of the chase for gold, and when a man was on the color, he could easily recoup his losses and some. But the uncertainty, as well as the miserable working conditions, made Danny confident that he'd made the right decision to pursue other means of making a living. Although, he wasn't doing much for a living at the moment.

"You know," James said between puffs, "Francis said you were bushwhacked the day he found you. He also said that you were leading a pack train with a load of stock for a store to the diggings."

Smoke swirled from James's lips and rose toward the rafters of the small cabin. It reminded Danny of how clouds infiltrated a mountain valley and slowly enveloped the surrounding mountains.

"Yes...my associates and I had eight mules on the Greenhorn Trail when we were attacked...first Ah Joe and Sam, and then me when I returned from scouting the route."

Danny felt his anger increase inside as he spoke of the event.

"As soon as I'm healed, I'm going after those men...the Roberts Boys," Danny said with a degree of vengeance in the tone of his voice.

Francis, James, and Albert felt the awkward tension in the cabin. The men looked for an opening to continue their tale.

"Peculiar thing James and I saw two weeks ago," Albert chimed in and picked up where James stopped. "As we were traveling from our camp to Keyesville, we came across a few different claims where the men had some mules that were new to them."

This interested Danny, and he sat forward with his elbows on his knees and his head cocked to the side. Albert had Danny's rapt attention.

"The animals looked out of place...not used to mining or the men who tried to control the beasts," Albert continued.

"Were they shoed? Branded?" Danny excitedly asked.

James, pleased with the information they had for Danny, raised his eyebrows and remarked, "Not sure about being shoed...but they were branded...on the left rump they had..."

"A JK brand," Danny and James proclaimed at the same time, one confident in what they'd seen, the other hopeful of what was to be.

A broad smile broke across James's face, "That's the one. We both saw it on all the mules."

Albert nodded in agreement, happy to affirm James' revelation. Both he and James were pleased that they had information that could be potentially helpful to Danny.

Danny explained to the men what the Roberts Boys looked like, hoping that maybe the men with the mules were his attackers. But they weren't.

On the bright side, their information gave him a starting point. Albert and James explained where the general location of the camps were. If anything, maybe the men in the camps could provide further leads that would take Danny to the Roberts Boys. Time will tell.

After dinner, James and Albert put on their coats and hats to stave off the chill of the cool fall evening. Their breath was visible as they mounted their horses, an indication that the season was moving quickly toward winter whether they were ready or not. Both Francis and Danny waved to the men and watched as they rode off into the encroaching darkness.

***

Ever since selling the mules and spare supplies, the Roberts Boys kicked around the Kern River Valley. They spent some time drinking in a makeshift saloon in Keyesville, harassed Chinese workers down on the Kern River, and gravitated toward other men bent on doing no good and who wanted a leader. Eli Roberts, with his twisted sense of morals and dark charisma, tended to attract such men.

Eli and his men had time on their hands. When your livelihood is dependent on the success of others, or at least for others to be unlucky and in the wrong place at the wrong time, work is a feast or famine. So, they found ways to waste time or keep themselves otherwise occupied. Turns out that George was adept at playing, and cheating, in card games. Many a miner gave up their gold dust and nuggets, or other valuables, to George. And if anyone suspected George of cheating, they were hesitant to call him out because Harry was always nearby and ready to back his friend.

With the change in weather, Eli decided to move his camp from the top of the mountain down to the Kern River Valley. It was a practical matter of comfort. The valley could get downright cold, but if snow did reach the valley floor it was measured in inches, not feet. And just like camping high on the ridge in the Greenhorn Mountains, they were able to camp in an out-of-the-way location and remain as isolated as they wished to be. But they were restless, and it wasn't long before they went looking for trouble.

***

After a month of convalescence, Danny was able to conduct himself in a mostly normal manner. He was back to chopping and carrying moderately heavy loads of firewood, getting up and down without much pain, and walking without having to stop to catch his breath and take a break from the discomfort. Danny also relinquished the bed to Francis, making a comfortable nest of blankets on the floor closer to the fireplace. It was the least he could do, but it was also warmer next to the heat from the burning logs at night.

With the change in the season, the world about the cabin in the meadow had changed. As fall gave up its gentle grip, winter moved in to spread its frigid fingers across the land. The leaves that'd turned from green to an orange-brown, and had gone from pliable to crisp and brittle, had fallen to the ground, creating a carpet of debris that became nearly impossible to walk upon without announcing your presence to every creature in the nearby wilderness. And the leaves in the trees, once concealing and obstructing the view for great distances, were no longer barriers, greatly altering the landscape. If each step presented a thousand different views during the spring, summer, and fall, then the winter, with the absence of foliage in the canopy of the trees, presented another thousand different views for and of you with each pace.

The animals had also changed. Squirrels and chipmunks worked feverishly to stockpile acorns and other seeds to finalize their preparations for the winter. The mule deer, their coats of fur thickened for the coming cold, began to run together in larger groups. Bucks, their necks swollen for the rut, jostled with each other for dominance and the right to breed with the does. And the birds, once plentiful as evidenced by their vocalization and presence, altered their behaviors, as well. Many of them, like the turkey vulture, migrated out of the hills during the winter, seeking warmer environs. Or they prepared their nests to better shelter them from the elements. The animals understood the ebb and flow of the seasons, their existence and habits instructed by eons of experience and survival ingrained within their genetics.

The time had come for Danny to venture back to that hanging tree; the scene of the crime where Sam lost his life and Danny nearly joined him. It had rained twice since Danny had been their last. He wanted to return to the place before any snow blanketed the ground.

If he wished to move on, to escape the pain and guilt over his friend's death, he needed to go back. Additionally, he wanted to retrieve his shotgun. At the very least he wanted it because his grandfather gave it to him and his brother, Seth, one Christmas. So, it had a great deal of sentimental value to him. And if he had his way, Danny also meant to put it to use soon.

Francis and Danny, once the sun rose and spread its warm glow across the frosty ground, ate some biscuits and bacon, and chased it down with hot, black coffee. It warmed their insides and prepared them for the day.

Outside, the temperature hovered above the freezing mark, so the men made themselves ready. Wearing union suits under their clothing, they donned heavy coats with the collar turned up, lined gloves, and hats to stave off the cold and dampness in the air. They topped off their protection by wrapping coarse-knit scarves around their necks, tucking the ends of the material into the top of their coats. They were as warm as they could be at the moment, a fact that they'd appreciate after spending time outside of the warm cabin.

It took an hour and a half for the two men to walk to their destination—from the cabin, over the rough track that led to the Greenhorn Trail, and then down the Trail. As they neared the large, ancient white oak tree, images and memories came rushing back to Danny. Instead of the greens and browns that he remembered from the late summer and early fall, everything was bathed in grey. Perhaps it was because the sun was lower in the sky due to the change in the season, or maybe it was because Danny's perception was skewed by the impending emotional stress of reliving the traumatic event. Either way, things were altogether different, but wholly the same.

What was once obscured, was now relatively open. There, in the distance, was the giant tree.

If only, Danny thought...if only the Roberts Boys had ambushed them at this time of the year Danny wouldn't have been caught off guard. Maybe Ah Joe and Same would have seen the men coming and escaped together unharmed. They may have lost the string of mules and the stock, but Sam would be alive. However, that isn't when, or the way, it happened.

As they approached the tree, there wasn't anything present to betray what happened to anyone who wasn't there on that day...at least at first glance. Understanding the gravity of the situation, Francis thought it best to hang back and give Danny some space.

Danny slowly walked to the tree. On the ground were tattered remains of the rope used during the lynching. He poked at the rope with his foot, at which point he was drawn to the section of a branch lying on the bare ground. It was approximately eight feet long, and it appeared to be solid, except where it was broken and splintered at its thickest end. He placed his hand against the craggy bark of the tree and felt a slight tug on the muscles connected to his healing ribs. His eyes looked skyward to where the branch broke. He followed the fragmented end back toward where the branch attached to the tree. Danny could see where the rope attached to Sam had stripped pieces of bark from the branch.

Images flashed in his mind—Sam hanging from the tree; the panic Danny had to cut him down; looking up to the sky and seeing Sam twisting in the slight breeze; blood running down his face, a slight ringing in his ears, and a searing pain in his side; choking and struggling against the blackness; and then the miraculous cracking of the branch. Danny felt a tingling from the rope burn on his neck that had mostly healed, and he could feel his heartbeat throbbing from the scabbed-over wound high on his forehead.

Danny leaned into his arm that now rested on the tree, and he began to sob. Tears ran from his eyes and wet the sleeve of his heavy coat. *What a sight I must be*, he thought. Francis must think he is some sort of a pitiful creature; even weak. But Danny couldn't help himself...he couldn't stop if he wanted to. He cried for Sam. He cried for himself. He just cried.

Francis apprehensively and awkwardly walked to Danny and placed a weathered, scarred hand on his shoulder, partly to announce that he was standing near, and partly to provide some sort of comfort.

"Listen, boy," Francis quietly said to Danny, "You've got every right in the world to be sorrowful...and there ain't nothin' wrong in crying."

Danny straightened and wiped the welled-up tears from his eyes, and he sniffed to stem the fluid running from his nose.

"But ya have to figure out what you want to do. The way I figure, you have one of two things you can do...you can let this consume you...let it eat you alive and become what is your ruin. It'll whittle you down...make you less than you can be. Or you can find a way to let it go. Now...how you do that is for you to decide. But I'm your friend...and I'll back your move."

Danny looked at Francis with a half-smile, the left side of his mouth curled up.

"Thank you, Francis...I'll find a way."

Francis slapped Danny on the back, "There ya go! Come on...let's head home."

The two men headed back up the Greenhorn Trail, eager to get back to the warmth of the cabin. The sun was now higher in the sky and warmed their faces as they walked.

They'd all but lost sight of the big oak when Danny stopped in his tracks, thinking hard about something. He turned around and got his bearings, looking at the trees, the Trail, and the bushes...looked down toward where the tree was standing. Scanning the ground, he began a slow walk back down from whence they came.

"What's wrong?" Francis asked. He began to follow Danny.

"Well," Danny replied as he neared a large clump of sage just off the Trail, "I kinda forgot to get something."

He looked toward the tree, and then back up the Trail. Danny figured he was in the right location. He bent slightly at the waist and made a wide sweep of the sage-covered hill. It didn't take too long until he found what he was looking for. Danny reached down into a clump of sage and pulled out what Francis originally took as a stick. But it wasn't. Danny found his discarded shotgun. Rust had formed on parts of the barrel, and the dark-colored walnut stock had a scratch etched diagonally across the grain. It had seen better days.

"I almost forgot to find this," Danny held the shotgun in the air and showed it to Francis.

Francis looked it over and relayed his assessment, "That's in a bit of rough shape. But it's not beyond saving."

Danny examined the rust on the barrel and brushed some of the dirt off the shotgun as the two men walked home. It'd take some work. He'd take some work, too. He vowed to find a way.

**

Petersburg was about four miles away from Francis' cabin. Located near the top of the Greenhorn Trail before it began its winding, treacherous descent down to the diggings along the Kern River country, Petersburg served as a waystation and offered a store, saloon, small hotel, and an unofficial post office for the large community of miners spread near and far.

Its founder, Peter Gardett, an immigrant from Prussia, joined in a financial partnership with Judge C.G. Sayles to find a bonanza by mining the miners. The town, if it can truly be referred to by that description, was an important location between the relatively civilized hamlet of Visalia and the wilds of the Kern River country, but it was hardly a bustling metropolis. Gardett could spend days without a single customer or visitor, and then experience weeks where he was busier than he could hope. It all depended on the whims of the miners themselves. Of course, rumors of new strikes and the rush of potential gold seekers helped stimulate his trade.

A light dusting of snow covered the ground on the day Danny, Francis, and Mick ventured over to Petersburg. Francis needed dry goods and an assortment of other supplies. As he had done with others in the past, he was hoping to barter with the pelts that he procured trapping and hunting over the last year—five bobcats, ten coyotes, six red and grey foxes, one grizzly bear, and two black bears. It was a fair amount of hides, and, depending on the value that Gardett placed on them, could be enough to acquire flour, sugar, salt, coffee, gunpowder, shot, and percussion caps. With any luck, he might even be able to procure a bottle or two of legitimate booze.

As the men approached Gardett's storefront, they could see that they were probably the only customers. The corral was empty, laughter and loud talking were absent from the saloon, and Gardett was lackadaisically carrying split pieces of wood into his store to feed the fire.

The structure that doubled as a storefront and saloon was recently upgraded from a tent to a tent with a false wooden-framed front, to a proper wooden structure. If it hadn't been for the fact that Gardett saw the men approach, he surely would have heard them; each step resounded with the cracking and breaking of innumerable ice crystals present in the snow. They reached the store, tied Mick's lead to a hitching post, knocked on the door of the storefront, and entered.

Inside, the room was warm and relatively pleasant for a remote store. Light from the fire, as well as from candle lanterns lit the otherwise dark room. There was a counter where business was conducted, and stock was stored on shelves or stacked on the ground in a secure corner. Two tables and two sets of chairs were over to the side in the small building, offering a place to sit, eat, and drink. The rich smell of stew emanated from a cast iron pot hanging over the low flames in the hearth.

"Halo vriends," Gardett said in his thick Prussian accent, "Vat can I do vor you?"

"Howdy," Francis cheerfully replied, "I was hoping we could do some trading for supplies...and my friend here was looking to post a letter if that was possible."

Gardett arched his eyebrows and assented that a deal might be worked out. And, as for Danny, he went behind his counter and fetched a piece of paper and a small envelope, a wooden pen tipped with a steel nib, and an ink well. Gardett set the writing supplies on one of the tables as he and Francis walked outside to look over the pelts.

Danny, not one for writing letters, was compelled to write to Jim Kinney, his business partner. He pulled out a chair, sat down, and then stared at the plain white sheet of paper. This was the difficult part of Danny's task, just thinking about what he wanted to place on the paper. He wanted Jim to know that he was well. And he wanted Jim to know that he intended to head back to Sacramento soon. But he also wanted Jim to understand that there was something he had to do before he left the Greenhorn Mountains. It was the wording, though, that tripped up Danny. So, Danny started with the envelope.

In the center of the envelope on the front side, he wrote, "Jim Kinney. J.K. Freighting Company. Sacramento, California." And in the upper left corner, he inscribed, "D. Vance."

With that done, he set it aside and continued to think. Thinking is what he called it, however, others might call it stalling. Danny drummed his fingers on the table. That didn't help. Then he placed his hands behind his head and fixed his gaze on the rafters of the small store. None of this was getting that letter written, and it would be an even more difficult task once Francis and Gardett returned.

Refusing to put it off further, Danny picked up the pen, dipped the tip in the black ink, and then started to scratch out his message.

December 2nd, 1854

Petersburg, California

Dear Friend,

I wanted you take a moment to write you a letter to let you know that I am well. My body is still a bit banged up, Jim, but I'm healing. By the time you get this letter, I imagine Gonzales has returned with Ah Joe and Sam's body. Please make sure Sam is taken care of, and that his family is helped out. Gonzales probably also told you about Francis Rutherford. He's been awful kind to me, and has willingly given me what I needed. In fact, he saved my life. Please send him $200 and a pair of breeding pigs. It's the least I can do to repay him for his hospitality.

I'll be heading home soon. However, I have some business to finish. The Roberts Boys need to be brought to justice, and I'm going after them. It's something I have to do or I'll never be at rest. Don't worry for me. I'm good however this turns out.

Your friend,

Danny

Just as he finished writing the note, folding it, and placing it in the envelope Francis and Gardett walked back into the store. They were laughing and appeared to both be pleased with the brokered deal. They'd already unloaded the pelts and placed them in a small storage shed adjacent to the store.

"Say...vell my new vriends join me for supper?" Gardett asked with hope punctuating his heavy accent.

Realizing he was hungry, Danny quickly replied, "I'd love that! The smell of those vittles have been torturing me while I wrote this here note." He held up the letter to be mailed and handed it to Gardett.

"Splendid!" Gardett motioned to a nearby table and chairs, "Please...sit down and let me serve you."

Francis and Danny, unwilling to be rude and desiring to get to know their neighbor better, eagerly sat down. It didn't take long for Gardett to place three tin plates with a pile of steaming stew on each onto the table. He added warm bread and three mugs of beer to the victuals. Francis and Danny couldn't believe how delightful the food was. Was it because Gardett added a European flare to the dish, or maybe it was the beer that excited their taste buds? Maybe. But it was probably a mixture of both, added to the fact that they were eating food that wasn't prepared by their unrefined touch.

It was an enjoyable hour. Francis and Gardett did most of the talking, telling stories of Gardett's time at sea and Francis' years traveling, exploring, and trapping. Danny took it all in, respecting the experiences of the older men. Eventually, the discussion did turn to the Roberts Boys and the stolen mules and stock of goods. Gardett expressed his sympathy for Danny's situation but added that he didn't have any news to offer on their whereabouts. He'd never seen any men with a string of mules matching the description, although he did admit that at times so many men passed through his store that perhaps they just didn't stand out in his memory. He remarked that he'd try to be more cognizant, both to provide Danny with information and for his own safety.

Reluctantly, Danny and Francis had to venture home. The three men packed the bartered dry goods and supplies onto Mick and into sacks that Francis and Danny slung over their shoulders. They heartily shook Gardett's hand and vowed to come back soon for a visit. Gardett waved at the men as they walked away.

Their visit was good for all involved, and Gardett truly hoped they'd come back soon. Alone, once again, he went back into his store to prepare for his next customer...whenever that would be.

***

As winter began to set in, mining operations began to pick up in the Kern River Canyon. The flow of the river and all of the little creeks that fed into it decreased, and despite the frigid, miserable working conditions, sandbars and other areas of the river normally submerged were now accessible. Although the amount of gold that'd be dug out of the Kern River Canyon and the Greenhorn Mountains wasn't comparable to that pulled from the earth in the Mother Lode, it still put money into the pockets and strong boxes of the miners and merchants in the region. It also kept the Roberts Boys pursuing their path of crime.

Chapter 6
Death in a Saloon

—————◆·◆·◆·◆—————

"Get another whiskey over here, barkeep!" George shouted across the room from the table he was lording over. He was well on his way to a bender, and the aggression and verbal assaults he waylaid the three men around the table made the atmosphere thick and uncomfortable for all present. All, except for Harry, George, and a fairly new member of the Roberts Boys named Johnny.

To them, this was entertainment; this was their element and a zone of comfort. Even without their leader, the followers of Eli Roberts were filled with vitriol and a desire to intimidate those around them. Others feared them, and the Roberts Boys knew this. They relished this fact, and they did nothing to discourage the dread of others.

"You going to stare at those cards all night?" he taunted one of the men. "I mean...come on...what are you waiting for? You want some cards?"

The man sitting across the table from George had beads of sweat forming on his brow. The temperature outside was in the thirties, and the drafty room of the saloon provided shelter from the elements outside, but it was still chilly enough for the men inside to wear their coats. The sheen of sweat was a nervous reaction, an apprehension of what was to come.

The day started simple and pleasant. He and his companions desired a break from working the frigid waters of the Kern River. Like others, they'd plucked and panned enough gold to make a living, but they were hardly wealthy. Their hard work was barely paying off, but it was an honest living.

And as many a miner did, they had an urge to blow off some steam. A hot meal, a bottle of booze, and an afternoon of gaming was what was in order. And it was a grand time...until three members of the Roberts Boys showed up. George barged his way into their friendly game of five-card draw, while Harry and Johnny lingered off to the side to watch and drink.

George was a decent card player, and without cheating, he was capable of drawing his fair share of lucky cards. He also possessed the ability to bluff his way to a winning hand.

But George's true aptitude for winning wasn't in his skill, it was in his penchant for intimidation. When he was winning, he taunted. When he lost, he made veiled threats and threw fits. His whim at the table was what mattered; the gaming was over when he said it was over.

And if his demeanor wasn't enough to cause unwilling players to maintain their positions at the table, the hovering of Harry and Johnny made them think twice about not only departing the game but also taking leave of this world permanently. Most men reluctantly chose to stay.

The man near George was holding three kings, a seven, and a two in his hand. Potentially, it was a winning hand. But to win in this situation might, in fact, be a losing proposition.

"I...I'll take two," the man stammered and tossed the two and the eight cards toward George. His friends both tossed three and four cards respectively toward George, less out of a desire to get better cards and more out of avoiding a verbal thrashing.

George distributed the required cards and took two of his own. Looking at the cards in his hand, he saw that he held a pair of tens. George looked around the table, trying to read the faces of the other men. Consternation. Concern. Pondering. That's what he saw.

"Your bet, lucky!" George barked at the man to his left. One after another, the three other men declined to raise the stakes.

"Check."

"Check."

"Check."

"You cowards," George said in a disgusted manner. "How can you even call yourselves men? Why, Sonorans and Celestial heathens have more guts than you! Sandwich Islanders, too! Hell...them Digger squaws are more manly than you sons of bitches!"

George tossed a ten-dollar gold piece into the pot, causing the other players to curse and groan to themselves. One of the players folded, causing George to kick his chair, almost knocking it, and the man in it, over. The other two men tossed in their gold pieces with trepidation.

"Let's see 'em!" George said with a smile on his face as he fanned out his cards revealing the pair of tens.

With relief, the player to George's left laid out his cards. He had nothing. All that was left was the man with the three kings...and a pair of fives that he picked up with the draw. It was a no-win situation. If he folded, he would draw wrath. But to win might be worse. His shaking hands displayed a winning full house.

"Ain't you a peach!" George shot to the winner, throwing his cards at the man. "Get your winnings...go on...take it!"

The man was confused. Should he pick up the money? Should he leave it? George settled the confusion by shoving the pot toward the winner. He drank down the last of his whiskey and lifted his glass toward the saloon keeper.

"George," Harry chuckled as he spoke, "take it easy on the boys...you can't win them all." He grew tired of hanging around the saloon and felt the desire to chase his primal urges.

"Well, I'm gonna go pay a visit to Molly up in Hogeye." Harry looked at the other poker players around the table.

"Say...don't let George there scare ya...he's usually harmless." He laughed at that thought as he walked toward the door.

"George...Johnny...see you back at camp."

And with that, Harry went outside, mounted his horse, and headed north farther into the valley.

George scooped up the cards in front of him and tossed them in front of the player to his left. "Your deal."

The men settled in for another round of testing George's temper, hoping he'd grow tired of the game before they ran out of money, luck, or a combination of both. It just wasn't their day.

***

"It might not look like much right now, but when that snow begins to melt in the high country…woo boy!" Francis said with wide eyes to emphasize the truthfulness of his claim.

"That trickling river turns into a frothy torrent of power! It can be a real bugger!"

Danny looked at the calm, lackadaisically flowing river up and down, admiring the steep gorge and smooth boulders cut by the water over ions of time. He stepped down off the bank and onto the sandy shoreline, crouched down, and placed his left hand into the water of the Kern River. It didn't take long until numbness overcame the warmth of his hand and a tingling sensation of pain radiated from his fingertips toward his palm. That water was cold, and it reminded him of his short time as a miner in the Gold Country to the north.

Mining was a miserable occupation, compounded by the fact that processing dirt for gold is often most productive during the winter months when water levels in the creeks and rivers were lower, allowing men to access gold-bearing gravel that was otherwise submerged throughout the rest of the year. Men toiled and bore the chances of hypothermia to make a living. They did this wherever there was a chance to find that yellow mineral and satisfy their lust for wealth. That is what drove men far to the north. It is also what attracted the large number of men accumulated along the Kern River.

Originating 13,600 feet above sea level from snowmelt and several small lakes in the Southern Sierra Mountains near Mt. Whitney, the Kern River flows south for about 164 miles. Both branches, the North Fork and the South Fork, joined together in the Kern River Valley and began its descent toward the San Joaquin Valley. After passing through the Kern River Valley, the river cascades through a rugged canyon carved by the erosive power of the water, as well as by the tectonic forces produced by the Kern River Fault that runs the length of the canyon. The river, at times appearing deceptively calm, is anything but that. Rapid currents, slippery rocks and boulders, undertows, and underwater obstructions proved the undoing of many a person. There is a reason why the river is referred to as the "Killer Kern."

On John C. Fremont's third expedition that took him and his entourage through the domain of the Kern River, Fremont gave the waterway its name. As the legend goes, his topographer, Edward M. Kern, misjudged the swift current of the river and nearly drowned. In honor of his service to Fremont and in recognition of not dying, Fremont ceremoniously dubbed the river the "Kern River."

This was the moniker that stood the test of time, but it wasn't the only name the river has gone by. Tubatulabal Indians, the original inhabitants of the Kern River Valley, called the North Fork the Palegewanap ("place of the big river") and the South Fork the Kutchibichwanap Palap ("place of the little river"). In 1776, Father Francisco Garces, a Franciscan, entered the San Joaquin Valley from the Tehachapis and traveled north. After following a Yokut Indian trail on the eastern side of the valley he soon encountered a raging river that he named "Rio de San Felipe." And later, in 1806, Padre Zavidea journeyed to the river and renamed it "La Porciuncula."

As California transitioned from the Spanish to the Mexicans to the Americans, the river continued to flow. The name applied to the river in the American period...the name engraved on maps...became the officially accepted title.

Danny stood up and stretched his back. It had been a long day that began early. Both he and Francis spent the morning packing two deer they'd killed, gutted, and skinned the previous day down the Greenhorn Trail to the mining camps along the Kern. Their mission was two-fold—sell the meat to eager buyers who were hungry for fresh protein, and look over the mules and supplies that Albert and James believed were from the J. Kinney Freighting Company. Mick made transporting the meat the ten or so miles from Francis' cabin relatively easy. It'd be the hike back up the trail that would be arduous. Until then, the two men focused on their task at hand.

It wasn't difficult to find willing buyers of the deer meat. They sold a hind quarter in the first camp, a whole deer in the second camp, and various portions in two other camps. Gold in hand and unencumbered by the meat, Francis and Danny felt free to search out the encampment containing his mules and supplies.

The directions supplied by James and Albert were easy enough to follow, and it wasn't long before they found themselves staring at three mules with the JK brand on their right rump. There was no doubt at all; these were some of the mules that were taken by the Roberts Boys. Mules that belonged to Danny and his company. Mules that were unlawfully taken.

Locating the mules was one thing. Getting them back could be a complicated process. Danny could plead and explain to the men in the camp that he was the rightful owner of the mules until he was blue in the face, but from the perspective of the men, they purchased the stock fair and square. They didn't know Danny, and as far as they were concerned, he may be a scam artist. It would require diplomacy, a delicate approach to the topic at hand, and a willingness of the fellows to be relieved of their acquired property.

"How goes it there, gentlemen?" Danny inquired as he approached the four men gathered around a small campfire while eating their dinner. Their meal was probably made of supplies they bought from the Roberts Boys, too; supplies that were intended to be delivered to Mr. Parker's agent in Keyesville.

The men eyeballed Danny, Francis, and Mick and concluded that they were there on friendly terms.

"Going well enough," the man who appeared to be the leader of the group stated between bites of cornbread. "Me and the boys are just catching a bite to eat and tryin' to ward off this damn chill that's grippin' the bones."

"Care for a nip?" Francis asked as he gestured to the jug of whiskey secured to Mick's trappings.

"Mister...it'd be mighty rude of us not to accept," the head man said through the upturned smile on his face.

Francis retrieved the jug, pulled the cork, took a snort, and then passed the jug along to the men in the camp.

"Whew! That's stout, friend!" one of the men exclaimed as one by one the men partook in the libation. They were all appreciative of the gesture, for it warmed their insides and was a neighborly thing for Francis to do.

They all made small talk—the weather, the river, the number of men along the canyon, how their claim was panning out—all part of the intricate dance leading up to the topic of the mules.

Motioning toward the mules, Danny felt it was now or never. "Mighty fine mules you have there."

"Thanks...some fellows came through a while back...maybe a month or two ago...and gave us a dandy deal," the head man offered. "Said they only needed them to haul some supplies over the Trail and into the valley...that they were more of a burden to them now...even sold us some bacon and beans."

"Hard to turn down a fair deal," Danny said as he took off his hat and rubbed the top of his head. He was nervous.

"These men...one of them 'bout my height, shaved head, and bad teeth? Maybe had two other fellows with him?" Danny inquired.

The men in the camp looked at each other and nodded. "Yes sir...that'd be them...seems you have a keen interest in them fellers."

"That might be an understatement," Danny grimly stated as he looked firmly into the eyes of the leader of the group. "Them men stole those mules and a shipment of goods from me...killed a friend of mine, and damn near did me in, too."

Danny adjusted the collar of his coat, revealing the still-visible rope burn around a portion of his neck. "They strung me up from a tree...if it hadn't been for the intervention of what I assume to be God, then I'd be done. Francis here came along and found me...brought me back to health."

"Now wait a minute here," the man defensively said, "we had no part of that...didn't even know 'bout that! We paid ninety dollars for that stock, and some twenty dollars for the bacon and dry goods."

"Relax, friend," Danny said as he lifted his hands to show his palms and diffuse the situation, "I ain't like them boys...it never crossed my mind to steal them long ears from you like they done to me. I aim to pay you fair and square. And them goods...well, nothing I can do 'bout that."

The men seemed relieved but still perplexed over the predicament. They were hard-working people, not cut from the same cloth as the Roberts Boys. Just hearing how the mules and goods were a product of an ambush and lynching made them feel physically ill.

"I hope that's fine with you men," Danny stated, but it sounded more like a question. "But what'd help me out a great deal is if you knew anything about those men...did they sell anything else to folks around here? Did they give any indication as to where they were heading? Any news of them would...."

"Hell, mister," one of the men in the group interrupted, "I just saw two of them fellers 'bout three hours ago down at the gamblin' house in Keyesville!" He pointed upriver as he continued his statement, "Just shy of a mile up that way."

"You don't say!" Danny exclaimed. He adjusted his hat and thought hard.

Surprised to hear this, Danny quickly contemplated his options. The slow burn of anger and justice grew hot within. He was eager to track down, not only his stolen stock but the Roberts Boys. It was difficult to let the opportunity slip away for the sake of safety.

"I'm much obliged for that information. If you don't mind, hold on to the mules and I'll come back for them soon."

Danny walked over to Mick and retrieved his shotgun. He looked to Francis and plainly stated, "I'll be back in a while." And with that, Danny set his bearings in the direction of Keyesville with a determined gait.

Francis called to Danny and pleaded with him to stop and talk. His words had no impact.

***

"You see this, Johnny? This boy here thinks he's got a winnin' hand?" George said with a snide tone in his voice.

He spit on the floor, reached for his glass that was nearly empty of whiskey, and then tossed back the remainder of the intoxicating liquid. George was heavily buzzed, the rot-gut whiskey clouding his mind and turning his normally bad temper even more disagreeable. His verbal barrage and body language, added to the kicking of chairs and throwing of cards, kept the other three players at the table on edge.

Johnny was a relatively new addition to the Roberts Boys, another one of the outcasts from society who periodically came and went from the gang. There wasn't much special about this man in his early twenties. He'd been in trouble back in his home state of Ohio, was kicked out of a company heading to California at the height of the Gold Rush for stealing and selling company supplies, and was run out of Visalia for his part in a shoot-out with some local boys over a horse that went missing. As with many individuals over the years, he gravitated toward the dark charisma of Eli Roberts, and he found a home...maybe for the long term...with a group of like-minded creatures bent on doing no good.

Johnny chuckled, "You're too much, George!" He, too, had consumed quite a bit of that tempered-down booze. Many a saloonkeeper in rural locations increased the amount of whiskey they had on hand by cutting genuine products with water, turpentine, cayenne pepper, and even gunpowder. It wasn't uncommon for homemade whiskey to also be offered that was comprised of raw alcohol, burnt sugar, and tobacco to add coloring; a truly devilish concoction that could blind, eat away at the stomach or just plain make a man ill. Surely, it gave customers a kick, but to consume any great quantity required an iron gut and a constitution bent on self-destruction.

"My belly done had its fill of that firewater," Johnny slurred to George. "I'm a steppin' out to the privy and then for some fresh air to clear my mind."

"Whatever you want, Johnny-boy," George called to his compatriot as he watched Johnny walk out the back door of the saloon.

He loudly tapped his glass on the table and hollered over to the keep, "I'm dying of thirst over here...do I have to kill a man to get a drink?"

The saloon keeper, a man by the name of Scotty, rushed over to the table with a bottle, half-filled George's glass with that firewater, and politely waited for payment. George looked at the glass, held it up, and slightly shook it to indicate that he expected it to be full. Scotty shook his head in disbelief as he filled the glass and then held out his hand. George tossed two bits into the air, which was adeptly caught by Scotty. He walked away muttering his disgust with the ruffian. George paid for his drinks, but he slowed down business by either driving other paying customers away when they discovered he was there, or unfortunate men found it necessary to moderate their drinking to save money and keep their tongues in check.

Once again, the men around the table laid down their cards to reveal what they were holding. And, once again, George had a winning hand.

"Woo hoo, boys! Looky my luck there! I suppose I'm just the winning kind. No offense meant, but you all aren't much fun! Grim faces and your sour countenance...I'm starting to think you fellas don't like me much!"

He said this to the men as he raked in his winnings. He laughed, gathered together the cards, began to shuffle them, and said, "Looks like it's my deal again."

The men around the table looked at each other. They didn't want to be there. Instead of spending a relaxing afternoon in the saloon, away from their claim, it had turned into an exercise of playing with fire, getting burned, and then pretending to like it to stave off further persecution.

With cards shuffled and a reluctant ante correct, George began to deal cards in a clockwise fashion. One after another, five cards in total. Even with a mind that was dulled by whiskey, George's fingers followed a familiar muscle memory as the cards slid off the top of the deck. But muscle memory can take you only so far. He still had to concentrate as he counted out the correct number of cards for each player. His attention was drawn to the task at hand, so much that he didn't hear the heavy, determined steps heading in from the front door. He didn't comprehend why the three players at the table suddenly scattered, springing to their feet leaving chairs, cards, and money in their wake. He didn't see the butt end of the shotgun cutting through the air until the last moment when he turned his head to the right.

The impact of wood against flesh; solidity versus tissue-covered bone. It was no contest. The momentum, coupled with a combination of anger, adrenaline, and revenge lust, drove the stock of Danny's shotgun into the right side of George's jaw with a degree of force that was greater than necessary. The smack of the hand-crafted walnut audibly illustrated to those in the room the devastating nature of the strike. Caught off-guard, George's head involuntarily whipped quickly to the left, slightly spinning his upper body out of his chair and toppling him to the ground in a heap. George was unconscious before he hit the wood-planked floor.

The men in the room—the three poker players and the saloonkeeper—didn't know how to react. They were incredulous. One minute they were begrudgingly playing cards with their tormentor. The next, a man they'd never seen before charged into the room, and, with vigor, turned George's world upside down.

"Lordy mister!" was all that one of the poker players in the room managed to say.

"Lord almighty! You picked a Hell of a hornet's nest to stir!"

With his statement, the flow of chatter in the room seemed to blend into a stream of questions and commentary on the situation, directed toward Danny at one moment, and to nobody in particular the next.

"Is that boy dead? Sure looks to be!"

"Looks to be...maybe not."

"Surely earned it, though...rotten to the core."

"What're you planning on doing now?"

"I'd leave right quick if I were him!"

"I'd never have the guts to do that from the start."

"Not with his temperament and who he runs with!"

"That's a fact!"

"Is he dead?"

"Naw...I think I see him breathing."

"That's a shame...."

"Where'd his friend take off to? Better watch for him."

"Out back to the privy and for some air."

"Could be a problem...they could all be a problem!"

"Say...what's your name, stranger?

Danny stood there, his fingers tightly wrapped around his shotgun, and his gaze transfixed upon George's body that was piled into a heap next to an overturned chair and the poker table. He could see George's shallow breathing, his chest slowly rising up and down. And he heard the men in the room talking and asking questions, but he wasn't listening. They were of no interest to him, as long as they weren't a hostile threat. Their actions revealed their neutral nature in this situation., so Danny ignored the other men in the room. His focus and his concern were first and foremost the task at hand. Asking George questions and getting answers. But most of all, he wanted justice, whatever that was and however it was meted out.

The men in the room were in a quandary. They didn't want to be here if George's friends came back. That wouldn't be a good situation, and they were bound to take out their anger and revenge on anybody and everybody. The Roberts Boys weren't too particular about making sure punishment was dealt to the correct party. The thing about dealing out pain and suffering, even if the right party isn't targeted, a message is sent. Men will stay in line, and a healthy fear will develop and continue to grow.

So, the men around Danny fought an internal tug of war, individually and collectively, about whether to stay or leave. To leave could be the difference between life and death for themselves. At the very least, it could save them a great deal of trouble and damage. But on the other hand, they had the desire to see how this situation played out. George had ruined their day and was a source of consternation. He was as unpleasant as a fellow could be, and this stranger had dealt George quite the surprise. Their curiosity was building, but so was the window of opportunity for them to escape in one piece.

Although it felt like a long time had passed, truly, it was only a matter of minutes. And their predicament, whether to stay or go, was a matter that was resolved for them as George began to slowly stir and emit a low groan. There was no way they were leaving now. This drama was about to enter the second act as George coughed once, sending a misty spray of blood onto the ground.

Danny stood at George's feet and waited for him to come to. He aimed his shotgun in George's direction, both as a sense of security, as well as a message to George that he meant business. It was hard to imagine that the butt-end to George's face didn't already make that clear.

"Aww! Wha...what the Hell?" George muttered.

He grimaced in pain and spit out a combination of blood and several broken molars. He was pretty sure that his jaw was fractured. As he regained his senses, his eyes rolled around in their sockets and began to scan the room. There was the man behind the rough-hewn bar craning his neck to peer down at George. And then the men he was playing poker with...meek men all. And then he perceived that a man was standing at his feet. George turned his head toward the man, and his eyes bulged with the realization that a dead man stood above him with a shotgun trained on his chest. A dead man, except he was there.

For a moment, George believed that he might be hallucinating. That man was swinging from a tree by the neck until he was lifeless! For sure, he was dead when the branch broke and he fell to the ground. But even if he wasn't dead, he was trussed up and would have succumbed to the elements or some wild beast. Yet, here he was. Alive. Flesh and bone, a determined look on his face, and the business end of a shotgun aimed at George.

George laughed and spit out more blood. His laugh was a cross between incredulity and hysteria, and he sounded like a madman.

"Boy," George said in mid-laugh as he settled his head back on the floor and stared at the trusses that held up the roof of the saloon, "you just don't know when to quit!"

Danny wasn't amused and he was hardly in the mood to ponder his tenacity with George. "Where's Eli and your friend Harry?"

George ignored Danny's question and pursued a tangent.

"I mean...look at you! You was dead last I seen you." Again, he interrupted his statement with a burst of laughter.

"Where's your camp, George? You men have to pay for what you've done," Danny stated.

His words were full of confidence, but he was a bundle of nerves within.

George lifted his head, glared at Danny, and yelled, "I don't owe you a thing! Hell, we don't owe you anything!"

Incensed, Danny, in turn, yelled back, "You men killed my friend! You nearly lynched me but for the grace of God! You stole my string of mules and all of the goods to be delivered to a merchant, and I suspect you killed him, too!"

As Danny shouted, the shotgun in his hands slightly thrust forward little exclamation points. He was in control of his emotions, but Danny started to feel as though his temper was now driving his actions.

"That's what this is about?" George almost sounded like he was truly surprised. "You're sore over that? It was just business, boy!"

He laughed, and the sound was that of defiance.

Danny had the incredible urge to just kill George. It would be easy. His taunting, his cockiness, and his general dismay over his current situation drove Danny to the edge. But Danny wasn't like them; he didn't want to be like them. No, he wanted to bring them to justice. Danny wanted to stop their savagery. However, that was the problem. He'd need to find the men involved like he found George, and then he'd have to detain them for authorities. That prospect made sending them to their maker seem more appealing and practical. That wasn't in Danny's true nature, though.

"George, your time's up," Danny calmly said. "Tell me where the others are. Don't make me kill you. I want to turn you and the Roberts Boys over to the law, give you a fair trial. It's the right thing to do."

Those words seemed to increase the boldness within George.

"The law!" George spit. "Look around you boy! Have you seen any constables? Marshalls? Rangers? Courts? Hell, boy...you're on your own and you're in over your head!"

He paused and then finished with, "Why don't ya just turn around and disappear to where ya came from before it's too late?"

George had a vile grin on his face as he finished his words.

It was what Danny feared most, that George wouldn't take him seriously and cooperate. He wasn't completely surprised, so the disappointment wasn't complete. Men like George and the Roberts Boys aren't given to surrender when the numbers are in their favor or there's a chance for escape.

Danny figured this is what it feels like for enforcers of the law every time they face their quarry. He didn't revel in the feeling, but in a way, it was also comforting. He might not have to deal with the logistics of capture, detention, and transport if George resisted. In the end, Danny's base instinct of retribution might be satisfied.

"That ain't gonna happen, George!" Danny firmly concluded, attempting to maintain control of the situation. "I'm taking you in. I might have to drag you to Visalia, or Stockton, or even Sacramento...but I'm taking you in. And if it takes me the rest of my life, I'll bring the rest of the Boys in, one by one if I have to!"

George began to edge his hand toward the Colt tucked into the front of his pants. Danny made a tactical mistake not noticing the handle when he had the chance to disarm George when he was unconscious. It was a mistake that he couldn't afford to make again.

"You ain't taking nobody in...as far as I see it, you won't see nightfall."

"Be smart, George! It's over for you...it's no use! You best back that hand away from that revolver!"

"Boy...you haven't the guts to stop me," George said between clenched teeth as he continued the motion toward his Colt.

"George...don't make me kill you! It doesn't have to be this way!"

Danny's words sounded more like a plea, than a demand. George's actions now commanded the situation. There was no chance that Danny could disarm George.

George had nothing, in his opinion, to lose. If, by some miracle, Danny was able to take him into the law, he'd be convicted and sentenced to hang. If he was able to draw his Colt, he might be able to secure his freedom and live another day. Or he might prove himself wrong and receive a load of buckshot from the shotgun that was aimed at his heart, and that would surely kill him. The decision was now up to George, and the outcome didn't look too bright.

"Leave here, boy...leave while you can." His hand was near to the handle of his revolver.

Danny stood his ground, strong and silent, and willing to let George write his fate. Whatever happened to George was now up to George.

"I'm going to enjoy killing you!" George said as he forced Danny's hand.

George's shoulder jerked as the tendons and muscles in his right arm tensed and sent his hand the last few inches to his beltline. He grabbed the handle of his Colt and pulled upward. George may have had a real chance to gain his freedom with the relative proficiency he had with his Colt, except for the fact that the hammer was caught on the heavy fabric of his trousers. There was no quick draw of the weapon, just an awkward tug and the realization that he sealed his doom.

Danny exerted several pounds of pressure on the trigger of his shotgun, eventually sending the hammer down to its resting place. The percussion cap struck steel, sending sparks down into the action, igniting the compacted load of gunpowder nestled deep within, creating a controlled explosion. The buckshot, propelled by the pressure from the ignited gunpowder, raced down the barrel and tore into George. It was no match—flesh and bone versus lead. George's body violently convulsed as the shot ripped through his chest. He was dead within seconds.

The smoke from the charge of black powder hung thick and sweet in the air, as the deafening sound of the blast echoed temporarily throughout the small room and within the ears of the men who watched the scene unfold. Even though the men knew something was going to happen, they were, nonetheless, startled. They jumped at the sound, both because of its suddenness and ferocity. Recovering from the concussion, the men intermittently looked at George, Danny, and then each other. It wasn't long before they began a chorus of conversation.

"Hell's bells!"

"Oh...he's dead for sure!"

"Earned that one, he did!"

"Rightly so...killed a man...almost two men!"

"Don't forget...stole his stock and wares."

"You had every right doin' what ya did! Justified, hundred percent!"

Full of amazement and good intentions, the men milled about and again talked amongst themselves, to Danny, and to nobody in particular. Their discussion was interrupted only by the sounds outside of horse hooves sprinting north away from the makeshift saloon. The men heard this sound, and it didn't take long before they made connections between the galloping of the horse and the dead body of George.

"Best watch your backside, friend...he had a friend here with him."

"More than likely was him that just rode off."

"They'll be gunning for ya for sure."

"If I was you, I'd take that Colt of his...you're gonna need it!"

"You earned it! Take his horse, too! Hell...his winnings are rightfully yours! Probably started out as your money!"

Danny listened to their chatter and took into consideration what was said. But it wasn't what was really on his mind. He killed a man. A man whose blood was now slowly soaking through clothing and dripping onto the floor of the saloon. Danny had never even pointed a weapon at another human being. Today was full of firsts. And the disturbing thing to Danny was that he felt no remorse. He didn't feel anything. George forced Danny's hand, and he would have killed Danny if he could have. If anything, George sealed his fate, and he earned it the hard way. George and the Roberts Boys started this war...Danny was going to finish it.

At first, Danny said nothing to the men. He reached down and twisted the Colt out of the waistband of George's trousers, and then rifled through George's pockets and claimed some caps, lead balls, and a small flask of powder for the revolver. He then grabbed a handful of the gold coins that were piled on the table, leaving a majority of them for the trio of poker players to recover.

Danny turned toward the barkeep standing behind the rough-hewn boards that divided the customers from the owner and calmly walked over. He leaned against the bar and motioned with his hand to Scotty, a universal signal that the barkeep had seen time and again. Scotty grabbed his cleanest glass, one of the fancy ones he had too few of, placed it in front of Danny, and then poured him a few fingers of his best stock.

"It's on the house, friend," Scotty stated to Danny.

Danny reached out and grasped the glass with a steady hand, raised it to his lips, and then sipped the strong, caramel-colored whiskey. It tasted rich and slightly spicy, and it burned his throat as he swallowed. But it was good, and the warmth that spread from Danny's insides to his outer shell was pleasant.

"Thank you," Danny spoke for the first time. He glanced over his shoulder at George's body on the floor. "Sorry about that...I don't mean to bring trouble to you folks."

"Well...perhaps we should thank you for relieving the world of that parasite. Trouble is...there's more of them!" Scotty finished his sentence by replenishing Danny's glass with whiskey.

"That's just the thing I'm after...those men," Danny said firmly. "They need to pay...they'll be held for what they've done."

Danny thought about that prospect for a moment, and then asked Scotty, "Do you know where their camp is?"

He looked at the other men in the room and asked the same.

Scotty shook his head, as did the other men. "Best I figure is they are holding out somewhere to the north, but if you don't mind my saying, and if you're in the mood for some advice, you should just get on that man's horse and ride away...ride as far and as fast as you can away from this place and their hatred."

"That ain't gonna happen," Danny said as he shook his head. "This is something that I need to do...for me, and for my friend. It's the only way I'll be free."

He finished the last drops of liquor from the glass, set it down, and then covered it with his hand indicating he was done drinking.

Scotty corked the top-end bottle of whiskey, turned, and placed it in a safe place. He scratched his head as if he was baffled by what Danny was saying. It didn't seem like this man could be reasoned with.

"Well, at the very least, you should get a better plan than this..." Scotty started and was interrupted in his thought by a man who shuffled, out of breath, through the south-facing door.

The man looked at the body on the floor, glanced at the men milling about, and then focused on the barkeep and Danny. He rushed up to Danny, who turned to see Francis with a face full of alarm and concern.

"Boy!" Francis started. "Looks like you're in deep now! We need to get out of here!" He said as he began to pull on the sleeve of Danny's coat.

"I can't...I have to find them!" Danny half shouted at Francis.

Francis grabbed Danny by both shoulders and violently shook Danny for a second. "Don't be a damn fool! It's not the time, nor the place! Get yourself a better plan, Danny! Come on, boy...let's go home. Let's get a better plan."

Danny respected Francis, and he knew Francis had experience that could be trusted. Reluctantly, he relented. Danny gathered himself and tipped his hat to the men in the room as he walked toward the door. Scotty reminded Danny about the horse. Before he left the saloon, he looked back one last time at George. A slight smile appeared on Danny's face. He felt a sense of relief. He felt no regret.

***

By nightfall, Danny and Francis made their way back up the trail from Keyesville to the cabin in the little meadow. They placed Mick, the string of mules Danny recovered and paid for, and George's chestnut-colored horse from the saloon into the corral. After the animals were unencumbered—bridle, saddle, and blanket removed from the horse, and the sawbuck packsaddles removed from the mules—a morral, also called a nose bag, was temporarily placed on each to feed them.

With the gear stowed, animals brushed, and the new editions to the corral appeared to be settled in for the night, Danny and Francis retired to the cabin.

Francis and Danny fed themselves and sat in front of the hearth, warming their cold bodies with the growing fire and the occasional sip of whiskey. They reviewed their day, focusing on the confrontation Danny had with George. As they talked, Francis listened to Danny's plan to go after the rest of the Roberts Boys. It wasn't a bad plan, but it wasn't great, either. Danny was outnumbered, outgunned, and out of his element. But, if Danny became the *hunter* and treated the remaining Roberts Boys as *prey*...well, his chances became better. They became even better if he accepted Francis' offer to help. However, Danny didn't want to risk his friend's life.

As the evening wore on, their desire for sleep increased. Tomorrow was the beginning of a new day, and possibly, an end to the Roberts Boys and their reign of terror. There was always a chance that it wouldn't turn out well for Danny, but that was a chance he was willing to take. Danny stoked the fire and then crawled into his bedroll on the ground before the hearth. He closed his eyes and was asleep in no time at all.

***

Hours earlier, Johnny entered the Roberts Boys' camp at a brisker pace than usual. Both he and his horse were tired, and it was obvious that Johnny was distressed and anxious. He dismounted, tied the lead of his horse to a small tree, and then went to find Eli, which was part of the reason why he was so high-strung. On a good day, Eli was sociable toward his men, but he could turn at the drop of a hat. Part of the reason they were so loyal and willing to comply with orders was the fact that they feared the repercussions of not doing so. This was one of those situations where Eli's temper could be unpredictable.

It didn't take long to find Eli. The camp, in contrast to their site high up on the ridges of the Greenhorn Mountains, consisted of three log cabins. Originally, it belonged to a company of miners, but with a little bit of encouragement and intimidation, Eli and his men convinced the miners that they were better off moving along. It didn't hurt that the nearby creek was played out and Eli offered them a small amount of money for their camp. Then again, the miners valued life more than their temporary homes.

Johnny opened a door to one of the larger cabins and saw Eli sitting in a chair with his feet propped up on a pine round. He was eating biscuits and beans, and drinking hot, black coffee tempered down with sugar. Eli was in conversation with one of his men named Jacques.

"I disagree," Eli stated. "These red kidney beans are much better than those pinto beans."

Jacques shook his head and interjected in a soft French accent, "Could be, but it's all in how they're cooked. Take these here red beans...straight from the can and cooked with bacon...everything's better cooked in bacon."

"Jacques...That's a good point. Maybe it's bacon that's the key...."

Johnny interrupted, "Eli...I gotta talk with ya!"

Eli looked at Johnny and then maintained his conversation with Jacques.

"This here cornbread...oh boy! Warm and smothered in butter. Not much to debate about that!" Eli said as he savored a bite.

Jacques nodded his head, "Cornbread is new to me. It is quite agreeable."

Johnny took a step closer toward Eli and, once again, inserted himself into the conversation.

"Pardon me, Eli...but I have something urgent that needs addressing!" Johnny plead.

Eli's good mood soured quickly. He set his tin plate down on the wood round as he stood up to dress down Johnny for disturbing a pleasant moment. His temperament bordered on turning into a tempest.

"Now, what's so damn important? Me and Jacques here was having a nice talk over some grub!"

Nervous and with no better way to tell Eli, Johnny blurted out, "We was down at Keyesville and someone shot George...he...he's dead!"

"Dead?" Eli questioned. "You sure?"

Johnny swallowed hard and continued, "I stepped outside the back of Scotty's Saloon for some air, then I heard a gunshot...I was a bit confused as to what was going on, but I took a quick look back inside the saloon and saw George on the ground...dead."

Anger swelled within Eli. George was a long-time friend and ally. And now, supposedly, he was dead at the hand of someone else. Eli quickly swung his arm at Johnny catching the side of his face with a backhand. The slap made a sharp sound and left a mark on the side of Johnny's face. The pain was sudden and unexpected, and tears welled in Johnny's eyes. He wanted to hit Eli back, but he was smarter than that.

"Why didn't you help him...you just left him there?" Eli yelled.

Johnny tried to defend his actions, stating "I didn't know what to do...I...I was drunk and wasn't sure how many of them were in there. So, I ran to my horse and high-tailed it to the camp. Please, Eli," Johnny stammered, "I just didn't know what to do!"

Eli grabbed Johnny with a hand on either side of his head. He looked away, took a deep breath, and then sighed as he looked Johnny in the face.

"Somebody needs to get his body, but it ain't gonna be you! You already failed George once. It's not gonna happen again! Besides...folks there know who you are. Go get young Will and bring him here!" Eli let go of Johnny's head and finished, "Don't disappoint me again, Johnny...never again!"

"I won't," was all that Johnny could manage. He composed himself and then dashed out of the cabin in search of Will.

"God damn kid!" Eli said to Jacques as he picked up his plate of food and sat back down. He took a bite of cornbread and beans, chewed it for a minute, and then swallowed. "Maybe pintos are a better bean, Jacques."

Five minutes later, Johnny returned with a lanky teenager who had collar-length hair. The boy was a fairly new arrival in the group, not yet trusted nor tested.

Eli glared at Johnny and then looked to Will, stating, "In the morning...first light, you're riding down to the saloon there in Keyesville. George is dead. I want ya to find out who killed him. Then, you're going to get George's body, pack it on a horse, and then bring him back to camp."

"Yes sir," Will replied.

"Try not to let me down, boy! Now you both get out of here!"

Johnny and Will left, and business returned to usual, but George and the mystery man weren't far from the back of Eli's thoughts.

Chapter 7
An Unpleasant Task

———————◆◆◆◆◆———————

E arly morning was Danny's favorite time of the day. The morning air was crisp, clean, and damp. On this particular morning, a heavy frost spread across the ground and sparkled like millions of crystals as the morning sun slowly climbed in the sky. It was at this time of the day that the world was coming alive, and with it, new possibilities and opportunities presented a chance to start over, again and again. The birds, squirrels, and other animals began their chatter and daily chores turning the quiet, dark night into a daybreak bustling with life. Nature had a way of reminding the world that God was present everywhere. It made Danny feel alive.

This morning was different, though. Danny was awake, enjoying a hot cup of coffee. And he took pleasure in the awakening world, but he had other matters on his mind. It was a day unlike any other he'd experienced. Today, he faced the very real fact that he was going after the Roberts Boys. Yesterday, he killed George; the rest of the gang was now within his sights. Of course, he didn't know exactly where they were, but he at least had confirmation that they were in the Kern River Valley or the innumerable drainages and nooks and crannies that dotted the surrounding landscape. They were out there...somewhere. However, Danny wasn't going to find them sitting around Francis' cabin.

Not knowing how long he'd be gone, Danny tried to outfit himself for at least a week. Packed into saddlebags, Danny had a supply of jerky, biscuit, and coffee for himself, and some oats for his newly acquired horse. He also had some basic cooking implements, a couple of canteens, and plenty of shot, gunpowder, and caps for his shotgun and the Navy Colt he was now carrying. Added to all of this, Danny had a bedroll and an extra set of clothes. Relatively speaking, he was traveling light. What he sacrificed in comfort, he could make up for in speed of travel.

Francis watched as Danny readied himself. He hoped that he could talk Danny out of this foolishness, but it was useless. And when Francis stated that if Danny was intent on going after the Roberts Boys, he'd go along as well, it produced a relatively heated argument between the two men. Francis cared for Danny, and Danny couldn't bear the thought that Francis could be hurt or killed in a fight that wasn't his. Danny was adamant, and despite Francis' protestation, Danny was going alone and wouldn't have it any other way. Francis glared at Danny with a mixture of frustration, anger, and admiration.

Danny had one last thing he needed to do before he left. In the realistic chance that Danny met his demise, he wanted to make sure that his affairs were in order. It'd make no sense if his financial holdings and worldly possessions weren't passed on to his family. And it'd be crushing to his mother and father if he disappeared without a trace, leaving them ever-fearful of his condition and agonizing over his unknown fate. It was bad enough that he'd been gone from home for a few years, and his letter-writing home was sporadic at best. So, Danny sat down a moment to scribble out a letter to his mother.

Dear Ma,

If you're receiving this letter, then I have died. It wasn't how I wanted things to work out, but I have accepted that it was a possibility. In previous letters I told you about the Roberts Boys and how they harassed Stephen and I on our trek to California, and how we had another run-in with them in Sacramento. Well, I ran into them again far from Sacramento while running a string of pack mules to a place called Keyesville. They ambushed my pack train, killing one of my men and nearly lynching me. They hurt me pretty bad, but as if by a miracle, I survived. I know you and pa always said it was best to forgive your enemies, but this isn't something I can let go of. The longer those men are out there, the more people they can prey upon, and it'll remain a ghost that is chasing me. Please forgive me, and see it as my way to make the world a better place.

Now, since I'm gone, I have a stake in life that needs to be tended to. You, Pa, and Seth are due all that I have, which is a partnership in the J. Kinney Freighting Company, my personal effects, and all of the money I have in the bank. Just contact Jim Kinney in Sacramento, he'll do you right. As I've said before, he's one of the most honest and genuine men I've ever met. He has all the information you'll need locked up in the company safe in our office.

Once you've settled all my affairs, please make sure to send money to Francis Rutherford in care of Petersburg down near Keyesville. He's the only reason I'm still alive to write this letter. He, too, is a good man. He's a bit rough around the edges, but he has a heart for the weak, and a kind and gentle nature. His appearance would fool you.

Please, don't be consumed in grief. I came to California to find myself, and that is what I did. I mostly like what I found. I'm a man, and I hope I'm remembered as a good and honorable man.

With all my love, your obedient son,

Daniel

With that task complete, Danny was ready to move on. He sealed the letter and handed it to Francis, instructing him to post it to his folks if he died. Francis wasn't happy about the situation, but what could he do other than cuss and mutter his protestations? Danny was as strong-willed and pig-headed as Francis, and if the roles were reversed, Francis would probably do the same as Danny.

Danny shook Francis' hand firmly and thanked him for all that he'd done. He walked with Francis to his horse, took the reins into his left hand, and then mounted. Danny tipped his hat to Francis and began to trot toward the connection to the Greenhorn Trail.

"Keep your powder dry!" Francis yelled to Danny, "And don't go getting yourself killed!"

He looked at the letter in his hand and shook his head in disapproval as he walked back into his cabin. Francis tossed the letter down on his table, walked to the shelf built into the wall of his cabin, grabbed his jug of elderberry wine, and then sat down on his bed. He pulled the cork out of the jug with an audible pop and then took a healthy swig of the fermented concoction. Francis unconsciously grimaced as he swallowed, and exhaled breath that was a mixture of reluctant toleration of the wine, and surrender to his thoughts. As he went for a second drink he muttered to himself, "You damn fool!"

***

Will woke up with a downturned countenance. He wasn't happy about having to ride into Keyesville to retrieve George's body. It wasn't picking up the dead man that bothered him, he'd seen dead people before. At an early age, he and his family ventured on the Oregon Trail to claim a plot of fertile land in the Willamette River Valley. Every day, it seems, fellow travelers died of cholera and other maladies. And it wasn't long before his baby sister, and then his mother, and then his father also succumbed to illness. He was alone...orphaned at a young age and grudgingly taken in by a family who were less interested in the love they could give Will, and more enthusiastic about the extra set of hands they had access to around their tiny homestead.

No, carting George's body wasn't the issue. His problem was the fact that this was Eli's friend, Eli partly blamed Johnny for the death, and Eli warned Will not to let him down. In Will's estimation, that wasn't a good position to be in.

He was a relatively new member of the Roberts Boys; still proving himself; wholly expendable at any given point. It wasn't a situation that inspired comfort or security. He felt that his existence, at this point, was hanging in the balance. It was, in a way, like the Oregon Country all over again. The family that took him in only wanted him for as long as he was useful. Once his need for appreciation, compassion, and family outweighed his usefulness, they cut him loose. For a few years, he bounced around families and odd jobs, until the California Gold Rush drew him southward. Will was eighteen years old, and he longed for a home and a sense of belonging, even if it meant falling in with the likes of the Roberts Boys.

He grabbed a cup of coffee from the pot that Harry brewed over a small fire outside the cluster of cabins. As he drank the hot and bitter liquid, Will ate a piece of bacon and a slice of sourdough bread that was too hard for his liking, but it was all that he had at hand. With any luck, he would find something more hearty when he reached Keyesville. Almost anything would be better than this grub, and the sooner he left, the sooner he might fill his belly.

Will saddled his Palomino and tethered a long lead to an unsaddled grey-colored mare. It wouldn't matter to George if he was draped across the mare's back.

He also grabbed the only other item that he owned that was worth anything, a .54 caliber Harpers Ferry Model 1841 rifle-musket, also known as a Mississippi Rifle. At nine pounds, it was a bit cumbersome, so as he mounted he tended to carry his long gun in the crook of his elbow.

What with the reins in one hand, the lead to the trailing horse in his other hand, and the rifle balanced precariously in his arm, he was as awkward as he looked.

There was no real hurry to retrieve George's body, other than the reality that Eli sent him on this errand. But the truth of the matter was that George's body wasn't going anywhere. Will doubted that any of the folks in Keyesville wanted anything to do with the corpse, and he couldn't blame them. George was a wholly unpleasant individual.

When he got right down to it, Will didn't like George because of his repulsive nature. Come to think of it, Will wasn't sure he liked any of the Roberts Boys. He was used to working for what little he had in life. Nobody would have labeled him a thief or a bully, let alone a killer. Simply put, Will was a boy without a home, and he was blinded by Eli's charisma and power. Maybe this wasn't the life for him. Either way, he had a task to perform and he was on his way.

However, it didn't mean he couldn't enjoy his time. Despite the overcast and cold morning, the scenery was beautiful. As he followed the north fork of the Kern River as it flowed south at times, and then southeast and southwest, twisting and turning as it tumbled over boulders in a torrent, only to appear as a glassy sheen around the next bend, he was caught up in the beauty of the snowcapped mountains that were evident in every direction. The pine and fir trees on the sides of the granite-choked slopes were dusted with snow and ice up high in their crowns. As the slopes merged with hills that ran down to the river, the oak trees, bare of leaves, stood sentry among the patches of snow that hadn't melted. It was scenery like this that intrigued Will and made him think that he could put down roots here, amid this splendor.

Will traveled on, picking his way around rocks and brush, trees and patches of ice, down the trail toward Keyesville. He passed through several mining camps in varying degrees of occupation. There were tents, shacks, cabins, and a lean-to here and there. Most of the men in these camps were working on their various claims. However, there were some inhabitants tending fires, mending clothes, and completing chores that were a necessity. They didn't give Will much attention, other than the courteous nod of the head or tip of the hat. He was no threat to them; just a boy heading down the trail.

This was something that wasn't lost on Will. Their reaction betrayed the fact that Will wasn't associated with the Roberts Boys in the communities at large. Men recognized Johnny, and they were used to seeing him accompanying both George and Harry. Many miners also knew the face and reputation of Eli and Jacques. Even though Will didn't possess an aggressive nature, and he didn't conduct himself in the manner of the other Roberts Boys, there were people in Keyesville who'd give him a wide berth out of fear if they knew he was acting on behalf of Eli Roberts.

Eventually, the north fork of the Kern River spilled out of its canyon and flowed into the Kern River Valley, joining with the south fork to continue its journey toward the San Joaquin Valley in the west. It was before this junction that Will diverted his path to the southwest to skirt the encampment of the Tubatulabal Indians that was located where the two forks combined. They weren't hostile people, but Will felt it was best to avoid the group that, for the most part, just wanted to be left alone. Not everyone was as mindful in that respect toward the Tubatulabal.

Will continued to amble in the direction of Keyesville. He rode on the trail that hugged the seemingly infinite number of crags, gulches, canyons, and draws that ran down from the snaking ridges of the Greenhorn Mountains to the valley floor.

At times, the trail was relatively flat, only to climb a rise or drop into a depression. It was on one of the rises where Will looked out across the valley. In some places, the river ran wide, creating what could be called a marsh, while in others it was definitely bordered by banks that had been cut through earth and stone throughout the eons of time. Someday, Will thought, this place will be mighty good farmland once the lust for ore died away. It had potential.

The closer he got to Keyesville, the more mining claims dotted the landscape. Just like the gold fields up north, miners worked the gravel and sandbars in the river, dug earth in the seasonal creeks that trickled down gulches, and tested dirt from dry pits that were panned, washed in a cradle rocker, or ran through a long tom. It was an interesting sight to see; the manipulation of land and water amid the natural setting of the river, granite boulders, and oak and pine trees. Ambition motivated men to move mountains. In some cases, that seemed true, as evidenced by the deep scars left on the land.

A few hours after he left the Roberts Boys, Will approached Scotty's Saloon on the outskirts of Keyesville. He could see that it was business as usual at the establishment. Smoke was rising from the stone chimney, and patrons occasionally walked in and out of the door he could see. But what drew his attention was the small crowd gathered adjacent to the saloon. From his elevated position on horseback, Will saw that George's body was propped up on a series of wooden planks, probably a door that was repurposed for the moment. The body, cold and of a grey-blue hew, was displayed for all to see.

The crowd of gawkers talked amongst themselves and peered at the body. George, as well as the other Roberts Boys, were infamous to many in the mining region, so, seeing one of the men dead inspired a hope for the future. Before yesterday, the Roberts Boys appeared to be untouchable; capable of running amok and unfettered. But now? Well, the Roberts Boys could die or be killed just like any other person...as long as the right individual, with the right temperament, came along. Of course, nobody in the throng of people believed that they were capable of being the bringer of justice. But they wouldn't get in the way of someone else trying.

As the mass of onlookers noticed the approaching rider trailing an empty horse, the mixture of curiosity and cheer that collectively ran through the gathering of individuals turned to minor panic. They turned in twos and threes, moving off a short distance or leaving Scotty's Saloon altogether, not willing to be caught up in any trouble that may happen.

Will looked around and let the mood set in. There was a degree of unearned deference that others paid to him because of his new association with the Roberts Boys. Barely eighteen, the respect made him feel like someone important; made him feel like a man. However, it was a conflicted feeling that betrayed the fact that he was just a boy looking for a place in this world where he could belong and earn the accolades of others.

Will sighed, dismounted, and tied his horse to a post. He looked at the people standing around and nodded his head toward them in greeting before walking over to George's reclining body. Several men, seemingly caught off-guard, raised their eyebrows and either tipped their hats in turn or docilely raised a hand and slightly waved. Others looked behind them before realizing the salutation was aimed at them, became flustered, and then skedaddled.

Will looked the body over. George was dead, alright. Coins covered George's eyes, and a coarse blanket was draped over the gaping wound on the dead man's chest.

He frowned and shook his head as he thought about George and the fate that he bought through the choices he made. It was a hefty price, one that came with the life of a Roberts Boy.

There was only so long that Will was interested in looking over George's body, largely because hunger began to gnaw at his insides. He was, after all, still a boy growing into a man. And with the urge to eat, he made his way to the door of Scotty's Saloon.

As he neared the door, he heard scraping along with the plopping sound of something plunging into water. It was rhythmic and provoked Will's curiosity. He opened the door to see the proprietor of the saloon, Scotty, on his hands and knees scrubbing the blood-stained floorboards with a stiff-bristled brush. He briskly ran the brush across the stain five times, dunked the brush into a bucket holding warm, soapy water, and then continued scouring. Scotty's vigorous efforts gradually reduced the stain from a dark crimson patch of blood to what appeared to be a light stain that could have been anything. Will stood in the doorway watching with a feeling that this wasn't Scotty's first time performing this task.

"Come in or go out!" Scotty said as he interrupted his task and looked at Will. "Either way, shut the damn door...you're letting the heat out!"

"I...yes sir," Will stammered as he stepped inside, quickly shut the door, and took his hat off, holding it in his hands. He looked around the room to see a man sleeping at a table, and two other men sitting near a window reading a newspaper and drinking coffee.

Scotty returned to his labor only to glance at Will who was still standing in place like he was unsure of what to do next.

"Well...whatcha need, son?" Scotty said between scrubs.

Seeing an opening for conversation, Will jumped right in, asking, "Got any food?"

Scotty stopped his work and sat back on his heels. He wiped the sheen of sweat from his brow with his forearm.

Satisfied with his efforts to remove the last traces of George from his saloon, Scotty dropped the brush into the bucket of water, and slowly stood up. There was an audible sound of his joints popping as he straightened his knees.

"I ain't really opened, yet," Scotty said as he walked to the door, opened it, and poured the water out, careful not to dump the brush onto the muddy ground.

"This fellow," pointing at the snoring man at the table, "he never left last night...and those vultures," he said as he nodded toward the two men reading a newspaper, "snuck in early to drink my coffee and read the news out of Visalia."

"Now Scotty, it's hardly the news when it's two weeks old," one of the men sarcastically interjected.

"As soon as you start payin' for that there paper...then you can complain!" Scotty quipped. "Otherwise, you know what ya can do with that paper!"

The men mockingly grumbled and returned to their diversion, content to read the happenings of California that were, at best, close to a month old, and news from back east that was described as dreadfully delayed and hardly current.

Scotty returned his attention to the teenager standing before him, shuffling his feet due to what seemed like an uneasiness and insecure nature.

"Ya mind leanin' that rifle of yours over in the corner and having a seat, boy? No need for that in here," Scotty said as he unconsciously looked toward the faded stain on his floor as he walked behind his bar and set the bucket down.

He wiped his hands on a rag that passed for clean, and then placed his palms on the counter, leaning on it in a relaxed manner.

"Now, I'm open. What can I do for you?"

Complying with Scotty's request, Will stowed his rifle and pulled up to a chair at a table.

"I'd love some fried chicken...or maybe a steak," Will enthusiastically replied, letting his appetite drive his response.

"I would too, son!" Scotty replied with disappointment in his voice. "I've got eggs and salt pork."

"That'll do...please. And, maybe some coffee. I got money," Will said in a voice that was shy of confidence, but eager for what was offered.

Scotty eyeballed Will for a moment, reaching for something in his memory; something familiar.

"I know you from somewhere?" Scotty queried.

"I don't reckon so," Will cautiously replied.

Scotty turned and gathered together a cast iron frying pan, a few eggs, and a small lump of salt pork, saying, "No...I got a thing for faces, and I've seen your young mug at some point. Where abouts you from?"

Will became worried about the direction the conversation was beginning to turn, but he realized that honesty, to a point, was the best line of response.

"Well...I came down from the Oregon Country in 1850 and bounced around San Francisco, then Sacramento, Stockton, Visalia, and then found myself along the Kern a few weeks ago."

He turned in his chair as Scotty walked to the wood-burning stove nearby.

"I'm running errands for some men upstream."

"Men upstream?" Scotty asked as he began to fry the previously soaked salt pork. "What men?"

Will was now walking on the edge of anxiety. He knew the Roberts Boys had a reputation, one that was well-deserved. And he knew that some men would cut and run if they knew he was associated with them. The fact that one of the Boys was killed in this very saloon the day before might get Will tossed out of the door by his britches. He hoped that wasn't the case.

"Well...I...I'm doing some odds and ends for Eli Roberts and his camp," Will calmly answered, smelling the aroma of the pork as it began to sizzle.

Scotty fumbled the fork he used to turn the pork when he heard Will's response.

"That's where I've seen your face! Boy, what're ya doing with them?"

"It's a long story, sir," Will began. "I don't rightly know how to explain it, but I'm all alone in this world, and I needed some work...someplace to be...he ain't been bad to me."

Scotty turned toward Will as he continued to cook.

"Son...I'm gonna go out on a limb here, but you can do a lot better than fall in with them fellas." He swallowed hard as he spoke. "You don't seem like their type."

Somewhat ashamed, Will tried to explain his predicament—being orphaned, a drifter, wanting to belong, and how he was now caught in a rough spot.

Scotty fried the eggs as he listened, dished up the food for Will and himself, poured some coffee into cups, and then sat down across from Will to continue the conversation and eat breakfast.

Will spoke as he shoveled food into his mouth.

"You see, sir...that's the trouble I'm in. Eli sent me down here to retrieve that body and to find out who killed him."

"I see," Scotty said as he sipped coffee. "I suppose I can help ya with one of them things. When we're through here, I can help ya with that body. But there ain't much I can do for ya as far as identifying who shot that man."

Scotty thought it over for a moment and then continued.

"Seems to me that he knew that feller...but it also seems that Roberts Boy brought his demise upon himself."

Scotty went on to explain that George and the other Roberts Boys robbed the man, killed his friend, and tried to lynch him. He also relayed the fact that George forced the issue by going for his gun. The man was in his twenties, well-built, had a nearly-healed wound on his head and what appeared to be a burn mark on his neck. He carried a shotgun, and last Scotty knew, he had George's revolver and horse. Also, he was practically drug out of the saloon by an older man with a beard. That was all he could help with. As far as who he was and where he went, that was a mystery to Scotty.

The two finished eating and drinking coffee, and Will reached into his pocket to get some money to pay for his meal. Scotty held up his hand, refusing to take anything from Will.

"I want ya to know that there're good people out here...honest people who'll help you. Give yourself a chance, son."

Will shook Scotty's hand and expressed his appreciation for the food and advice. Will grabbed his rifle, and they walked outside. Scotty dispersed the small crowd around George's body as Will brought the spare horse over. Together, they lifted George's body onto the horse and tied it securely into place.

With the task that Eli ordered mostly accomplished, Will mounted his horse and prepared for the trip back to the Roberts Boys' camp. Will pulled the reins to the side to turn his horse toward the trail he needed, and he slowly headed away from the saloon.

Scotty watched Will slowly ride away. Before he got too far away, Scotty imparted one last thing.

"Boy! Remember...you can do better!"

Will looked back at Scotty, and with a smile on his face replied, "I'll keep that in mind!"

***

One hundred yards away from Scotty's Saloon, huddled on the side of a hill among boulders and a cluster of scrub oak, Danny watched the young rider leave the saloon while leading the horse carrying George's body.

Danny waited until he was sure the rider couldn't see him, mounted his horse, and then began to trail the rider.

Chapter 8
Hurry Up and Wait

———— ◆ ————

"**I**f I'd only stayed behind...then maybe...maybe George would still be alive!" Harry mournfully said as he sat around the small campfire in the center of the Roberts Boys' camp. He was George's closest friend, and the loss hit Harry especially hard.

"Don't beat yourself up over it...mistakes were made...we move on," Eli said as he looked toward Johnny with disdain in his eyes.

"But he was like a brother to me," Harry managed to say.

He was choked up and intermittently took swigs of whiskey to ease his sorrow. Eli walked over to Harry and grabbed the bottle out of his hands.

"You've had enough, Harry," Eli firmly stated. " I need ya to keep your wits sharp."

"I need to get drunk!" Harry slurred back with an edge to his voice.

Eli took Harry's chin into his left hand and moved Harry's face so he looked directly at Eli. The grip was uncomfortable for Harry, and he began to realize that Eli's patience was quickly fading.

"Drunk?" Eli paused. "Being drunk is what led to George's death. I've told you men...all of you...that you need to control yourselves! It's just fine to have a nip here and there...but to lose your sensibilities? That gives an edge to the other fella...the fella that hates you, and wants you dead because you took his belongings, or gave him a thrashing, or killed his friend, or whatever! You need to be smart! Now, drink some coffee and sober up."

Eli released Harry's chin, bent down, picked the cork up off the ground, placed it back into the bottle, and then tossed it to Jacques who placed it into a nearby cabin.

Johnny grabbed a cup and poured some coffee from a pot that had been brewing the strong elixir for several hours. He handed the cup to Harry, who took a sip of the steaming, murky liquid. It was hot and stout. A cup or two of that concoction would have Harry back into shape in no time at all.

The men continued to sit around the small fire, poking the glowing coals with sticks. The fire provided comfort from the cold. The sky was still crowded with dark clouds, adding a menacing tone to the already somber situation.

They talked about what their plans were. Harry wanted to ride down into Keyesville and shoot the place up. Johnny expressed his hope that the Roberts Boys would pull up camp and head to the desert where nobody knew their name. Jacques wanted to stay put, but he was perfectly happy to be anywhere. And Eli? He didn't tell the men what he thought at that moment. He was lost in his private thoughts as he took slow draws on a pipe and stared at the flickering yellow flames.

From outward appearances, Eli seemed to not have a worry in the world. But within, Eli battled a knot of conflict and uncertainty. He'd lost George, who was an obedient soldier. George was quite the dimwit, but he was dead now, so it didn't matter much. There were still three capable men under his control. And the kid, Will, who wasn't seasoned, and who Eli doubted as being the type of individual who'd fit in with the group. Either way, he was responsible for all of them as a leader.

At heart, Eli recognized that, ultimately, his top priority was himself. But being a leader and all, he had to at least feign concern for the Roberts Boys. Sometimes, Eli wished he could just quit this business and live a straight life. That was easier said than done. He was a wanted man back east, along the Overland Trail, and now out west. Maybe, Eli thought, his only place of refuge was in the south...or even farther south, down in old Mexico. Whatever happened, it'd probably need to wait until spring.

Eventually, talk around the fire turned to how long Will had been gone. He left that morning, and it was now late afternoon. The men hoped they'd get George's body back early enough in the day to give him a proper burial. They didn't relish the thought of having the body in camp overnight. In their estimation, the sooner he was in the ground, the better. It was the right thing to do.

Earlier in the day, Johnny was sent just outside the camp with a pick and shovel to dig a hole in the ground. He worked on the project for a few hours, chipping away at the frozen earth until it gave way to dirt that was easier to move. The trench ended up being about six feet long, three feet wide, and about four feet deep; large enough to be an adequate resting place for George. None of the men were carpenters, but Jacques and Harry were able to fashion a coffin of sorts out of spare lumber that was piled up behind one of the cabins. It was nothing fancy, and it looked more like a crate than a vessel for George's remains, but it'd do the job it was intended for.

It wasn't until the late afternoon when the day passed to early evening that the men clustered around the fire heard the sounds of someone approaching the camp. Jacques and Johnny both jumped up to investigate; Jacques with a shotgun, and Johnny with a revolver. They scrambled up to an elevated vantage point near the trail and leveled their guns where they anticipated a rider would soon make an appearance. It was Will. He had his hat off and smiled at the men he knew would be waiting for him. Jacques and Johnny lowered their weapons and returned to the campfire as Will entered the encampment with George's body draped across the backside of a horse.

Will dismounted and stretched his legs, arms, and back. He shivered against the cold and longed for the warmth of the campfire.

"Say...pour me a cup of that there coffee," Will said as he grabbed a cup. "I'm 'bout frozen to the core! That was a cold ride back along the river."

Harry grabbed the pot and poured coffee into the cup that Will eagerly held in an outstretched hand. Once full, Will brought the cup to his lips and took a sip. Carelessly, he slightly burned his tongue, but the hot fluid radiated a momentary sensation of heat down his throat and into his stomach. It helped to reduce the chill, but only slightly.

Eli watched the boy and patiently waited for him to sip coffee. He rose from the stump he was sitting on and walked to George's body. Eli pulled a knife from the scabbard on his side and cut the ropes that bound George to the back of the horse. He sheathed the knife and asked for Johnny to help him place George on the ground. They lowered his body, and the Roberts Boys gathered around.

After a moment of reverence, Eli took off his hat, knelt, and looked George over. George had a lifeless, lax face that was bloodied around the mouth, a jaw that wasn't set right, and a messy wound that was obviously the result of a shotgun blast. It was a pitiful sight to see. This man...his friend...dead on the ground. Eli stood up and focused his attention on Will.

"Well, boy...what'd you learn?"

Between sips of coffee, Will cheerfully relayed what he'd learned at Scotty's Saloon. Too cheerful, in Eli's estimation. Will's jovial countenance was in stark contrast to the gloomy mood of the other men, and that began to eat at Eli. But, at least at that moment, what was important to Eli was the information the boy had.

Of course, what he was able to tell Eli was somewhat limited. He didn't know the name of the man who killed George, and there was nothing that indicated where he came from or where he went. However, there was some useful information that Will was able to glean from his mission, namely, the fact that the man took George's horse and gun, and what the man's basic physical description was.

And it was that man's description that got Eli thinking, especially the observation that the man had marks, like a burn, around portions of his neck. Eli reviewed in his head all of the men who'd been victims of the Roberts Boys; the men who were killed, and the men who were left alive. He could only recall a handful of men who fit the age, height, and build that the man had. But there was only one man...one man who would also have burn marks on his neck, and Eli truly believed that there was no possible way that man could be the same man who was lynched for his string of pack mules. He was strung up by his neck until he was unconscious. And even if the branch used to suspend the man above the ground broke, he was still bound and was left to die of the elements. He was practically dead. Or was he? That prospect left Eli with something to mentally chew on.

As Will told of what he'd seen at the saloon, and the conversation he had with Scotty, he let it slip that he took the time to eat a meal. For some reason, this infuriated Eli. Maybe it was because Will took his time bringing George's body back. Or perhaps it was because Will didn't exert force to extract more information. It could be that Will just didn't fit the mold of a Roberts Boy. He wasn't cruel, a killer, or a thief. Will was just a boy; a kid who had a chance in life under the right circumstances.

"You stopped to have breakfast?" Eli roared as he slapped the cup out of Will's hands. "You're telling me...George's body was out there for all to see...and you took the time to eat?"

Eli's voice shook with disbelief and anger.

Will was surprised by Eli's sudden outburst, and his good-natured attitude quickly turned to fear.

"I didn't mean anything by it...I...I was cold and hungry," Will pleadingly said. "I figured it wouldn't hurt nothin'...I got the information you wanted."

Eli cut Will's explanation off, shouting, "That's not what I told you to do! You were to go to the saloon, find out who did this, and bring George back! Nowhere in those orders did I ask you to just do whatever you want!"

He punctuated his statement by striking Will across the face with an open hand.

Will held back tears, but his eyes became watery.

"I'm sorry, Eli...I didn't mean...I didn't think...."

"Damn right, you didn't think! That's your problem, boy! You can't follow orders!" Eli snapped at Will. It was a reprimand meant as much for the boy as it was for other members of the gang.

"I'll do better! It won't happen ever again!" Will tried to explain and regain the trust of Eli.

Eli shook his head. "You let me down...I told you not to disappoint me. You ain't cut out to be a Roberts Boy!"

"Please, Eli...I'm sorry," Will said as tears began to roll down his cheeks. "Just give me a chance...I can be a Roberts Boy!"

Eli turned his gaze from Will to Johnny. "Get rid of him, Johnny."

With that order, Johnny pulled his revolver, cocked it, and started to raise it toward Will's head.

Terrified, Will dropped to his knees, covered his head with his hands and arms, and cried out "No!"

Just as quickly as Johnny pulled and raised his revolver, Eli reached out and grabbed the barrel of the revolver and pushed it to the sky.

"Not that, you jackass!" Eli scolded Johnny. "Get him out of camp! Jacques...take the boy's rifle and horse."

Will scrambled to his feet in protest. "I'll leave, Eli! I'll go far away...but please, leave me with my horse and rifle...it's all I got!"

Eli walked a short distance away and turned his back to Will. It was a silent statement that his mind was set. It was also a way he concealed his true feelings. The boy hadn't done anything all that bad, but Eli was giving Will a chance he never had. Eli never had someone to set him on the right path. Perhaps losing everything and being run out of camp was the nudge Will needed to stay away from people like the Roberts Boys. Underneath the tough persona, shaved head, and bad teeth, a little bit of good existed.

Resistant to being separated from his worldly possessions, Will struggled with Jacques over his rifle and horse. He tried to wrench the rifle away, but Jacques had a firm grip. The struggle continued, kicking up clumps of mud and snow, causing Will's horse to become skittish and unsuccessfully pull against the rope that tethered the animal to a tree.

Will fought with Jacques over the rifle, stopping only when he felt a white-hot sting across his back. And then another burning sensation on his shoulder and upper arm. Again and again, pain shot across his skin. Howling in pain, Will turned toward the source. Johnny and Harry both wielded quirts and took turns whipping the boy. Even though Will wore several layers of clothing to shield him from the cold, it wasn't adequate protection from the slashing of the rawhide quirts. Attempting to ward off the whipping, Will received the brunt of the trauma across his forearms and hands.

He finally had enough, and through tears and great pain, Will ran out of camp and back down the trail he rode up with George's body just thirty minutes before. Alone and dispossessed, Will disappeared with the shrinking light of day.

Their deed complete, Johnny and Harry put away the quirts. Resisting Will's attempts tired the men out. They breathed hard and tried to recover from the exertion. Jacques, too, was tuckered out. He leaned the rifle against a tree and began to unsaddle Will's horse.

By the time Will was run out of camp, Eli turned back to his men. He was satisfied with their efforts and refocused on what needed to be done. In the fading light of the evening, the men carried the rough coffin and placed it next to George. Unceremoniously, Jacques and Johnny grabbed George by the arms and legs and placed him in the wooden box. Harry placed the lid on the coffin, and Eli, hammer in hand, drove the nails that sealed the body away from the open air.

With two short lengths of rope placed under the coffin, the four men each took the end of a length and lifted the coffin from the ground. They walked the short distance out of camp to the freshly dug grave. Upon Eli's word, the men lowered the coffin, in an orchestrated manner, inches at a time, until it rested on the earth at the bottom of the hole.

No further words were spoken. No prayers were said. Eli uncorked a bottle of whiskey, took a drink, and passed it on. He bent down, grabbed a handful of dirt, and tossed it onto the top of the coffin. Each man followed suit until all four had followed Eli's lead.

The bottle emptied, Eli dropped it into the grave and ordered Johnny to finish the job while he and Jacques returned to camp. Harry sat on the ground and by the light of a lantern he watched Johnny fill in the hole.

***

Following the rider out of Keyesville wasn't a difficult endeavor for Danny. For several miles, the trail paralleled the Kern River before entering the Kern River Valley. It twisted and turned, but Danny was able to keep the rider in sight as he kept a careful distance to avoid detection. Eventually, though, Danny had to employ even more caution.

As the trail entered the Valley, the trees Danny used as cover were not as plentiful, so, he had to put more distance between himself and the rider. And, with more distance, Danny began to lose sight of the young man and his cargo when the trail sporadically dipped into gullies and ravines. It'd be different if there was more traffic on the trail, but that wasn't the case. As a result, Danny did the best he could.

It was a stressful task that lasted several hours, wearing on Danny's stamina and nerves, producing a long day in the saddle, full of slow riding and covert maneuvers. As far as Danny could tell, the rider had no idea he was being followed, and if Danny's plan played out as he figured, the rider would lead him directly to the Roberts Boys' camp.

The plan, for a plan that was made up while Danny sat on the side of the hill watching over George's body, appeared to be foolproof until the rider veered off the trail before the river split into a north and south fork. At that point, where the rider was going was more difficult to discern. Danny employed the same tactics he'd used for another mile or so, but as the canyon walls narrowed, and the river banks became crowded with vegetation and boulders, Danny began to lose sight of his prey.

A few times while trailing the rider along the north fork of the river, Danny, unbeknownst to him, rode into a mining camp. He began to think twice about the veracity of his plan, especially since he was unfamiliar with this country. As far as Danny knew, he might stumble into the Roberts Boys' camp at any turn in the trail. That wouldn't do much for the element of surprise that Danny counted on, especially since he was riding on a dead man's horse...a horse the Roberts Boys surely knew.

Reluctantly, Danny decided to continue his task on foot. This allowed for more flexibility. It was much easier for a man to remain concealed than it was for a man and a horse. At this point in time, being on foot wasn't much slower than being on horseback, especially since Danny had no idea where he was headed. At least he'd have the ability to edge around the trail and hide in vegetation as he trailed the rider and sought out the camp. He could also be much quieter.

But this decision also came with trade-offs. On foot, he all but eliminated the ability to escape quickly, for it is much faster to ride away on a horse than it is to run. Then there was the issue of endurance. Danny was in great shape, with well-toned and exercised muscles. He was used to walking long distances, but it came with a cost. How long would he have to follow the rider? What toll would it take on his body? Would he have the energy to engage the camp? These were important questions that Danny couldn't answer until he found the camp.

And then there was the fact that having a horse allowed Danny to carry a great deal of gear—food, ammunition, his bedroll. On foot, sacrifices had to be made. Danny had a knapsack, so he could carry powder, primers, and shot. He could also carry some basic rations, and maybe stuff a blanket into the pack. But that was about all he could carry in the brief moment he had to prepare.

Danny tied his horse to a tree, allowing enough play in the lead for the animal to graze, donned the knapsack, grabbed his shotgun, made sure the Navy Colt was securely tucked into his belt, and continued the task of following the rider.

The light of day began to slip away as Danny darted from tree to boulder to bush in an attempt to stay hidden and spot where the rider went. He repeated this process, over and over for at least a mile, and in all of that time, he only saw the rider once, and that was when he diverted from the trail and rode through a stand of pine that covered the side of a hill and low ridge. Danny couldn't ascertain where the new path headed. The low ridge was over a quarter mile away, maybe further. But he did see wisps of smoke that he guessed was from a campfire. If his hunch was correct, the Roberts Boys were somewhere over that ridge.

He was close, and the time for immediate action was best delayed. Danny knew that he needed a plan. There was no way he could just waltz into the camp and expect to come out alive, specifically because it was his goal to not be neighborly. No...this was a delicate matter. Danny had one shotgun and one revolver with six shots. Each weapon could be reloaded with a degree of speed, but whether he had time to do that once the shooting began was questionable. He would have felt a bit better if he had a rifle with him, and, perhaps, a small army. That wasn't in the cards, though. This was his burden to bear alone.

Being this close to Eli and the Roberts Boys required a new line of thinking and planning. Counting the rider, Danny figured that there were at least three men in the camp. Chances are, though, there were more. With that potential, it was best for Danny to reconnoiter the place. That, unfortunately, meant that Danny would have to approach the ridgeline with caution and a greater degree of patience. And, coupled with the approaching dusk, Danny's chances for a bout with the Roberts Boys today were improbable. Originally, according to Danny's estimation, the perfect line of action was a swift attack at dusk; he could hit them and disappear into the night. However, that necessitated knowledge of his target...knowledge that Danny lacked. With that in mind, Danny hoped to at least get an eyeball on the camp before nightfall. Exacting revenge on the Roberts Boys would have to wait.

Danny picked his way toward the ridge, which was a painstakingly slow process. He was part crawling, part squatting, part kneeling in place, and wholly concentrating on his efforts. It was already a cold afternoon, but the wind began to blow. Danny couldn't help but feel a chill that gripped his body. His slow movements didn't do much to fend off the chill. Perhaps the only thing that made it slightly bearable was the adrenaline coursing through his veins.

He was desperate to reach a vantage point before it was too dark to see, but it was a race against the turning earth that he was destined to lose. The sun fell behind the rocky precipices to the west, and a grayness enveloped his surroundings. Being within a river canyon, the absence of light intensified the coolness of the breeze, and it robbed one's eyes of the ability to see far.

Impending darkness is a magical time. Many creatures, big and small, increase their activity during this transitional period. Whether it is to reach bedding areas or nests, feed before nighttime, or cross from one area of cover to another, there is typically a flurry of goings-on in the last light of day. And then nothing. A hush is ushered in over the land; a stillness that can become unnerving.

As Danny traversed the land toward the top of the ridge, he couldn't help but notice the increased activity, expressly because his senses were already heightened due to the sensitivity of his mission. There was the sound of the river a short distance away, its icy flow tumbling down rocks toward a distant destination. Birds flitted about, the sound of their wings and singing to one another filled the air.

Danny also made noise as he moved up the slope. It was the sound of grains of decomposed granite grinding against each other with each footstep, mixed with the slight crunching of ice crystals that formed in clustered patches. It was a sound audible to Danny alone, but each step was an explosion to Danny. Then there was nothing...except for the sound of the river and the sound of Danny's movements. And another sound, faint at first, but growing louder as the seconds ticked by.

Danny stopped, cocked his head, and listened. It sounded like something running. Something large, like a deer or a small horse. Maybe a man. Danny couldn't afford to take any chances, so, he hid behind a large manzanita bush beside the path he was following. Waiting. Watching. Anticipating.

He didn't have to remain crouched in his hiding spot for long, perhaps a minute or two, before he saw the shadowy form of a person briskly moving down the trail, heading right toward Danny. The man was moving quickly, and Danny could hear what he believed to be whimpers. Danny's legs tensed, the muscles like springs ready to be unleashed. And he pounced on the man as he passed near.

It was a violent act. Danny, in one fluid motion, tackled the figure, firmly placed one hand over the man's mouth, and tightened the forearm of the other arm across his throat. The man thrashed about, his terrified, muffled screams filling the little space in the brush alongside the trail where the men struggled. But this was no man. It was just a boy, still in his teens, and no match for Danny's strength. Danny had a firm grip on the boy, and he felt wetness on his cheeks, like tears. They were tears. Danny could now tell that the boy was crying.

"Shhhh! Shhhhhh! Calm down, boy!" Danny whispered into the boy's ear. "I ain't gonna hurt you! Ya just have to trust me!"

The boy continued to struggle, but his resistance began to wane as he realized that Danny was in control of the situation and fighting back was futile. Danny's repeated reassurance that he wouldn't harm the boy also helped.

"Listen to me...I don't know you...and you don't know me. If I wanted ya dead, we wouldn't be havin' this here conversation," Danny reasoned with the boy.

The boy relaxed even more, the tension in his shoulders lessened, and he exhibited all of the signs that he relented to Danny.

"Now...I'm gonna remove my hand," Danny continued to whisper, "and I'm gonna ask you some questions. When I'm done, you'll be free to go...but God help ya if ya start to scream or fight! I've no intention to hurt you, but I will if need be!"

Shaking his head in the affirmative and issuing a muffled agreeance, the boy removed his hands from Danny's forearm and raised them in front of his body. Danny noticed that there were bloodied stripes along both of the boy's hands and wrists. With a gentle and slow movement, Danny removed his hand covering the boy's mouth and loosened the stranglehold he applied with his forearm.

"What's your name?" Danny questioned.

"I'm Will...Will Watkins," the boy answered as he sniffed back the snot produced from his crying.

"Ok...my name's Danny Vance. Now...where're ya coming from?" Danny inquired.

"A camp over that ridge and down in that gully, but I ain't ever going back! They horse-whipped me...took my rifle and horse," he stated as he pulled up the sleeves of his jacket to reveal bloodied wounds. "It was all I had...everything I owned!"

Will began to sob again.

Danny released the boy, turned him around, and examined the stripe marks left by the rawhide quirts. He shook his head in shock and felt a bit bad for the fright and tussling he'd given Will.

"Someone did a number on you...who did this?" Danny truly felt bad for the boy.

Will looked at Danny, somewhat fearful of the words he was about to utter, especially since he didn't know the man in front of him.

"They call themselves the Roberts Boys," Will managed to say. "They're real bad men, mister...I'd steer clear of them if I was you!"

A smile spread across Danny's face, which seemed odd to Will, causing his sobs to dissipate. Will was puzzled to the point that he wondered if the man in front of him was touched in the head.

"You just made my job a bit easier," Danny said, pleased at the stroke of luck he had by running across Will.

"I've been looking for that bunch. How many men are in the camp?"

The remaining reluctance Will had disappeared as he asked, "What in the world you trying to find them for? You ain't one of them, are ya?"

"No...not even close, Will," Danny said with a little chuckle in his voice. "Those men...they stole from me, murdered my friend, and tried to lynch me," he explained as he pulled down the collar of his jacket and shirt to reveal a healed-over burn mark that was barely visible in the increasing darkness. "I already killed one of them over at the saloon in Keyesville."

Surprised, Will exclaimed, "That was you? Lordy! You've got them more riled up than a cornered rattler! I spent the day hauling George's body back to camp."

"I figured that was you...I spent the day trailing you back to these hills," Danny interjected. "Why're you running with them?"

Will felt ashamed, and he dropped his head to stare at the ground as he answered.

"That's a good question...one that ain't easy to answer. Maybe I don't rightly know, myself! I was all alone with nowhere to go and no place to be. Eli seemed like a nice feller...well, until recently. I've only been there a few weeks running errands for them men and doing chores. That ain't the case now...I hope to never see them again!"

"I aim to make sure you don't," Danny stated, both as a fact and to ease Will's trepidation. "That said, tell me about that camp."

Over the next few minutes, Will relayed what information he could about the camp. Four men currently made up the Roberts Boys—Eli, Harry, Jacques, and Johnny. George would've been five, but he was, by now, cold and in the ground. They were holed up in three cabins that were loosely clustered around a fire pit. Off to the side, there was a small barn attached to a small corral. They had six horses and two mules. And, altogether, Will believed they had two shotguns, two rifles (including the one taken from Will), and at least four revolvers. Harry and Johnny shared the cabin on the left; Jacques slept in the middle cabin that doubled as a cook-shack; and Eli occupied the cabin on the right. Other than that, Will didn't have any information that Danny deemed to be pertinent.

Danny expressed his thanks for the knowledge that Will imparted. It gave Danny a better idea of what to expect in the camp, as well as confirmed to Danny that he was inevitably in over his head. It was a reality that he chose and that he accepted. All that was left now was action.

By the time Danny and Will finished their conversation, the night had arrived, bringing with it a quality of darkness that was tempered only by the light provided by the half-moon that alternatingly shined brightly in the sky and hid behind passing dark clouds.

Will was eager to be on his way. He hoped to make it to Scotty's Saloon and the only other person who'd shown kindness to him since being here.

Danny told Will about the horse he had stashed down the trail, and that he wouldn't need it anymore. Either he was riding away from the Roberts Boys' camp on one of their horses after he finished his deed, or he'd be dead and no longer in need of a horse. Will was impressed by the gallantry Danny exhibited. Danny was on a mission, determined to fulfill an uncertain destiny.

Will stood up and turned to leave, but stopped after taking a few steps. He turned and looked back at Danny as he, too, stood up. Will reached out with his right hand. The welts and streaks of blood were prevalent and impossible to miss. In turn, Danny reached out with his right hand and clasped Will's. They shook hands like men, even though the act was painful for Will.

"Good luck, mister!" Will imparted in a hushed tone, and then he disappeared into the night.

***

Twenty minutes after Will's departure, Danny was at the top of the ridge looking down into the gully containing the Roberts Boys. There wasn't much to be seen, what with the trees and darkness of the night. But from his perch, Danny did see the flickering of a campfire and the shadowy light that the flames cast onto the nearby cabins. He was able to spot the occasional movement of men down below, and he heard voices and laughter. But Danny was unable to specifically identify any of the men. Without a doubt, they were the Roberts Boys, Will confirmed as much. And Danny had a hunger to send down a hail of bullets, but to do so at this time would be negligent.

If his goal was to end their reign of terror, it'd be a nearly impossible task under these conditions. Sure, he might be able to hit one or two of the men if Danny was able to edge his way down the side of the ravine to get closer to where they were. Chances are, though, the remaining Roberts Boys would quickly escape into the darkness. Outnumbered and outgunned, with the element of surprise spoiled, Danny would be in a heap of trouble.

Danny thought over his options, settling on the idea that it was best if he hunkered down for now and got some rest. Then later, in the dead of night, he might slowly pick his way down to where the horses and mules were kept, and then he'd turn them loose. When the shooting began, at least the Roberts Boys wouldn't have the advantage of being mounted and more mobile.

Until then, Danny crawled up under the protective overhanging branches of a pine tree. He made a bed of pine needles, pulling great heaps of the substance into his temporary shelter, as much for comfort as it was for insulation against the cold. Danny laid his shotgun and revolver next to where he, himself, was to lie and pulled a small woolen blanket from his knapsack. He reclined on his needle-strewn bed and covered himself up, settling in for what would be a long and unkind night.

Chapter 9

Bacon, Beans, and a Dead Man

———— ◆ ————

If Danny hoped to get some rest on the side of the ridge, he was sadly mistaken. Even with the insulating layer of pine needles and a small woolen blanket, Danny was infected with a chill that went straight to his soul. No matter what he did...no matter how he positioned himself...his body shivered in response to the elements. It was a cold that he couldn't remember ever experiencing.

Danny had spent many a cold day and night back in Missouri, on the Overland Trail to California, in the Gold Fields along the American River, and in Francis' cabin. But none of those experiences matched the situation he was now in. Sure, it was probably just as cold and damp in other areas he'd been. And, the gusting wind intensified the cold, just like it could anywhere. But Danny didn't have the luxury and comfort of having a fire to combat the frigid air.

Fire. That miracle of civilization that can build and destroy, sustain and kill, comfort and terrify. It was something that Danny longed for. Unfortunately, it was something he couldn't have, not if he hoped to catch the Roberts Boys by surprise.

So, Danny suffered through it, his body violently convulsing, at times, to generate blood flow to warm his extremities. Miserable hardly described how he felt.

As the hours slowly and painstakingly slipped away, Danny waited and contemplated when it was the right time to make his move and release the horses and mules. Too early, and the Roberts Boys might still be awake; too late, and they might easily wake up. It was a conundrum that had no easy solution.

Regardless of when he decided to make his move, nothing was going to happen until he moved from under the shelter of the tree. If anything, Danny reasoned that if he made his way down the hillside and down into the ravine, he might be able to generate some warmth.

He pulled the woolen blanket from his body and then tucked it back into the knapsack. After hours in the cold, Danny found it difficult to use his fingers without any type of agility, but he was able to reposition the blanket, the gunpowder, the shot, and the primers so he could get to them in a hurry if needed.

Danny crawled out from under the tree, the Colt revolver tucked into his belt, the shotgun in his left hand, and the knapsack in his right.

He never, not even once, believed this was going to be easy, and as he surveyed his surroundings in the dark grey of the night, he confirmed as much. The path he planned to take down to the camp, and more specifically, to the corral, was strewn with boulders, loose decomposed granite, brush, and dead trees and branches that fell over the years and created a wilderness obstacle course. Picking his way down the mountain required slow, measured movements, which paired well with his desire to remain undetected. It was a task melding care and patience.

Twenty minutes later, Danny reached a pile of rocks situated about forty yards from the nearest cabin. It was twenty minutes of climbing over fallen trees, dodging low-hanging branches, slipping on loose dirt and rock, and generally trying to reach his destination without injury or being exposed. He decided to make the pile of rocks his new hideout. From that position, he could barely see the doors of two of the cabins through the limited light.

With the light of day, he'd be able to see them. He could also see the third cabin, but its doorway was obscured from view.

The distance from the rocks to the cluster of cabins was far enough to be hidden from plain view but within shotgun and pistol range. If all worked according to Danny's ever-developing plan, he'd be able to ambush and eliminate the Roberts Boys before they knew what hit them. It was a plan based on many factors Danny had no control over, and he was all too aware of best-laid plans and how they could turn out.

Danny looked over the cabins and corral, his breath coming out in puffs as the warm air from his lungs met the chill of the night. All was quiet. Not a soul was to be seen, and the animals were calm. With any luck at all, things would remain in that state.

He took off his knapsack and placed it and his shotgun amidst the pile of rocks. Danny didn't need to be further encumbered while trying to release the horses and mules pinned up in the corral. All he needed was a knife. The corral might be tied shut, or the animals may be tethered to a post or have their legs hobbled. He would still have his Colt if any shooting needed to be done, but that was a last resort. And if that happened, then his chances of success were smaller than they already were.

With unsheathed knife in hand, Danny crouched down and made his way in a roundabout manner toward the corral. Skirting the camp to get to the corral was a slower option, but it was much safer than cutting through the camp itself. It was also taxing on Danny's cold body.

Each step was planned out. Danny peered through the muted darkness at the ground ahead of him, assessed how he'd place his foot in the space, looked around to determine if all was still well, and then gingerly raised his leg and set his foot down, the toe of his boot first, and then slowly shift his weight to the rest of his foot.

Maintaining balance, restricting movement, and walking in a slow-motion crouch expended more energy than most people realized. By the time he was thirty yards from the corral he was breathing hard and Danny felt the strong, elevated thump of his heart in his chest.

At twenty-five yards, Danny quickly held his breath and felt his heart race, even more, when his careful step went wrong as he lost his balance on the uneven ground and his hastily repositioned foot landed on a branch. The snapping of the dry wood sounded like thunder to Danny, and all he could do was freeze in place. He crouched as low as he could, trying to blend into the background.

Danny watched the camp, mindful of any movement. He felt a degree of relief when nobody emerged from the cabins. However, a few of the horses did turn their attention his way.

Fairly certain that all was well, Danny tried to slow the flow of adrenaline through his body. He saw the dull glint of moonlight on the blade of his knife. The point of the knife led the way toward the corral, seemingly slicing through the late-night air.

Surprisingly enough, the horses and mules weren't alarmed by Danny's presence. It wasn't uncommon for animals to be somewhat skittish around an unfamiliar person, especially when that person was sneaking around in the middle of the night. Maybe it was because Danny was acting in a non-threatening way, with slow movements. It could also be the fact that the two mules were the property of the J. Kinney Freighting Company. They were familiar with the smell and sight of Danny, and their acceptance might have pacified the horses. Either way, all of the animals looked to Danny and tolerated his existence.

The corral was a simple structure, made of split rails that were stacked on top of each other. Where the ends of the rails met, they crisscrossed in an alternating fashion, making neat angles as the pieces of timber snaked around an irregular oval until both ends met at a gated opening that was tied shut.

With a few efficient strokes, the razor-sharp edge of Danny's knife made quick work of the rope. Danny quietly lifted the unsecured end of the gate and slowly pivoted it open. The horses breathed hard and lightly brayed, less out of alarm and more out of confusion. That worried Danny, but he wasn't in a position to stop what he was doing. There was no going back now.

As quick as he dared, Danny approached the mules and gathered in both of their leads. He led them out of the corral and pushed them toward the trail that led back toward the Kern River Valley. One by one, he did the same thing with each horse. He didn't want to stampede the animals, which would generate a great deal of commotion. Ultimately, Danny just wanted the animals to be inaccessible to the Roberts Boys. Danny moved behind the horses, raised his arms in a shooing motion, and made audible clicks with his mouth to move them along.

Satisfied with his effort, Danny began to creep back to the tree line to retrace his steps back to the pile of rocks.

His line of travel, however, was cut short when he spotted a figure exit the door of the cabin closest to the corrals. Quickly, Danny concealed himself behind a large pine tree. Once again, his heart began to race, and a minor sense of panic encompassed Danny's thoughts. Did the man hear Danny release the horses and mules? Was Danny's movements louder than he perceived? Danny didn't have the answers, but the man's actions dictated what he'd do next.

The man stood outside the door to the cabin and scratched his head. He was still half asleep and his head swam from a combination of recent slumber and the whisky he'd consumed earlier in the evening. With a staggering gait, the man walked to a tree that was fifteen feet from where Danny was hiding. It didn't appear that the man was looking for anything in particular.

Danny's concern was reduced a fraction as the man, undid the fly on his trousers, leaned forward to brace his left forearm against the tree, rested his head against his forearm, and then began to relieve himself. He was so close that Danny could hear the steady stream of urine hit the tree and sprinkle down onto the ground. It was too close for comfort, but not to the point that'd spur Danny into action. Doing that may spoil any surprise that he planned for the Roberts Boys. Danny patiently waited out the man, repositioning his head bit by bit so he could spy on the man with his right eye.

The man finished up his task, swayed as he straightened up, and turned away from the tree as he buttoned up his fly. He was about to return to his cabin when he noticed something on the bend of the trail leading out of camp. Standing there, partially hidden by distance and the darkness, was an indiscernible animal. It was bigger than a deer and smaller than a horse.

The man rubbed his eyes in an attempt to clear his vision. Unbeknownst to the man, Danny was watching and hoping that the man would let his curiosity go. But that wasn't the case. The man muttered something, and then slowly stepped forward to get a better view of the animal. He passed right by where Danny was hiding, unaware that an invader had infiltrated the camp.

"C'est une mule," the man softly said to himself. He was confused and not entirely clear-headed, and it took longer for him to process what he was seeing. As reality took hold of his perception, the man cocked his head and crinkled his nose with the thought that a perfectly good mule was on the loose. He thought it was odd, and his first compulsion was to round up the mule. But he was tired and drunk, and the chill night air was cutting through his clothing. The cabin was warm, and the comfortable bed inside beckoned him home. In a dismissive gesture, he put off chasing the mule and turned to walk back to the cabin.

Once again, he passed by the tree where Danny was hidden. His focus was on returning to bed until he glanced to his right where the corral was. He stopped in his tracks and stared at the corral as he contemplated what was different. Something was out of sorts. Even in the dark, and in his inebriated state, the man discerned that there was a problem. And then it hit him...the fact that the horses and mules weren't within the enclosure.

"Les chevaux!" the man said and then repeated a bit louder than before. They were the last words the man would ever say.

Before he knew what was going on, Danny grabbed the man from the back. And just like he'd done with the young man who called himself Will, Danny firmly covered the man's mouth with his hand. But, unlike Will, this man was full of strength and fight, even though his agility and coordination were compromised by drink. The man twisted and turned within Danny's grasp. His screams and exclamations were hushed by the hand that doubled as a gag, but just barely. It was an epic struggle—Danny trying to prevent his plans from falling apart, and the man fighting for what could be his life.

Like a cornered animal, a man faced with his potential demise has a way of mustering a degree of power and vigor that manifests itself with flailing arms and legs. But Danny had a few things in his favor, besides the obvious element of surprise and sobriety. Danny was taller than the man, by a good five to six inches, and he was at least twenty pounds heavier. The height, muscle, and sinew gave Danny leverage over his opponent. So, containing the struggling man wasn't easy, but it was easier than if the roles were reversed. The knife firmly grasped in Danny's right hand was also advantageous, even if it was a last resort.

Danny didn't recognize the man he was battling. He wasn't one of the three Roberts Boys he'd encountered on the Greenhorn Trail, but there wasn't a doubt in his mind that he was one of the Roberts Boys. The boy Danny interrogated provided details of the men in the camp. Danny had no particular issue with this man, but he was a Roberts Boy. He'd be loyal to Eli. Surely, he'd send up an alarm just as soon as Danny released him. There was no doubt of what needed to be done.

It was a very personal act, one that Danny had never performed before. And it didn't require any degree of skill. Many a man of lesser quality than Danny had done a similar deed for less. No pleasure was derived from the act; it was a means to an end.

Danny plunged his knife into the man's chest to the hilt. The first strike met some resistance as it tore through layers of cloth to meet flesh and deflect off of bone. His knife was sharp and well-maintained, designed for cutting and slicing. Danny repeated his actions twice more, driving the implement deep. He gripped the knife, and with great effort he kept it buried in the man's chest, pulling it upward as much as he pulled it inward.

The man resisted the best that he could, and he screamed out in pain and with alarm that nobody, except Danny, could detect. His resistance, once strong and spirited, faded with each strike of the blade, and it completely disappeared as the lifeblood poured from his body. There was nothing left but to succumb to death. The man's body went limp, and Danny eased him to the ground when he was sure that he had given up the ghost.

He pulled the knife out of the man's chest, and he experienced a feeling he'd never had before. What he noticed wasn't the racing of his heart or the slight trembling of his body that was a result of adrenaline. And it wasn't guilt. That required reflection, and Danny hardly had the opportunity for that. It was an odd sensation; one hand cold and dry, the other warm and sticky from the man's blood. It wouldn't be long before the blood dried in the cold night air, crusting on his skin, marking Danny for the deed he'd done. The blade of the knife was also wet and discolored, no longer reflecting the light of the moon.

Danny wished to distance himself from this personal act as soon as he could. He wiped the blade of the knife on the man's trousers, and he followed it up by doing the same thing with his hand. The blood that'd seeped under his fingernails and into the crags of his hands refused to wipe clean; it'd be a reminder of what had transpired. And even when he could find the occasion to wash his hands, he'd never be fully clean. Not with the death of an unknown man on his hands, regardless of whether the man deserved it or not.

From where he grappled with the dead man, Danny gauged his surroundings. The struggle with the man hadn't alarmed anyone. The rest of the Roberts Boys were probably as much into their cups as the dead man was, which was beneficial for Danny.

He sheathed the knife, stood up, and then grabbed the dead man by the armpits, careful to avoid the blood-soaked portions of his garments. Dragging the body backward, Danny pulled the dead weight away from the trail toward a cluster of manzanita where he secreted the body away the best he could.

Danny looked the man over one last time. He still felt no shame or regret. The man was a Roberts Boy. There was now one less Roberts Boy for Danny to deal with.

Retracing his path to the pile of rocks wasn't difficult. No branches were stepped upon, no rocks were loosed, and no men stepped outside the nearby cabins. All was as well as Danny expected.

He climbed amid the rocks and found a spot that was as comfortable as it could be, and then he sat down. From the knapsack, he pulled out his powder, shot, and primers and placed them within easy reach. He leaned the shotgun against a low rock, pulled the Navy Colt from his belt, and set it down on the knapsack.

The events of the preceding hour had warmed Danny, but he was now fixing to remain motionless for quite a while, and he was bound to once again catch a chill. He pulled the woolen blanket from the knapsack, mindful of the revolver poised on the sack, and then covered himself up the best that he could. Danny reclined against the cold, smooth granite boulder behind him and settled in for the rest of the night.

***

The morning dawned, just as every morning did this time of the year—frigid and damp. Frost covered the patches of grass on the surrounding hills, and small pools of standing water were frozen over. It was an unfriendly environment to be in until the sun came up. Unless you were fortunate enough to wake up in a cabin.

All three of the cabins in the Roberts Camp were rigged with the necessary comforts that comprised adequate shelter. Each had a bed or two, a table and at least one chair, a door to shut out the elements, a glassless window that could be sealed by a wooden shutter, and a fireplace. As long as the fire was stoked, and the door and window were kept closed, a man might find some warmth, even if cold air filtered in through the gaps in the chinking between the logs that comprised the walls. The heat from the fire and the glowing coals provided just enough comfort to make a man feel at home.

Johnny opened his eyes as he lay on his side in bed. He was as snug as a bug sequestered under the heavy quilt, just like when he was younger at home with his Ma and Pa. Most of his slumber had been pleasant, except for when he crawled out of bed to stir the embers in the fireplace and throw on another log. It was a task that was typically easy but made more difficult with a bellyful of drinks. He also had to deal with the sounds emanating from the man he was now staring at. Harry was sound asleep in the bed across from Johnny. His mouth, wide open, was a factory of noise. Like a bucksaw slowly drawn repeatedly across a block of wood, Harry poured forth a chorus of sporadic snoring that was second to none. Or so Johnny thought.

There was no going back to sleep, even if he could. It was morning, and some things had to be done—take wood into the cabins, start the coffee to boiling, help Jacques cook breakfast, and care for the animals. For the past few weeks, Johnny was able to pass on the mundane tasks to Will. He was the new fish, and so, Johnny was able to push him around some. There was an advantage to having seniority, but that seniority was driven right out of camp the night before.

Reluctantly, Johnny pulled the quilt off of his body, swung his legs over the side of the bed, and sat up. With his elbows on his knees, Johnny placed his head in his hands and rubbed his temples to wish away the slight headache that he had. It was a reminder that there are consequences to drinking, a fact that is easily forgotten. And it wasn't a legitimate reason for Johnny to not begin the day. Eli wouldn't stand for that. Johnny was determined to stay on Eli's good side if there was one.

He stood up and stretched as he looked at Harry and wondered how in the world that man was able to sleep so soundly. Johnny grabbed his trousers from the end of the bed and put them on over his union suit, stepped into his boots, and grabbed his cleanest dirty shirt to wear for the day.

Desiring to quench his thirst, he walked over to the small table where there was a canteen and drank his fill. It was refreshing, and it'd probably go a long way in killing that headache. Washing his face might have a positive impact as well.

Johnny was thankful that the miners the Roberts Boys ran out of this camp had thought to build some creature comforts into the cabin. Within the fireplace, they installed an iron bar where pots and kettles were hung for cooking. Most of the cooking for the Roberts Boys was done in Jacques' cabin, so Johnny and Harry preferred to hang a large cast iron kettle over the fire to both produce steam to humidify the dry air of the cabin and warm water for washing.

Johnny ambled over to the kettle, poured an ample amount of water into a wash basin, and proceeded to wash the memory and smell of last night's drinking bout off of his body. It was refreshing, and perhaps, would be the highlight of his day.

Now that he was freshened up for the day, Johnny placed a few small logs on the fire, slipped the suspenders over his shoulders that held up his trousers, put on a coat and hat, and opened the door to his cabin to step outside.

As he closed the door, Johnny looked back at Harry who was continuing to snore away the morning. Johnny shook his head and headed into the brisk morning.

The sun was just beginning to rise behind the mountains, dropping the temperature as the light of day gradually burned off the darkness. Johnny heard the stirring of birds and other critters in the woods, and he could faintly hear the running of water down in the river. He was looking forward to spring, with the green grass, warmer weather, and the potential of the Roberts Boys to move on to new territory. But for a winter morning in the ravine, it wasn't too bad. He might even describe it as a handsome day in a beautiful setting. It was a good day to be alive. Then again, any day in his line of work was a good day to be alive.

Johnny headed to the woodpile to restock the supply of cut logs and split wood in front of each cabin. One after another, he carried an armful of wood to the smaller piles outside each cabin door. The stacked piles for each cabin became larger as the main pile became smaller. Johnny frowned at the prospect of spending a few hours later in the day bucking logs and splitting them for future use. It made him regret that Will wasn't around anymore. The timing could've been better.

With that task done, Johnny walked to Jacques' cabin, opened the door, and stepped inside. Usually, Jacques was already awake working on break-fast for the Roberts Boys. For a killer and bandit, Jacques was a decent cook. He became the designated chef shortly after he joined the gang, and he relished the role. Granted, the quality of the food was relative to the hunger of the men, but warm grub was appreciated by most men. Johnny was looking forward to the biscuits, bacon, and beans that were the usual offerings in the morning.

To Johnny's disappointment, the inside of the cook shack that doubled as Jacques' cabin wasn't filled with the aroma of cooking bacon and burn-ing coffee. In fact, there wasn't much going on in the cabin at all. There was a slight chill in the air, and a quick glimpse at the fireplace revealed that the fire hadn't been stoked in a while. Ashes and partially burnt wood surrounded the low pile of glowing coals that yearned for additional fuel.

Johnny, seeing that Jacques wasn't in bed, began to feel annoyed. What? Is it his job to cook all the food and do all the chores, too?

He placed a few small sticks on the glowing coals and got down on his hands and knees to blow on the embers until they caught the sticks on fire. It didn't take too long for the dry sticks to produce tall flames, at which point Johnny added a few larger pieces of wood to the growing fire. Soon, there'd be a sufficient base of heat to prepare breakfast.

Johnny added water and several spoons of coffee to a pot, placed it near the fire to boil, and then thought about what needed to be done. He had a lot of work ahead of him.

Probably the most labor-intensive task to be completed for breakfast was making biscuits. Measuring flour, adding water and salt, mixing it all, placing dollops of dough into a greased Dutch oven, placing it on some coals, and then monitoring the biscuits to make sure they didn't burn took a lot of work. And that was just one portion of the meal. He'd also need to cut some strips of bacon from the cured pork belly that was kept on a shelf, wrapped and protected from insects, drain the water off of the beans that soaked overnight to soften them, and then cook and season the beans so they'd be edible.

Johnny helped Jacques on numerous occasions, so he knew what to do, but that did little to allay the displeasure that he felt.

"Where is that fool?" Johnny thought to himself as he got to work. Jacques was relatively dependable, and unafraid of work, especially the type of work he enjoyed.

It could be that he slept late and then had to visit the privy. Johnny could've just missed him, and he could have walked into the cook shack at any moment. Or perhaps Jacques rode down to Keyesville for a night of gambling and drinking. He'd done it before, but Johnny couldn't recall that happening without everyone knowing.

Johnny had a fleeting urge to go ask Eli if Jacques went somewhere. That wouldn't go over so well, though. Eli would be in a foul mood if Johnny woke him up.

The only recourse he had was to carry on with preparing breakfast in the hope that Jacques would show up soon. It was bad enough that he had to make the food and then do the rest of his chores. It'd be worse if he had to eat his own food, too. There is only so much a man can stomach.

Forty minutes later, and the coffee was done, the biscuits were cooked, the bacon was fried, and the beans were hot. Johnny could be polite and sit around and wait for everyone before he ate, but that wasn't the way of the Roberts Boys. Eat what you can, when you can. Besides, the only truly important rule to follow is to have food ready when Eli is there. And with that, Johnny poured himself some coffee, placed two biscuits, some bacon, and a few scoops of beans on his plate, and then sat at a lonely table for a quiet breakfast.

That struck Johnny as odd. It was, perhaps, too quiet. He could hear quail calling to each other outside, but it was otherwise a very still morning. Maybe it was nothing at all, but he was used to chatting with Jacques and the other men while eating. Johnny could remember eating alone plenty of times in his life, and quite a few times while a member of the Roberts Boys, but it just felt different. Maybe he was just having an off day. Perhaps it'd feel different if he had some company.

Johnny sopped up some beans with a biscuit and took a bite as he stood up and walked to the door. He walked outside and stopped in his tracks when it hit him. Damn, it was cold! Or at least that was the way it felt after spending some time in the confines of a warm cook shack and having some hot food in him.

Quickly chilled by the moist, cold air, Johnny wasted little time contemplating the change in environs as he walked to the door of the cabin he shared with Harry and entered. Harry was still in a deep sleep, the sound of his snoring keeping time with the rise and fall of his chest.

"Hey!" Johnny said as he nudged Harry's bed frame. "Hey! Harry! Grub's on!"

Harry slightly stirred and turned onto his side, but remained in slumber. Sure enough, Johnny thought, it was going to be one of those days that'd feel longer than most, and that he'd wish were over sooner, rather than later. He kicked the bed with more force.

"Hey, Harry! Wake up!" Johnny kicked the bed a few more times. "Come on, you worthless cow! Get your ass up! I don't wanna eat by myself."

That seemed to do the trick. Harry's eyes cracked open, one at a time, and he began to focus on the rascal who'd just startled him.

"Wha...what's the problem?" Harry asked.

"Nothin's wrong...it's...I got some beans and the such ready...thought maybe you'd want some food." Johnny tried not to sound desperate for company.

"My God, son!" Harry said as he stretched in bed. "If I wanted food, then I'd be up!" He rolled onto his other side in an attempt to get back to sleep. "Christ...go eat with Jacques!"

"Well, he ain't there!" Johnny replied with irritation in his voice. "Why ya think I had to make grub?"

Harry rolled back toward Johnny, one eye closed in an effort to slip back into unconsciousness. "He go into town or sumptin'?"

Johnny gestured with his shoulders and hands, "Hell...I ain't know where he's off to. He was gone when I got up."

"That ain't much like him." Harry rubbed his eyes and slowly sat up in bed. "You cooked that grub yourself?"

"Had no choice," Johnny sighed as he replied. "You know how Eli wants his morning. I ain't gonna be the one to disappoint him."

"Well, shit!" Harry growled as he pulled the covers from his body. "I best go see what type of damage you've done. I'll be there in a few."

Naked as the day he arrived in this world, he got out of bed and looked for his clothes. Johnny had to bear the brunt of chores, cook breakfast, and now witness Harry in all his glory. He exited the cabin and returned to the cook shack, half expecting to see Jacques there. Just like before, Jacques wasn't there.

Johnny didn't need any more confirmation. It wasn't going to be his day.

A disheveled Harry joined Johnny in the cook shack several minutes later. If it was possible, Harry looked even worse than when he was awakened, but that could be cured with coffee. As Johnny had done, Harry fetched himself some food and drink and then sat down in the chair across the table from Johnny.

"Lord almighty!" Harry exclaimed after taking a drink of coffee, "That there brew'll curl your toes! How long did you boil it?"

"Not long...started it with breakfast. It ain't that bad," Johnny said in defense.

"It ain't that great either," Harry quipped. "And the bacon, it's kinda burnt...the biscuits are a bit dry...."

"Look here," Johnny interrupted, "I did the best I could when I came in here! Jacques wasn't here, and it needed to get done, so I did it. If ya need to blame someone, you just point that finger at Jacques!"

"I'm just saying," Harry managed between bites, "Eli will probably kill you over this food, although the beans might be your saving grace...they're pretty good." Harry half-smiled with that last bit of critique.

"Speakin' of Jacques...he tell ya he was going off somewhere?" Johnny inquired.

Harry shook his head in the negative as he took another drink of coffee and winced as he swallowed.

"God...that's like drinking bitter mud! He said not a word to me...that Frenchie...it ain't like him to up and leave like that. Eli must've set him to a task or sumptin' like that."

"I guess," Johnny responded, growing a bit tired of the criticism, even if it was relatively good-natured. "We'll just have to wait for Eli and find out."

He took a drink of coffee and muscled it down. "Coffee ain't that bad."

They sat around for a good half hour talking and eating, and generally killing time as they waited for Jacques to get back or Eli to wake up. They talked about nothing in particular, and nothing consequential. Although George did come up in their ramblings, Harry wasted no time in changing the topic. The loss of George cut Harry deep, like no other loss he'd experienced before; the bond between boyhood friends can be stronger than anything imaginable. Harry accepted the fact that he'd need to drink a lot of whiskey to dull that pain.

The men, following routine, poured hot water into a wash bin, soaked their tin plates and spoons for a few minutes, and then proceeded to wipe them cleaner than they were before. They then turned to one of the best time killers they knew—a game of cards. If they had to sit around and wait, then they might as well get some pleasure out of it. Sure, they could be doing other things, but it wasn't like the camp was a working camp. They weren't raising any crops or stock animals. Their pursuit wasn't mining, freighting, or producing anything at all. The upside-down world they occupied depended on the productivity of others. The horses and mules needed tending to, but they'd be just fine left alone for a bit. They had some feed in the corral, but they'd need to be brushed and looked over. There was time for that later when the day warmed up. So, to them, a game of cards was the natural order of things.

It was a friendly game between friends; no high stakes, no tension, no drama. They played for dried beans. Men were less liable to take the game too seriously and kill each other if they played for something like beans. Gold dust or coin was too risky. To lose a handful of beans that you never intended to keep longer than it took to play cards was meaningless. Losing something of value had a way of simmering tempers and spiking emotions to the point where men, friends even, were willing to damage each other. They didn't want to risk that.

For twenty minutes, the two men engaged in a friendly game of cards. Hand after hand, the pile of beans in front of each man shifted. The piles grew, and then shrunk, especially as the wagers increased when each man believed they had a winning hand. It almost felt like a real game, with real stakes.

More than anything, the men were enjoying themselves and were quite relaxed as they wasted the time away. The comfy and quiet cook shack was a place where food was prepared, men ate, and camaraderie was had. Life was sustained here. A glimpse of enjoyment and happiness was found. If the men sought some sort of normality in their lives, it was more than likely found right there. But it was also where the chaos began.

Harry was holding a pair of jacks in his hand, and he believed to have bested Johnny. He was watching his face for a tell-tale sign that he was bluffing. A twitch of an eyebrow; a slight curl of the side of the mouth that hinted at a smile; maybe a bead of sweat trickling down from the brow. Johnny pushed forward five beans. He meant business, and he had what he figured to be a winning hand. Or did he? Was it a bluff? Harry pulled the same rouse in a previous hand. There is a reason why poker and other card games are referred to as a game of skill. Surely, there is a bit of luck needed in drawing a winning hand, but the skill comes in reading and fooling your opponent, as well as knowing when to fold and when to increase the bet enough to pad the pot, but not scare away other players.

Unfortunately, both men wouldn't find out who won the hand. A loud bang echoed outside the cook shack, and both men, startled by the noise, stiffened their spines. They looked at each other, confused and somewhat alarmed. In times of crisis, the sensation of slow motion is often experienced. Hesitation often meant the difference between life and death, survival and defeat. What felt like minutes, was, in reality, only a second or two.

They looked around the cook shack for the stash of weapons the Roberts Boys kept in each cabin. On a shelf near Jacques' bed lay a pistol. Leaning against the wall was the rifle the men took from Will. Heavy footsteps, angry and determined, raced toward the door of the cook shack. Harry and Johnny sprang out of their chairs for the weapons nearby. But they were too late in their actions. The door was kicked in, slamming open with a deafening bang.

"Where the Hell are the horses?" Eli demanded. He was infuriated, practically frothing at the mouth with rage. His revolver was drawn, and he was looking for a fight.

"The goddamn horses aren't in the corral! The mules are gone, too!" Eli roared.

Both Harry and Johnny were even more confused than before. This was news to the men and was particularly worrisome to Johnny. Tending to the animals was part of his chores for the day, and he would've done it sooner if he hadn't been tasked with making breakfast...and if he hadn't been involved in a game of cards. Johnny felt that he was primed to be the target of Eli's wrath. It was a place he always sought to avoid. And now, he was firmly within Eli's sights.

"The horses ain't there?" Johnny asked with great concern in his voice.

Eli pointed his revolver at Johnny in response, "That's what I said! You was supposed to check on them!"

"I aimed to, but I had to get breakfast cooked like you always want," Johnny pleaded in defense of his actions.

"That's what Jacques is for," Eli continued.

"Well...he ain't here...wasn't here in the morning, wasn't here to cook, and wasn't here all the time we were. The cabin fire was practically dead when I came in," Johnny explained.

All of a sudden, things started to make sense to the men. Eli lowered his revolver in understanding, and both Johnny and Harry either wrung their hands or rubbed their head in frustration. It seemed clear to them now.

"That son of a bitch!" Eli proclaimed. "All this time he was one of us, and it was a ruse to steal our horses...and who knows what else! Look around the camp...see if anything is missing...check the corral for tracks...see if you can tell where that French bastard went!"

The men raced out of the cook shack to grab their revolvers and to look into the disappearance of Jacques and the horses.

Eli, visibly upset, set his Colt on the table, grabbed a cup, poured some coffee, grabbed a biscuit and several pieces of bacon, and then sat down at the table to reflect on the events that were moving too fast for his liking. Eli lost George, who was careless and too stupid at times, but he was a friend and a Roberts Boy. His killer was still out there, and there was a chance that the killer was a ghost from their past. Will was whipped out of camp the previous night, which Eli felt a little guilty about, but it was for the boy's own good. He was too soft. And now, their mobility was gone, and so was Jacques.

Eli fumed over the thought that somebody...one of his own...stole from him. That bit at Eli hard, and he thought about what he'd do to Jacques when they ran him down. It wasn't pretty.

He took a swig of coffee, swallowed it down, and then looked long and hard at the liquid in his cup. Jacques was going to pay...but Eli sure would miss his cooking.

Chapter 10
The Murder Hole

———— ♦ ————

Vigilance. That is what is needed when lying in wait to spring an ambush. Patience. You must be willing to wait an undetermined amount of time for the perfect moment to attack. Concealment. There is no point in planning a surprise attack if the target can see it coming. Willingness. The conditions might be perfect, and the victim might be completely unaware of their impending crisis, but it is all for naught if the attacker hasn't the heart to carry out the deed. Asleep. It's not what a person should be if they are hoping to spring a successful ambush on a person, let alone three people.

Danny was asleep.

It isn't too difficult to understand why Danny fell asleep while watching over the Roberts Boys' camp. He hardly slept the night before, the cold and anticipation of what was to come saw to that. And then there was the rush he experienced with releasing the horses and mules. Of course, Danny also experienced the highs and lows associated with taking the Frenchman's life, especially the rapid flow, and then dump, of adrenaline within his body.

When Danny nestled into his perch among the pile of rocks, his body had more than it could handle. It wasn't that his bed among the rocks was more comfortable than the one under the tree on the hillside because it wasn't. The rocks were cold and hard...unfriendly in every sense. He wasn't any warmer than during the middle of the night. In fact, the closer it was to dawn, the colder the surrounding air became. No, his body sought sleep, and that is what it did.

Danny resisted the urge to sleep for as long as he could. He watched the camp, eyes darting from cabin to cabin, ever mindful of the slightest change in the scenery and sound. But his eyelids became heavier and heavier, and his head bobbed as he fought against the urge to sleep. More than once, his body was suddenly zapped into consciousness, like he was falling in a dream, and then abruptly awakened, in his attempt to resist falling asleep. Finally, Danny gave in and slipped into a restful, if not uncomfortable, slumber.

Of course, most good things come to an end. Danny's much-needed sleep was interrupted by an explosive sound coming from the camp below, not once, but twice. The first sound startled Danny. His eyes quickly opened, and he was temporarily confused as to what was going on, as well as disappointed that he'd fallen asleep. To his credit, he didn't spring to his feet in alarm. That could've ruined any chance of an ambush. Instead, he clutched his shotgun tightly and focused on the camp.

It wasn't difficult to figure out what was going on. The door of one cabin was wide open, and within seconds a man emerged on a mission. He stormed from that cabin to another and then caused the second explosive sound by kicking the door open. Danny only saw the man for a second, or maybe two, but there wasn't a doubt in his mind that it was Eli. He'd recognize that man anywhere; the way he walked, his shaved head, his face.

Danny thought to raise his shotgun and place a bead on Eli, but it all happened so quickly. Eli was there, and then he was gone. Danny also realized that if he hoped to ambush all of the Roberts Boys, taking a haphazard shot at Eli wouldn't bring him anywhere near that goal. Neither would taking a shot at the other two men who, one after another, left the cabin Eli was now in and scattered separately to various places around the camp. They were looking for something, no doubt associated with a missing camp member and horses.

At first, the men weren't armed, but somewhere along their hustling and bustling about the camp they acquired weapons. Both of the men carried revolvers, which made the most sense. If it was called for, the shooter had six chances of hitting their target before there was a need to reload. That was an equalizer, of sorts, in armed combat. What the revolver lacked in range, it gained in shear output. However, a shooter still had to hit their target.

Danny watched the two men dart around camp. They didn't bunch up together, which would've presented an opportune time to shoot them. So, Danny waited. Once they finally came together at the corral, they were out of shotgun range.

Perhaps the pile of rocks Danny chose wasn't as perfect as he thought, at least with the weapons he had in his possession. He'd have to wait, or at least revise his plan. But that, too, seemed to be the least of Danny's problems at the moment.

The men at the corral were talking in earnest, pointing at tracks on the ground. They followed the tracks, all the while surveying the trees around the camp. It wasn't a surprise to Danny that they'd try to figure out where the horses and mules went. What was a sudden concern, though, was the recognition that the Roberts Boys might soon discover evidence that one of their comrades was dead in the brush.

***

"Look," Johnny whispered to Harry, "someone pissed here...probably Jacques."

"Yeah, and then he walked over yonder," Harry said in hushed tones as he followed the tracks on the ground. He squatted down on his haunches and called Johnny over.

"This doesn't look right at all," Harry continued. "Somethin' happened here...the ground is all churned up...kicked-up dirt and rocks."

"And look at that...blood!" Johnny excitedly stated as he pointed at a small pool of coagulated blood on the ground.

Blood. That changed their perception of what had transpired. It may be that Jacques slipped away into the night with the horses and mules, but there was now the chance that something else happened. Maybe Jacques hadn't taken the animals. Maybe he tried to stop the theft in the middle of the night. Or maybe that wasn't his blood at all. It could've been someone else's blood, or it could have even been animal blood. The two men couldn't tell just by examining the blood.

"I don't like this at all...not one bit." Harry held the revolver in his hand with more earnestness as he noticed the drag marks that led into the trees and brush.

"Coulda been a cougar."

Harry and Johnny both stood up and followed the drag marks. The grooves in the ground, undoubtedly made by the left and right heels of a pair of boots, snaked their way sideways across the side of a hill, rounding trees, boulders, and brush. As they followed the marks, drops of blood sporadically peppered the path.

With each step, the men continued to warily look around. If it was a cougar that attacked, and then dragged Jacques into the woods, they didn't want to be the next victims. And, if it was a man, or men, that did this, they didn't want to be easily picked off because of their carelessness.

It didn't take too long for the men to spot a pair of boots sticking out from behind some brush. They walked up to the body and identified it as Jacques. All of their speculation—whether it was an animal or man that'd done this—was answered by the stab wounds in Jacques' chest. He was attacked and killed, and then his body was placed out of sight.

This changed everything. Jacques didn't steal the horses and mules. It looked like he might have interrupted the act, struggled with the horse thief, and lost his life doing so. However, the fact that two of the Roberts Boys were now dead wasn't lost on Harry and Johnny.

"Son of a bitch!" Harry muttered. He scratched his head in deep thought. "You best go tell Eli about Jacques, but keep quiet...whoever did this might be around...might be waiting to kill us all. No need to send up an alarm."

Johnny nodded in agreement and then retraced his steps back to the corral. He kept to cover, darting from place to place, until he reached the side of a cabin. Hugging the side of the structure, he continued until he reached the cook shack. Quickly and silently, he opened the door and entered the structure.

Harry took more time than was necessary to look over Jacques. There wasn't much more to see or understand; he was dead. Jacques was killed in the middle of the night and his body was stashed in the brush. That was the puzzling thing about the whole affair. If someone was after the horses and mules in the corral, and Jacques interrupted whomever it was that was doing the deed and got himself killed in the process, why take the time and trouble of moving his body? That was more effort than it was worth. When there was a need to make a quick and clean getaway, any delay was tempting fate.

Harry thought about that and put himself in the place of the horse thief. It just didn't add up. He kept pushing the thought out of his head, but it kept circling back to the forefront—they weren't out to steal the horses. That was a diversion; a way to eliminate a fast escape. Maybe? Stealing the horses wasn't their main objective. In Harry's mind, moving Jacques' body proved that theory. And if the perpetrator acted the way Harry would, then they were lying in wait somewhere. To do what was anyone's guess, but Harry had a pretty good idea that it was nothing good.

George was dead. Jacques was dead. Their only means of quickly escaping the camp was gone. The dominance of the Roberts Boys was being challenged, and someone, maybe more than one person, had killing on their mind.

Working off of that theory, Harry believed the only course of action was to find the killers before they found him. In other words, turn the tables and surprise those who planned on staging their own ambush. It was a task that required stealth and a bit of luck. They could be anywhere, armed with the most modern weaponry available.

Maybe they were men just like the Roberts Boys—thieves, bullies, killers, social pariahs. There was also the possibility that these ghost killers didn't exist at all. Someone took the horses and mules, and Jacques was collateral damage. Maybe they moved his body to give them a little extra time for their escape. Either way, Harry decided to work off the premise that there was someone out there.

Armed with a pistol and knife, Harry kept low to the ground and searched for tracks. In soil composed mainly of decomposed granite, it wasn't easy. Here and there Harry was able to find the deep impression of a boot heel or toe, and then there was nothing for yards. It was an exercise in patience.

He slowly moved, picking his way along the probable path. It was all about being silent, looking ahead and all around for danger, and planning his next move. Was someone hiding in a stand of trees, in thick brush, among the numerous piles of boulders and rocks that dotted the hills and knolls around the camp?

There were an innumerable number of places to search, but Harry tried to think like a man lying in wait. Where he secreted himself would largely depend on the type of weapons he had. If he had a rifle, then the roost could be a hundred or more yards from the camp. A competent man with a rifle could reach out and touch someone. But a perch with the requisite line of sight didn't exist in this ravine. So, the man hunting the Roberts Boys might have a rifle, but he is close to the camp, especially if he was only armed with a revolver, shotgun, or musket.

Harry convinced himself that the killer, if he was still in the area, was hidden where he could see the cabins, had a clear line of fire, and was close enough to where a shotgun or revolver could be used to kill or injure the men in the camp. In his estimation, the only places that fit the bill were the rocks that were located on a hillock to the side of the camp. That had to be the spot. That was where he would be. That was where Harry was heading.

Harry closed the distance to the rock pile rather quickly and quietly. He crouched low and moved with a degree of ease and grace. His breath was steady, coming out in visible vapor puffs. The closer he got to the rocks, the slower and more cautious his approach became.

It was the perfect place—elevated and secure; a miniature fortress and murder nest. Even as Harry reached the side of the stack, he could see that it was impossible to clearly see every nook and cranny where a shooter might hide. There was no way around it, Harry had to climb up into the rock pile; a pile that was a study in contrasts. Some were smooth, others jagged. Many were seemingly secured into the earth, but some were loosely stacked and would make a hollow scraping sound if he climbed atop of them. They were all cold to the touch, though.

He inched his way up into the rocks, ever-ready and aware, prepared to launch his attack. All it would take was one, maybe two well-placed shots from his revolver to dispatch the would-be sniper. Unless there was more than one man. That'd be problematic, but not an impossible one to overcome. He'd just have to be quicker and fire multiple shots at multiple targets.

Harry figured the shooter or shooters would be bunched together and focused on the camp below. An attack from the side would be unexpected, a surprise of sorts. And it was a surprise...for Harry. He was careful and methodical in the way he climbed into the rocks. His silence provided a necessary factor for an ambush. But it was all for naught.

As Harry was just about to crest a boulder that'd allow him to peer down into the pile, a man, vaguely recognizable as someone Harry knew, appeared from amid some rocks sixty feet away. Panic ensued. Harry raised his revolver at this unexpected target, but he was too late and too slow.

The sound of a shotgun echoed off of the rocks and boulders as the lead shot tore into Harry's side. The momentum spun Harry onto his back, and the force of impact, as well as gravity, caused him to tumble down the hard surface he had ascended. An involuntary groan emanated from Harry as he was shot, with more each time his body pounded against the hard granite.

At some point along the way, he lost grip of his revolver and it skidded and skipped into a crevice between some boulders, lodging deep and forever lost.

Harry landed on the uneven ground with a loud thud, knocking him silly. But Harry's desire to survive urged him to lift himself off of the ground to escape to the safety of the cabins.

There was no doubt that he was badly damaged. He clutched at the wound in his side caused by the lead shot, the blood running out of the wound soaking his shirt and coat, and running down into the waist and upper leg of his trousers. He limped the best that he could, tripping and falling several times along the way. On his way to the safety of a cabin, Harry heard the sounds of additional shots, and little clumps of dirt kicked up beside him.

With great relief and exhaustion, Harry reached the door of the nearest cabin. He fumbled with the mechanism keeping the door closed, finally opened it, and then collapsed on the floor inside.

In his last bit of strength before he slipped into unconsciousness, Harry muttered, "Dammit! Not this way!"

Somehow, he managed to kick the door closed.

***

Danny watched the two men searching the area around the corral, and he understood, almost immediately, that he'd made a mistake. He was so concerned about being quiet and undetected, as well as hiding the body of the man that he'd stabbed, that he didn't think to cut a sprig from a fir or pine tree to erase evidence of the struggle and the drag marks that were plain to see. It was an error that could spoil his plans for an ambush.

On edge, Danny watched the men follow the drag marks up into the trees and brush, right to the body. He wiped the stress-induced sweat on his brow with the coat sleeve of his right arm and noticed the dried blood on his hand and under his fingernails. Danny quietly sighed and shook his head in disappointment. This killing thing, Danny thought, it isn't an easy business.

His concern heightened as the men split up—one dodging his way back to the camp, and the other picking his way along the trail Danny took back to the stack of rocks. This wasn't what he planned, nor what he wanted. The man heading back to camp would alert the only other man who was supposed to be there, Eli. And the man on the trail, heading right to where he was sequestered, was an immediate threat.

Danny focused on the man heading his way. He recognized him as one of the men who'd lynched his friend, Sam, stole his pack train, and tried to hang him, too.

And now? Now he was coming straight to him. This wasn't part of the scenario Danny thought over in his head. It wasn't conducive to an ambush of the whole group at all. Sure, Danny shouldn't have any trouble dispatching this man with a gunshot from his hidden and elevated position, but that would alert the rest of the Roberts Boys. However, there was a chance that Danny could circle the man, sneak up on him from behind, and then stab him to death. It was the only way Danny could see his plan staying on track without too much deviation.

Danny was still kicking himself for making his trail from the body in the brush to the hiding place in the rocks so obvious. Hopefully, this was one of those live-and-learn situations. Hopefully.

He checked on the progress of the man that was approaching the stack of rocks. The man was still coming, clearly intent on getting to the rock pile.

Leaving his knapsack, Danny grabbed his shotgun with his left hand and pulled out his knife with his right. He quickly looked down into the camp to make sure the men in the cabin hadn't emerged. Satisfied, Danny stayed low and climbed up the backside of the rock pile to spring a trap on the approaching man. It was a decent plan, except for the fact that he wouldn't be able to see the man until he rounded the side of the rock pile.

Danny began to think this was a bad idea, but there was nothing to do but move forward, literally and figuratively.

After climbing up and down a series of boulders and rocks of various sizes, Danny believed he was elevated high enough in the pile that he could cut over and be in the correct position to watch the man and attack him from behind.

Carefully, he started to pick his way through the maze of granite. Danny's anxiety was greater than he could remember. Then again, he'd never been in this situation before, and with any luck, he'd never have to do anything like this ever again. He moved with confidence and a quiet determination, expecting to see the man climbing up the rocks ahead and to the left of where he was. And if the man moved quicker, or Danny had traversed the rocks slower, that probably would've been the case. But it wasn't.

There'd be no attack from behind, no surprise, and no remaining clandestine. Danny and the man, both climbing up a different series of rocks, and both planning their own ambushes, topped their respective slabs of cold stone and spotted each other.

Danny's saving grace was that he saw the man a second before the man saw him. It was enough of an edge to make a difference.

The man raised his revolver, intending to shoot, but Danny was one step ahead of him. He'd already dropped his knife and shouldered the shotgun, squeezing the trigger before the man could fire his weapon. The shotgun bucked against the bunched muscle of Danny's right shoulder, and he witnessed the impact of the shot. A mist of blood and dust rose from the man's side before the impact propelled him out of sight.

It wasn't a solid hit, and Danny wasn't sure it'd even kill the man. Panicked, Danny abandoned his knife and half-ran and half-scrambled across rocks to where the man had stood when he was shot. Down below, he saw the wounded man struggle to his feet and attempt to flee. This wouldn't do.

There was no longer a pretense of surprise. That shotgun blast was anything but unnoticeable. And if that man got away to the safety of the cabins, even if he was wounded, he'd still be a threat.

Danny pulled the Colt from his belt and began firing at the fleeing man. Shot after shot, six in all, pierced the ground around the man. Hitting a moving target proved to be more difficult than Danny believed. Maybe it was the excitement and desperation of the moment. Perhaps it was because the man was slightly out of range. It could have been the simple fact that Danny wasn't that experienced with a six-gun. Either way, Danny watched as the man fell several times, but eventually staggered to the safety of a cabin.

All Hell was bound to break loose now, and here was Danny with two unloaded weapons, his plans for an ambush ruined, and no other options but to flee or fight. Running away would never destroy the haunted thoughts Danny had. The Roberts Boys would continue to live and terrorize the innocent. They'd remain a threat to Danny.

Fighting the Roberts Boys created the chance that Danny would have peace from the turmoil and feelings of guilt inside. He'd be liberated from the burden by either killing the Roberts Boys or by dying trying. For Danny, there was no question about what he was going to do.

Danny hurriedly climbed back up into his hiding place and reloaded his Colt revolver, and then the shotgun. It didn't take but a few minutes, yet, the lapse of time felt heavy and slow. And when the passing of seconds and minutes could mean the difference between life and death, especially his own life or death, Danny became self-aware of his situation. An ambush was no longer possible. He'd now have to take the fight down to the Roberts Boys. The perceived advantage he'd once had hidden among the rocks was now gone, and Danny had to, once again, revise his plan. It wasn't an envious position to be in.

He slung the knapsack over his shoulder and secured the Colt within his belt. With the shotgun held firmly in his left hand, Danny traversed more boulders, not in the direction he'd originally taken into his hiding place, but the opposite way. Might as well try to keep the men in the camp guessing where he was. If Danny was going to die, he wasn't going to make it easy.

***

Johnny peered around corners and tried to remain as flat as he could against the side of the cook shack. Seeing that the coast was clear, he rounded the building and entered the structure to report back to Eli. The abrupt opening and closing of the door to the cabin startled Eli to the point that he fumbled the cup of coffee he held, spilling some of the hot liquid on the table.

"Dammit Johnny, busting in through a door like that can get a man shot!"

"It's Jacques!" the out-of-breath Johnny managed to blurt out.

"What about him?"

"Up in the brush, we found him," Johnny gulped air and tried to regain his composure. "He's dead."

"Wait, what? Dead? Slow down...tell me what you found."

Johnny took a few more deep breaths and leaned on a chair to steady his nerves and recover from the excitement.

"Harry and me, we searched around the camp, didn't find anything. Nothin' missing that we could see, except for the horses and mules. We looked around the corral and found some tracks, then some blood."

Eli listened intently and patiently.

"Damnedest thing, we saw some drag marks and followed them up into the trees and brush. And sure enough, there was Jacques lying dead...stabbed."

"Stabbed?" Eli pondered as he placed the cup of coffee on the table.

"Yes sir! Maybe two or three times, right in the chest. He ain't the one who took them horses, far as we can tell."

"Did it take you long to put that together?" Eli asked with heavy sarcasm in his tone. He was bewildered by the stupidity of Johnny.

"Well, I was just..."

"Just stop, Johnny! Christ! Where's Harry? He staring at Jacques wondering how he done stabbed himself to death?"

"No, I don't think Jacques..." he stopped himself after the sudden awareness that Eli was mocking him. "Harry...he said he was gonna look around some more, maybe see if he can find more tracks."

Eli felt the rage building within. He wanted to throw chairs and destroy everything in his reach. He'd love to beat Johnny to death, just to relieve the pressure inside. But that'd be a tactical error on his part. Eli might need another gun if someone was after the Roberts Boys.

No, Eli thought. Soon enough, he could shed the dead weight from his clan, but right now, Johnny might be a useful idiot. Eli let his anger subside to a manageable simmer.

"Ok, seems we have a thieving killer to deal with here. Johnny, I want you to round up all our guns...long arms and revolvers, shotguns, muskets, rifles...whatever we got around here. Gather up all the powder, shot, and primers, too. Everything we might need...bring it all back here to the cook shack. If you see Harry, get him to help."

Knowing better than to question Eli's instructions, Johnny acknowledged the order and set to carry it out. Johnny walked to the door and extended his hand to open it. Just then, a loud blast, more than likely from a shotgun, echoed throughout the ravine. Johnny readied his revolver and opened the door just a crack.

"Wait!" Eli commanded.

He, too, armed himself and rushed to the door. Eli pulled Johnny out of the way and looked out of the narrow slit made by the barely open door.

At first, there wasn't anything to see except for the empty yard of the camp. And then a series of shots from a small caliber revolver came from somewhere he couldn't see. He repositioned himself at the door, straining to see something. Anything. In a matter of seconds, he saw Harry, bloodied and fleeing for his life. Eli was tempted to call Harry his way, but he was already moving toward another cabin. Eli lost sight of Harry as he tumbled through the door of the cabin, falling to the ground. The door of the other cabin abruptly shut. Eli did the same with the door to the cook shack.

"Change of plans," Eli bluntly stated to Johnny who grew antsy from the activities outside.

"What now?"

"Well Johnny, seems we have some son of a bitch out there that'd like to kill us! Harry got hit!"

The turn of events put Johnny into a tailspin of distress. He grabbed a tuft of hair with his free hand and began to pace.

"No! No, no, no, no...this ain't happenin'," Johnny lamented.

"Calm down, dammit!" Eli snapped at Johnny. "I need you to keep your head!"

Johnny watched as Eli tipped the heavy wooden table onto its side, creating a barrier he could take refuge behind if necessary. He grabbed the rifle that used to belong to Will, as well as powder, shot, and primers, and placed them behind the table. Eli remained calm. His demeanor reduced Johnny's fear.

"What do you want me to do?" Johnny inquired.

Eli checked his revolver to make sure the cylinder was loaded. He did the same with the rifle. Eli sighed and looked around the room. There was one door and two windows. The windows were opposite each other, one in the wall facing where the shots came from, the other facing toward the corral.

"Here's what I need you to do. Johnny, you're going out that window." Eli pointed to the closed window facing the corral.

"I think there's only one man out there, and he's up that way," Eli said as he pointed away from the corral. "I'll keep him busy down here. You'll circle to the side. One way or another...we'll get 'em! You got it?"

"Yeah, if ya think it'll work," Johnny replied with a slight hint of uncertainty in his voice.

"If ya see someone that's not a Roberts Boy, shoot! We'll sort out the details later!"

Johnny walked over to the covered window. It was attached to the frame of the cabin by a series of wooden latches, one on each side. He rotated the latches and lifted the wooden cover away.

Looking out toward the corral, Johnny didn't see any gunman or threats of any type. Johnny grabbed a chair and placed it under the window, climbed atop, and waited for Eli's signal.

Eli was armed with two revolvers, and he had a rifle in the room. Seeing that Johnny was ready, Eli moved back to the door and opened it just enough to see out.

He needed to create a diversion, something to draw the attention of the man or men who were out there away from the window Johnny was waiting to exit. Although he couldn't see any targets on the hillside, he knew approximately where Harry was fleeing from and where he was shot.

"Now!" Eli alerted Johnny.

With the command given to Johnny, Eli opened the door and stepped halfway out of the cabin to get a better view of the hillside above. He aimed his revolver at a likely hiding spot for a shooter and then fired. One after another, six shots at six different random targets, Eli pulled back the hammer and squeezed the trigger. He glanced back into the room to see Johnny climb out of the window. And with the rounds in the cylinder of that revolver emptied, he pulled his other revolver and did the same thing. It was a waste of ammunition, but Eli had plenty in the cook shack. However, he was gambling on having enough time to reload.

"Come on down and get us, if ya think you're man enough!" Eli shouted after his last shot.

Just as he closed the door, six shots in succession rained down from somewhere and pinged off the side of the cabin, making a dull snapping sound as the lead burrowed into the logs.

"I'd be careful with what ya ask for!" Eli heard shouted in return.

Eli wasted no time as he raced to the open window, replaced the cover, and secured it with latches. No point in making this easy for whomever wanted him dead. He then kneeled behind the table and reloaded the revolvers with a speed that demonstrated his experience.

"Maybe we can work something out! No use in any of us getting shot up! I see you've already taken out a couple of my men!"

Eli was hoping to give Johnny more time to circle and flank the enemy. It was foolhardy to believe he meant a word he yelled.

"Nothin' doin'! I'm here to make you pay, Eli!"

For the first time in recent memory, a shiver shot down Eli's spine. The man doing this knew who Eli was. This was personal. A vendetta. Retribution for some wrong. Which wrong was anyone's guess? There were so many. But whoever shouted down those words was there to collect on a debt.

"You know who I am!" Eli shouted. "Who're you?"

Eli waited for a response. Seconds passed, and then a minute. A response resonated down from a new position on the hill.

"I'm death, and I've come to take you!"

That didn't bring any comfort to Eli.

Chapter 11
No Easy Way to Die

———— ◆·◆·◆ ————

D anny made sure his weapons were fully loaded and readied before he entered the camp. He was now playing a game of cat and mouse, except he knew where two of the mice were. Eli was in the cabin that Danny took fire from and fired upon. And the man that he shot up in the rocks was badly wounded and was in a cabin across from where Eli was. Danny wasn't too worried about him, though. Chances were good that he was either dead or dying on the floor.

The unknown factor in all of this was the Roberts Boy Danny saw with the man he eventually shot. He saw him by the corral, and when they discovered the man up in the trees. Danny lost track of where he went, but Danny surmised that he either circled the camp, staying on the hillside to get the jump on Danny or made his way back down into the cabins. Sooner or later, Danny would find out.

Sticking to cover, Danny moved down to the backside of the cabin the wounded man was in. He listened carefully but heard nothing that would be alarming. It'd be smart for Danny to enter the building to make sure the unaccounted-for man wasn't in there, or, at the very least, to make sure the wounded man was no longer a threat. The problem, of course, was that the cabin faced the door of the cabin where Eli was holed up. That was too risky. Danny decided against that effort.

There were three cabins and a small barn in the camp. Two of the structures were occupied. The third cabin seemed like a probable location where a man might be lying in wait. It was worth looking into, especially if it meant Danny could eliminate another Roberts Boy.

If he moved quickly, he'd be able to cross the yard of the camp without exposing himself too much. There wasn't a better way to approach the situation under the circumstances.

With the revolver in one hand and the shotgun in the other, Danny sprinted from the safety of his hiding place beside a cabin, across the empty yard, and to the door of the cabin near the corral.

Wasting no time, Danny kicked the door open and rushed inside. He aimed his revolver around the room as he ascertained whether or not a Roberts Boy was there. Nobody was there. It was a somewhat large cabin compared to the other two cabins, maybe thirty feet by thirty feet. But it was still small enough to be quickly searched.

It was sparsely furnished with a bed, a small table and chairs, and a couple of trunks containing clothing and personal items. And their weapons. Two shotguns, several old-style single-shot percussion cap pistols, and a broken rifle. Every weapon, except for the rifle, was loaded, which might come in handy if Danny had to make a stand in the cabin. However, it wasn't practical for him to lug all of those weapons around with him. He wanted the extra firepower, but it wasn't worth the burden. He placed the two shotguns against the log walls just inside the door in case Danny needed them later. He left the pistols where he found them.

Not wishing to make himself any more of a target than he already was, Danny stole quick looks out of the doorway at the cabin where Eli was. Getting to him wasn't going to be easy. Eli knew he was gunning for him, so he was already on high alert. There was only one door, and going through that would be like racing into a hornet's nest.

There was always the option to use fire to flush out his adversary. The fear of fire, especially burning to death, was universal. If Danny set the cabin on fire, then he could shoot Eli down as he fled the cabin. Or, at the very least, Eli might succumb to the smoke. That was too good for Eli, though. And then there was the undeniable fact that the logs of the cabin were damp. Fire wasn't a feasible option when quick action was essential.

The cabin did have one window that Danny could see, and he recalled that there was another window on the opposite side of the cabin. Breaking through the cover over the window might allow him to catch Eli off guard. It was worth a try, as long as Danny remained vigilant against an encounter with the unaccounted-for man or the chance that Eli would pour out the door and go on the attack. Danny would never know unless he gave it a try.

Danny quickly scanned his surroundings for immediate threats. None were found. He took several deep breaths to bolster his nerves and then pushed off with his right foot to run as fast as he could to the side of the cabin protecting Eli.

As he reached the cabin, he crouched and leaned hard against the pine logs. The stress and fatigue were beginning to set in. With several more deep breaths filling his lungs, Danny stood up and crept a few feet to the window.

To allow himself more leverage and dexterity, he leaned the loaded shotgun against the cabin, retaining the Navy Colt in his right hand.

Settlers employ many tactics to secure window coverings. Some builders have the luxury of metal hinges and clasps to secure shutters, while many more use leather hinges. There is no one way to do it, so Danny was unsure how these shutters were secured, if at all.

Carefully, Danny smoothed his left hand across the logs to the wooden panel that covered the window. Testing the strength of the panel, Danny gently pushed against the upper right-hand corner. There was no give, and it didn't budge. He applied more pressure with the same result, except that the wood made a little creak that sounded louder than it actually was.

The noise startled Danny, and it alarmed Eli, too, for not two seconds later three rounds of lead punctured the wooden cover inches from where Danny's hand was. He snatched back his appendage before his fingers were blown off. Danny almost returned fire, but that would've been a wasted effort. To shoot through the cover with any control meant squaring up in front of it. That was unwise, and it was an excellent way to get shot. Firing through the logs wasn't an option, either. They were too thick, and the chinking between the logs was narrow, affording a poor line of sight on potential targets, supposing he could see anything at all.

Things were growing ever more intense, what with Danny's realization that Eli knew he was just outside and the fact that the only way to get to Eli was by breaching the door. Odds were good that Eli, and whomever else was in the cabin, recognized this fact and were ready for the man on what appeared to be a suicidal mission. Danny hated those odds. Hate them or not, they were the only plausible, and unfortunate, options that he had. It was mid-morning, and it was turning out to be an ugly day.

Grabbing his shotgun, Danny stayed close to the side of the cabin and maneuvered to a position just left of the framing for the door. Resigned to circumstances, Danny steadied himself for the assault.

***

Crawling out the uncovered window wasn't too much trouble for Johnny. The bottom sill was only a tad taller than waist-high. He moved through the opening, hopping to the ground, and then scurried to the corral. Johnny vaulted over the skinny, but solid corral railings, and then worked his way to where he and Harry found Jacques.

Hearing the exchange of gunfire, Johnny hoped to join the firefight. With any luck, Eli could distract the shooter enough to be careless and oblivious to Johnny's approach. And as long as his thoughts were occupied with contemplation, Johnny also hoped that Harry wasn't badly injured and could fire on the enemy, too. Regardless, he had a job to do.

He ran through the trees, stopping every thirty yards or so to search for the shooter. Johnny repeated this over and over, seeing nothing, until he finally spotted movement ahead. There was a man, armed with a revolver and what looked to be a shotgun. To Johnny, it looked like the man was weighing his options and deciding on a course of action. The man had no idea that Johnny was there, a mere fifty yards away. It was an opportunity that seemingly fell into Johnny's path, a stroke of luck that was bound to both eliminate the threat to the Roberts Boys and please Eli.

Johnny firmly gripped the revolver in his right hand as he began to put the sneak on the man. He wanted to be closer before he shot. He wanted to make sure his target was within range of his sidearm. He wanted to kill the man.

Johnny made quick work out of the distance. As the man a short distance away came into range, Johnny became pleased with himself. A small, mischievous grin spread across his face.

I've got you now, Johnny thought to himself as he raised his long-barreled revolver, steadying it with both hands. He pulled back the hammer and eased his rough right index finger into the trigger guard as he looked down the sights at the man he intended to make dead.

***

Making what could be the last decision you ever made was never an easy thing to do. Danny stood beside the closed door with his back against the log siding of the cabin. Luckily for him, the door swung inward. If it was locked or barred, then Danny might be able to kick it in. But that was only part of the equation. When Danny got the door open, then he'd have to deal with the quarry inside. They were, there was no doubt, armed and willing to kill.

A cool breeze kicked up in the ravine, hitting the sheen of sweat on Danny's neck and forehead. It was an odd sensation. He was so concentrated on the Roberts Boys that everything else was a distraction. But the little shiver it produced reminded Danny that he was alive. The collective bundle of muscle, nerves, bone, tissue, and organs yearned to continue living and thriving. Danny wouldn't mind that at all, but it depended on what happened in the next minute.

Danny looked over his weapons and made sure all was in order. They were loaded and the percussion caps were all in place. He stepped away from the cabin and stood at an angle in front of the door. Danny took the floppy felt hat from his head and tossed it to the side. It was one less thing that could get in his way or obscure his vision.

He lifted his right leg and bunched his muscles, shifting his weight and energy from the left leg to the right as the sole of his boot rammed the flat space next to the door handle. The solid exertion of force exploded the locking mechanism, and the door swung open as splintered wood spat into the cabin.

Within a fraction of a second, as he took cover to the side of the door frame, Danny looked into the cabin to see that Eli was behind a table turned onto its side. Through the light cloud of dust created by the breached door, both men raised and aimed revolvers at each other. There was no careful aiming. No outdrawing the opponent. No advantage because of caliber. Each man, in that fraction of time, was reacting. Danny fired two shots at Eli, both of which hit the table with loud claps. He ducked behind the door frame as Eli fired three shots that either hit the door frame with popping sounds or zipped out the door like angry bees.

Hearing the clicking of a hammer hitting empty chambers, Danny swung his arm and revolver around the frame again, firing two more shots toward Eli. Tin plates and cups on a small shelf to the side of Eli jumped as a bullet penetrated the thin metal. The pinging sound mixed with the heavier noise of Eli dropping the expended revolver he held in his hand.

Eli picked up his other revolver, fully loaded, and returned fire. His thumb and index finger worked in conjunction with each other, squeezing round after round at the man outside. The rounds of hot lead kicked up splinters of wood and were buried deep into the log walls and door frame. Eli and Danny took turns firing at each other until the sounds of metal hitting metal came from each man's revolver.

Reloading a firearm during a gunfight is a luxury, especially when it is a battle in close quarters. The fog of war, or in this case, combat, typically obscures useful information about the participants. How many weapons did they have? Were there more enemies than could be seen? Was anyone wounded or killed? It was all about chance, and nerve, and grit.

Both men, with empty revolvers and not knowing what was to come next, weren't willing to take the time to reload. That would make each man feel vulnerable. An easy target without any defense. Inevitably, neither man wanted to be in that position. Both men wanted this to end. Both men switched weapons.

In Danny's left hand was the shotgun. He held it by the smooth, wooden forestock underneath the barrel. Dropping the revolver, he placed his right hand at the groove that married the stock with the hammer, action, and trigger.

Danny cocked the hammer back and placed the butt-end of the stock into the valley between his shoulder and right chest muscle. He swung around the door frame just as a volley of gunshots opened up from somewhere he couldn't see. The noise caught him off guard, putting a stutter into his step. Forward momentum continued, the barrel of the shotgun moving toward its target. Looking down the cold metal barrel of the shotgun, Eli came into Danny's sightline. At the same time, Danny also saw that he, too, was being aimed at. Both men discharged their weapons nearly at the same time; Danny the shotgun, and Eli a rifle.

With two controlled explosions from the weapons, the smoke from burning black powder charges, already thick in the air, became even more dense. The sharp report of the Mississippi Rifle announced the delivery of a lead projectile traveling over 1,000 feet per second. Almost as soon as Eli fired the shot, it plowed into the wooden stock of Danny's shotgun, splintering the shaped walnut. It was a good stock, made of strong wood that was built to last. But it wasn't designed to withstand the impact of a .54 caliber rifle ball fired at what was essentially point-blank range. The impact sent wooden splinters and bullet fragments into Danny's right shoulder as he fired the shotgun, skewing his aim.

As the smoke and dust settled in the room, the two men, now unarmed, looked at one another. Danny grasped his shoulder in pain and rolled onto his side. Eli, on his knees, reached up to the left side of his head to feel the warmth of blood trickling from a flesh wound.

Astonished at his luck, Eli looked at the blood on his hand and wiped it on his shirt. For the first time, he looked at the man lying on the floor in front of him and recognized his face. He cocked his head to the side and let out a half-sigh, half-laugh that summed up his disbelief.

"You got more fight in ya than anyone I ever met, boy!" Eli exclaimed as he rose to his feet. "But your problem is you ain't figured out how to quit!"

Danny said nothing. He wouldn't give Eli the satisfaction of conversation. He glanced at his shoulder and saw that the fabric of his coat was punctured and turning crimson.

"I can't fault you for killing George, he was a mean pain in the ass. You saw him. You had revenge on your mind. But you coulda walked away after that."

Eli righted a turned-over chair and dragged it across the floor toward Danny.

"But no. You couldn't stop there...you had to kill Jacques. And it looked to me that you did Harry in, too!"

He stood above Danny, glaring at the injured man. There was a fire in his eyes.

"What makes you think you're any better than me?" he punctuated the question as he swung the chair down onto Danny, breaking one of the wooden legs. Danny writhed in pain.

"You know what? I coulda killed you back in Missouri. I coulda tracked you down on the trail, or in Sacramento, and killed you, but I didn't. You weren't worth it!"

Eli hoisted the broken chair above his head again and swung the piece of furniture down, striking Danny. He stumbled and fell to his knees in the process.

Danny, groaning in pain from the impact of the chair and the gunshot wound, tried to crawl away. Unfortunately, the effort was difficult with Danny's injuries. Pushing with his legs and dragging his body with one good arm wasn't fruitful.

Growing tired from the gunfight and the pummeling he was giving, Eli rose to his feet. He slightly swayed from side to side.

"Granted," Eli continued, "I thought we did kill you on that mountain trail. And now that I've had time to think about it, I apologize for that."

He steeled himself and stood tall, gripping the chair and preparing for another strike.

"But now...," he said with a smile, "right now...I mean to kill you, and it'll feel good!"

Eli once again hauled the chair over his head in an arch and started to swing it downward. The partially broken chair tracked toward Danny's head. The blow would have a devastating impact, maybe even be enough to kill Danny. But the impact never happened.

Before the chair could complete its path, a shotgun blast raged from the open door and hit Eli in the hip. The force of the discharge propelled Eli to the floor and the chair skidded to a corner of the room.

A man stood at the entrance to the cabin holding a shotgun. Little wisps of smoke rose from the barrel of the gun. He stepped into the room and kept his gaze fixed on Eli.

Incredulously, Danny looked to Eli and then back to the man. He heard a familiar voice.

"Eli, I told ya to leave my men alone!"

It was Jim Kinney, Danny's partner in the freighting company. Jim had previous dealings with Eli back in Missouri and on the trail to California. He knew Eli Roberts, and he detested what the man was, even more since he and his gang had killed an employee and robbed the company.

But it was more than a disgust in the man. Jim Kinney hated Eli Roberts and the Roberts Boys because they brought harm to Danny. He and his wife saw Danny as the son they'd never had.

Buckshot shredded cloth and flesh, and smashed bone, especially at close range. The shot fired from Kinney's shotgun immobilized Eli, breaking his hip and opening wounds that bled profusely. He was in poor shape.

"J...Jim? How...how?" Danny stammered through pain and fatigue.

Kinney looked from Eli to Danny, leaning his shotgun against the wall of the cabin. He drew the holstered revolver he wore.

"Save your strength, boy," Kinney urged Danny, "you're gonna need it."

Danny exhaled heavily and dropped his head back to the floor. He momentarily stared at the ceiling, trying to ignore the sharp pain pulsing in his shoulder.

As Kinney walked with a pronounced limp toward Eli, Danny turned his head to watch.

"It's all over now, Roberts. Your murdering and thieving."

Kinney examined the chambers of his revolver, rotating the cylinder to see each round.

Eli watched Kinney and thought the situation over. He was injured, but not dead, so he had that going for him. But he was unarmed. Every weapon near him was unloaded. A fraction of hope did cross his mind, though. There was a chance Johnny or Harry was still alive.

"You had your run, Eli. And you've had more than enough time to walk the straight and narrow, law-abiding path of life."

Eli laughed at the thought.

"I've had time enough to make all kinds of choices," Eli replied. "Some good, some bad. But they were all mine."

"It's a shame, really. All that talent and charisma. Eli, you coulda been something more."

Eli pushed himself into a sitting position, tolerating the pain from his hip.

"I was all I ever wanted to be."

He looked around the room and saw a bottle of whiskey lying just out of reach. Kinney took a step toward the bottle and gently kicked it toward Eli.

"Much obliged," Eli said as he uncorked the bottle and took a big belt.

He swallowed and offered the bottle to Kinney. Kinney brushed the offer away with a wave of his hand and shook his head in the negative. He wasn't there to drink.

Eli took another big drink and rested the weight of his upper body on his free arm.

"So...Kinney. What now? You round us Boys up and take us into Visalia or Stockton or Sacramento? Take us to the law for trial?"

"Boys? There's no Boys left. Just you."

Eli looked confused and disappointed.

"One fella...he ran into us on the hillside. He thought he had the drop on one of our men. He was wrong. We cut him down before he had a chance to fire." Kinney chuckled as he recounted that fact.

"And another man, he's dead in the cabin across the way. I suspect young Danny here gravely wounded him. So, it's just you, Eli."

"So, you take me in...hold me accountable for all that's been done?" Eli inquired.

Jim Kinney leaned in a bit closer to Eli and looked him square in the eyes.

"Oh, you'll be held accountable alright. But you ain't goin' nowhere. There's no law, no judge, no trial, no jury. Just me."

Eli tried to stand, but that damaged hip gave way and he dropped to the ground. He scooted backward using his arms and one good leg until he butted up against the overturned table. Out of options, Eli turned defiant.

"Damn you, Kinney! Damn you! I'll see you and your boy in Hell!"

And with that, Jim Kinney raised the revolver and aimed it at Eli Roberts. He cocked the weapon and fired all six shots into Eli's body.

With each shot, Eli convulsed and the remaining life that coursed through his body faded. When it was over, Eli slumped sideways and came to rest on the floor. Eli was dead, and the Roberts Boys were no more.

Danny watched it all unfold as he started to flutter in and out of consciousness. Just before he passed out, in the fuzzy glare that became his vision, he saw three other people enter the cabin.

***

After Kinney dispatched Eli, there was a new and more urgent task at hand. Danny was wounded badly, and he couldn't travel until it was addressed. There was no way he could even start to mend until the shrapnel and wooden splinters were removed.

Danny regained consciousness as he was carried out of the cabin into the sunshine. Scotty, the saloonkeeper, was at his feet, Francis carefully carried Danny's upper body, and Will supported Danny's midsection. Danny weakly smiled at his porters and looked at his destination. Jim was standing next to the table that used to be inside the cabin. It was covered in a blanket.

The men placed Danny on the table and covered him with another blanket to ward off the cold. A campfire was burning steps away, the crackling wood doing its best to warm a pot of water. It wasn't the optimum location to tend to Danny's wounds, but there was more light outside, and it was a good deal cleaner.

"Now, I ain't got no medical training, Danny, but I've done a great deal of frontier doctorin'," Francis explained.

Waves of pain shot through Danny's shoulder. However, it didn't stop him from listening to Francis with great interest.

"And I ain't got no fancy tools, just a sharp knife. But we gotta do this. You understand?"

Danny nodded his head in the affirmative, clenching his teeth against the throbbing injury.

Francis took an uncorked bottle of whiskey from Scotty, put a hand behind Danny's head, and placed the brown-colored bottle where Danny could see it.

"You need to drink some of this down...get yourself a little liquored up to numb ya from what's to come."

Francis placed the bottle against Danny's lips and gently tilted it for him to drink. Most of the liquid made it into his mouth, but a small stream of whiskey spilled out the side of Danny's lips more than once. This was repeated for several minutes until Danny's head was swimming. The pain, once an intense stabbing sensation, was but an echo of discomfort; a shadow of agony.

"Is it time?" Jim asked Francis.

Francis let out a deep breath reflecting his apprehension.

"Unfortunately, yes. Really, the sooner the better."

Scotty soaked rags in the hot water and wrung them out. They had already removed Danny's coat and cut away his shirt. Scotty dabbed at the wounds, removing all of the dirt and blood that he was able to, continuing the process until it was reasonably clean.

Jim cut a strip of leather from strapping he found in one of the cabins. He placed one of his hands against the side of Danny's head to provide comfort, and he raised the piece of leather to where Danny could see it.

"I'm gonna place this in your mouth. Bite down on it when you feel pain. It'll help some, and I'll be right here."

"Danny...I ain't gonna lie. This'll hurt like Hell," Francis said with sympathy in his voice.

And with that, Francis poured whiskey onto the wounds, producing a groan from Danny. He could see from Danny's jaw that he was clenching his teeth tightly against the leather.

Armed with a sharp knife and the fact that he'd done similar tasks to other people on more than one occasion, Francis started to cut and probe Danny's wounds. Wooden splinters and fragments of lead were removed amid Danny's stifled screams.

"You're doin' great, boy! Hang in there! Francis is almost done." Kinney encouraged Danny, trying not to be overwhelmed by the tears spilling out of Danny's eyes and rolling down his cheeks.

It took more than ten minutes. Ten long, intense minutes that all involved would never forget. Nobody likes to see one they care for in excruciating pain.

More than once, Scotty felt his knees become wobbly and his head began to swim with the sensations associated with fainting. He sat down and gazed at the surrounding scenery to shut the happenings out of his mind. They didn't need two patients.

Jim took Danny's face into both hands and turned his head away from Francis.

"Danny...hey, Danny! Look at me! I want you to focus on me. We're almost done here, then we can think 'bout gettin' on home. But I need you to think about anything other than what's happening here...try as hard as you can!"

Jim moved his eyes for a fraction of a second to look at Francis. Danny didn't detect the nearly imperceptible nod he gave Francis.

Francis frowned and moved to the fire burning close by the table. He put a heavy leather glove on his right hand and picked up a long knife that'd been heating up in the flames. It was hot. Not glowing red or orange or white hot, but hot enough to do what needed to be done. It would be an unpleasant task. It was a necessary task.

Scotty and Will both looked away and steadied themselves for what was to come. Jim looked at Danny with compassion and a touch of pity.

Stopping the flow of blood from a wound is paramount to the survival of a patient. If the proper materials are available, stitching the wound typically provides a proper seal and will eliminate the loss of blood, at least externally. But in an emergency situation, the only feasible option is cauterization. It's not a pleasant task for either party. However, it saves lives.

Moving quickly, Francis placed the hot knife against Danny's wounds. One by one, for short periods, the heated blade did its job, burning the tissue and stemming the flow of blood. The smell of singed flesh wafted upward. The sizzling sound turned the stomachs of those who heard it, and Danny's muffled screams seemed to pierce the sky until he passed out from the pain. If one could see his face, they'd see that sweat intermingled with the profuse amount of tears Danny had cried.

Chapter 12

Reunion

———◆ ∙ ◆ ∙ ◆ ∙ ◆———

Several hours later, Danny regained consciousness. He was now lying in a bed in the cabin that hadn't experienced any violence that day. His right arm was immobilized in a sling made out of an old shirt Francis found in one of the cabins in the camp. The room had a slightly musty smell to it, but it was warm and the bed was comfortable. Sitting in a chair nearby was Will.

Danny licked his dry lips and blinked hard to clear the fog of sleep and alcohol that clouded his head. He snickered a little when the image of Will became clear.

"I thought I was dreaming," he weakly said to Will.

He shifted in the bed and the pain in his shoulder reminded him that this was entirely real.

"Oh...it's no dream," Will replied in a friendly voice as he leaned in closer. "You got yourself a bit shot up, but those Roberts Boys are no more."

Will got up from the chair and ladled cool water from a keg into a tin cup. He helped Danny take sips to quench his thirst and moisten his parched lips. The sensation of the cool liquid running across his tongue and down his throat was welcoming. Danny noticed the bandages covering Will's hands.

"I never thought I'd see you again, not alive anyway," Will quipped to Danny.

"I'm a bit surprised, myself," Danny proclaimed.

He looked around the room that was lit by a series of candle lanterns to see a fairly well-furnished cabin containing all of the requisite comforts of a home and workplace in the wilderness.

"Where's Jim and Francis? And that saloonkeeper?"

"Out burying the Roberts Boys, which is probably more than they deserve. I'll...I'll go tell them you're awake."

Will left the cabin, leaving Danny to wallow in a haze that continued to border on what felt like reality and sleep. It was ten minutes before Will returned with Jim and Francis, but Danny hardly noticed the passing of time.

"I'll go help Scotty finish with the graves," Will told Jim as he exited the cabin.

Mostly snapped out of the previous fog, Danny was still in disbelief that Jim and Francis both showed up, out of nowhere, when he needed them the most. *God truly works in mysterious ways*, Danny thought.

The clanking sound of furniture moving was loud in the room as both Francis and Jim pulled up chairs and sat down to talk with Danny.

"Sorry about the whole mess with your shoulder, Danny. How're you feeling?" Francis inquired.

He smiled at Francis, saying, "It feels terrible! But I understand. You all just surprised the heck out of me! Francis, I can understand how you're here. But Jim? How'd you get here?"

Jim leaned back in the chair and crossed his left leg across the right, and he began to relay how he came to be here.

"It all started with Gonzales and Ah Joe. After they recovered Sam's body from Francis' place, they took almost a week to reach Visalia. There, Gonzales contracted an express rider to bring news of Sam, you, and the ambush to the office in Sacramento. And even though it was an express service, it still took close to a week to deliver a message."

Jim reached into his pocket and pulled out a clay pipe and bag of tobacco. He packed a load of tobacco into the pipe and lit it as he continued his story.

"Turns out, one of the riders was delayed when his horse went lame on an isolated stretch of the Stockton Road. He walked until a man with a buckboard came along and took him to the next station."

"There are some lonely lengths of road heading to Visalia," Danny interjected in agreement.

"When the message reached the office, there was another, unfortunate, delay. We were shorthanded, more so than normal, and all hands were on deck making deliveries...including me. I was up the American River drainage making a three-week run to the far-flung camps. By the time I got back to the office and read the message, it'd been sitting on my desk for two weeks. I about jumped out of my skin when I read what happened."

Danny thought about asking about Julia but then thought better of it. If he got a chance, he'd privately ask Jim later.

"If it was just me with no business to operate, I would've dropped everything and rushed to the Greenhorn Mountains. But responsibilities are responsibilities. You understand? I had to make sure loose ends for the business were tied up before I could leave. I felt better about the situation knowing that were being cared for by Francis."

"I also needed to shore up everything with the wife. She looks at you like a son, too, so she was eager for me to leave. All of this put the trip off for a couple of days."

"And you know I adore her, too, Jim," Danny said.

"I know," Jim reassuringly said and then continued his story.

"Taking a stage south, I believed, was the quickest manner to reach the jumping-off point for the Greenhorn Trail."

Jim sighed, signally further disappointment in what had transpired.

"Unfortunately, all of the stages running out of Sacramento were booked, so I had to ride over to Stockton to find a stage that still had a seat available and was scheduled to make the run south. It's one of those situations where nothing was happening quickly or smoothly, but finds a way to work out in the end."

He took a few drags from the pipe and blew smoke into the air. His tale kept the attention of both Danny and Francis.

"The stage ride south wasn't abnormal in any way. Despite the suspension on the stage, every bump and small rut rocked the vehicle back and forth, and side to side. Without fail, every time the stage met another wagon or horse on the Stockton Road, dust filtered into the compartment."

"Hold on a moment," Francis said as he got up and looked around the cabin. He found three empty cups and an unopened bottle of whiskey. Francis poured booze into each cup and gave one to Jim and Danny. He reserved one for himself.

"For Danny's pain, you know?" Francis said in defense. "And, well...this is turning into a long story!"

They all got a pretty good laugh over that but didn't mind sipping the whiskey as Jim spun his yarn.

"I shared the ride a great deal of the way with a woman and her son, and a snake-oil salesman who tried to peddle his cure-all formula to anyone he could. I'm sure you're not shocked, but I was in no mood to be flim-flammed, so I shut that sales pitch down rather early on the ride."

"Now, I was polite, but firm. But it sent a strong message to the salesman. The only time we heard a peep from that man about his potion was when the stage made a stop in a town or at a ferry crossing, and a new batch of potential victims emerged."

"Mostly alcohol in them bottles, so I hear," Francis quickly interjected.

"The whole ride, the only thing that was really on my mind was getting to the Greenhorn Mountains. That, and looking at every wagon we passed as the stage headed south. I was looking for Gonzales and Ah Joe. So, I sat by the window and stuck my head out of the stage upon the approach of every buckboard. Time and again, mile after mile."

"At times, it was a tedious process, especially as the stage neared towns, river crossings, and trading centers. Other times on lonely stretches of the road, it was a game of waiting."

"Finally, somewhere between Visalia and some other remote station which I cannot recall, our stage approached a buckboard wagon with familiar faces aboard. Now, when I boarded the stage I talked with the crew, informing them of my intentions, and striking a deal with them to stop when they encountered the buckboard I was seeking."

"So, seeing Gonzales and Ah Joe, I called out to the driver, and the stage came to a halt as it passed the wagon. I felt a bit bad for the other passengers, and I apologized for the momentary delay, but I needed to get more information."

"Me and Gonzales and Ah Joe somberly greeted each other and shook hands. We briefly talked about what happened on the Greenhorn Trail, and I looked over Sam's encased body in the wagon. It was a sad sight and made me downright angry."

Danny's countenance temporarily turned gloomy thinking about Sam.

"I sure wish we would've been able to build him a proper coffin for the trip. He deserved better than what we had," Danny sadly stated.

"You done ok, Danny," Jim said to comfort Danny. "Sometimes, you just have to go with what you have."

The men all took another sip of whiskey before Jim continued.

"Before continuing on our way, Gonzales gave me a more detailed description of how to reach the cabin where you were and what Francis looked like. After that, we parted ways, and the stage and wagon continued on."

"Once I reached Visalia, I was on my own to make the trip up to Linn's Valley, to Poso Flats, and then up the Greenhorn Trail. I was able to rent a horse from a Visalia stable, and I also secured provisions there."

"Using the information provided by Gonzales, I headed up the Trail and ambled around in the mountains until I eventually found Francis' cabin. As luck would have it, I missed your departure by a handful of hours."

"Funny thing is," Francis added, "when Jim rode into my yard, I was preparing to leave and go find you to give you a hand. So, together we rode down to Keyesville. It made sense to stop into Scotty's saloon to ask about you and the Roberts Boys. And that is when we met Will."

Francis excitedly told this portion of the story, partly the result of the whiskey, and also because he wanted to be involved.

"Will was being tended to by Scotty. After meeting him and learning what the Roberts Boys did to him, we thought we struck gold! And it got even better when Will relayed how he ran into a man who was gunning for the Boys."

Francis gestured with his hands as he talked to Danny.

"Putting two and two together wasn't difficult, so Jim and I had a general idea where you'd be found."

"With the information Will provided," Jim took back over, "we could've found the camp, but luck was with us when Will volunteered to lead the way back to the Roberts Boys. It was also helpful that Scotty offered to help."

Francis looked a little put off when Jim took over, but he got over it quickly as he poured more whiskey into his cup.

"It was dusk before we were ready to move on, and the group decided it would be best to get some rest. Collectively, we decided to wake in the early morning hours, when it was still dark. From Will's figuring, we'd reach the camp around daybreak or thereabouts."

"And that's just what we did. Led by Will, we rode through the dark, in the cold, toward our destination. Although, by daybreak, we still hadn't reached the camp, but we were getting close."

"Damn, that was a frigid night!" Danny remembered.

"By the time we were within shouting distance of the camp, we heard shooting. Apparently, that was you blasting away."

"Well, we agreed to spread out a bit and approach the camp. That's when one of the Roberts Boys, a younger man that Will identified as a boy named Johnny, thought he had the drop on Scotty. In essence, he did, but he didn't count on me and Francis jumping out from some trees and bushes. He was too slow and too stupid to survive that matchup. We both dropped him where he stood."

"So the battle was on, and we snuck down into the camp. The shooting had stopped. We quickly searched around, found Harry dead, and then found you being beaten. You know the rest of the story."

Jim emptied his cup and then held it out to Francis for a refill. Francis promptly filled his cup and topped off Danny's.

"It's probably best we stay here in camp for a couple of days until Danny here is fit to ride," Francis stated to the two men in the room.

"Reckon that'd be the appropriate thing to do," Jim chimed in as he took another sip.

"I wouldn't mind not moving for a while," Danny said with a partial smile as he, too, took another drink to ease his pain.

"Hey Jim, a couple of our mules were mixed in with their horses when I ran them out of the corral last night."

"Let's not worry 'bout that right now. They're not far off, I imagine. We'll get them soon enough."

Before Jim finished telling Danny how he'd wound up at the Roberts camp, Scotty and Will came into the one-room cabin. They were both tired and dirty. Feeling the warmth of the fire, they crowded near the hearth. Digging graves in the cold ground was unpleasant. But they weren't unciv- ilized. Even men like the Roberts Boys deserved a proper burial. Granted, some men earn their graves sooner than others.

The men lounged around the cabin that night. Will and Scotty sat around a table and talked with Francis. Danny was lying in bed and Jim tended to him. Despite the circumstances, everyone was having a relatively good time. The roaring fire in the fireplace kept the men warm.

Supplies of food and coffee were salvaged from the cook shack, and Scotty prepared a stew for dinner. The men had a natural camaraderie and felt like old friends. They didn't mind if the moment lasted forever. Except for Danny. He didn't mind visiting, eating, and chatting. But as the evening wore on, the stabbing pain in his shoulder intensified. He could do without that.

As the time trickled past, separate conversations emerged within the room.

"What're you gonna do now?" Francis asked Will.

"Well, Scotty here said he'd take me on, give me a job at the saloon until I can figure things out."

Scotty slapped Will on the back and beamed with pride.

"I can always use a hard worker, one with integrity and potential. Like Will."

Will blushed a bit at the compliment and grinned a grin wider and brighter than he'd had in a long time.

"What'll happen to this place, the Roberts Boys' camp?" Will pondered with genuine interest.

"Here's the thing," Scotty quickly answered, "I know of them boys who built this place and worked their claims nearby. Good chance they'll want to know that the men who ran them out are no more. Maybe they'll come back. At the very least, they may want to collect their belongings and sell the place. Guess it's up to them."

Francis looked around the room and thought of the other two cabins, the corral, and the small barn.

"I know that if'n this were my place, and I worked so hard to build it, I'd want it back. They've a fine setup here if they can ignore the fact that a bit of violence occurred."

The three continued their conversation, vacillating topics, moving from the camp to Keyesville, to hunting, and a variety of other topics. On the other side of the room, Jim and Danny were deep in conversation.

"I'll see to it that Sam is taken care of in whatever way his family wants," Jim said. "Not real sure of their customs...if it means being buried, or burned, or shipped back to his homeland...I'll make sure that he's done right."

Danny was happy to hear that, and, a bit morose, too.

"He was a good man, and a hard worker, too. I couldn't understand much of what he said, though."

"Me neither!"

Both of them got a good laugh out of that admission. It felt good to laugh, and Danny reveled in Jim's company.

"Think you'll be headin' back home to Sacramento when you're fit to travel?" Jim asked with a tint of seriousness in his voice.

Danny didn't immediately answer. That was a tough question, and he hadn't given it any thought during his convalescence with Francis, nor his hunt for the Roberts Boys. Revenge and justice consumed his thoughts. And to tell the truth, Danny hadn't thought much about the future because he wasn't certain he'd have one after finding the Roberts Boys.

"I ain't given it much thought. I...I suppose I will. Maybe for a time...or longer. I might come stay with Francis from time to time."

He raised his good arm and rubbed his head. Mixed emotions occupied his thoughts and tugged at his allegiances. He was conflicted over what to do and where he should call home. On the one hand, Danny's stake in the J. Kinney Freighting Company, his source of income, naturally influenced his thoughts about going back to Sacramento, as did his affinity for Jim and his wife.

And then there was Julia. He was still smitten with her. However, it was foolish to have such thoughts about a married woman. She still occupied his thoughts, though.

Then there was Francis. He'd saved Danny's life, nursed him back to health, been his friend for these past months, and, in a very real sense, was responsible for saving his life once again. It was Francis who encountered Jim, and brought him to Scotty's where they met Will. Danny felt obliged not to abandon Francis and the friendship he had there. Perhaps there was a way he could do both.

Jim recognized the inner turmoil. He understood how it felt to want to be somewhere and everywhere all at once.

"Well," Jim said with kindness in his voice, "The decision is really yours, and I couldn't fault you for any thoughts or actions you might have. Hell, I wouldn't mind coming back to this country from time to time, maybe bring the missus to escape the hustle and bustle of the city."

Jim found himself thinking of the sprawling southern San Joaquin Valley, the meadows and timber of the Greenhorn Mountains, the potentially wild and wooly Kern River, and the prominent walls, domes, and peaks of granite that protruded around the Kern River Valley. He found himself enamored with thoughts of the scenery. Jim imagined himself looking out across that gray stone every day. He could easily spend the rest of his life in these mountains. He could fall in love with this country. Jim wasn't the first who possessed those thoughts, and he wouldn't be the last.

Danny's voice drew Jim away from his daydreaming.

"Guess I got time to figure it out. Maybe I'll even travel back to see my folks in Missouri."

That statement seemed to jar Jim's memory. He hastily got up from his chair and crossed the room to where his coat was hanging on a wooden peg in the log wall. Rummaging around a bit, Jim pulled a letter from the inside pocket and returned to the chair beside Danny.

"I got so caught up with everything today, that I completely forgot about this."

Jim handed the letter to Danny.

"It was at the office when I returned from my run up the American River. The funny thing is, I was in a bit of a panic about you, and I was eager to get down here. I didn't know what sort of shape you'd be in. Hell, you might've been dead by the time I got to you. But I saw that letter and thought *I'd better bring your post.* Kinda peculiar what we think and prioritize during stressful times."

Danny took the letter and immediately recognized the handwriting. It was from his mother, addressed to Danny in the care of the J. Kinney Freighting Company, Sacramento, California.

He opened the letter, unfolded it, and shifted his body so he could get a better angle of light to read by. The movement lit his shoulder on fire with an edge of pain. Danny winced. The paper crinkled as he awkwardly held it open with his left hand and turned it toward the light.

September 23, 1854

Dear Daniel,

It is my hope that this letter finds you well and healthy. From your previous note it sounds like you've found your place in California, working with Mr. Kinney. That is wonderful news. It's a far cry from what you originally set out to do with Stephen, but, from what I hear, it's mighty better than digging for gold. I heard from Stephen's folks that he's still at it, working claims all up and down the mountains. He's made some money, but most of it just covers expenses. As long as he is happy, then that is what matters. Maybe your paths will cross soon. I think you should keep on with freighting. Do you have other close friends besides Mr. Kinney. Are there other fellows you consider your friends?

Have you settled down and bought a house there in Sacramento? It's always nice to have a place you can call your own. And what of your prospects for a wife? Have you met any nice, respectable lasses? I'm sure a successful young man like you could have his choice of young women for a wife. You will let me know before you marry, I hope.

Your father and I are doing well, as is Seth. But things in Missouri are beginning to sour. I'm sure you've heard of the troubles generated by the Kansas-Nebraska Act. I cannot imagine that Mr. Douglas and Mr. Butler believed that their law would stir the passions of so many people. Radicals from both sides—a pro-slave state and anti-slave state—have flooded into Kansas. They're well-armed and impassioned. The perils of democracy are realized with popular sovereignty. It seems that not a day goes by that we don't hear of fistfights and worse breaking out in Kansas Territory, and even in the border regions between Missouri and Kansas.

It is getting to the point that your father and I are afraid that the disputes over the slavery question are reaching the point of no return. One side or the other will have to give, or violence will become the norm. And we are, we believe, too close for comfort.

We are especially worried that young Seth will be caught up in the to-do, regardless of his intentions.

And that is why I'm writing to you. Seth, your father, and I are going to sell the farm, pack up our belongings, and come to California. Your letters paint a lovely picture of that state, a real land of opportunity. And we long to see you. I hope this isn't too much of a surprise for you, and I hope we will not inconvenience you in any way. It's just our desire to get out of the gathering storm. And you know your father. Just like you, he has that wanderlust. Truthfully, I'm still shocked he didn't hit the trail with you and Stephen when you went to California on your great adventure. Maybe this is just a good excuse to try something new. Regardless, we are all looking forward to the challenge of the trip, and of starting over...again. We also look forward to being a complete family again.

As of now, we plan on leaving in the spring, just as soon as it is feasible to do so. When we are prepared to leave, I shall write to you word of our departure. Until then, may God be with you and protect you.

With much love, always,

Your Mother.

Danny set the folded letter down on his lap, thought about it for a moment, and then lifted it to the light to read it again. The words resonated in his head as he read through the lines of the letter. Jim became concerned by the look on Danny's face.

"What is it, Danny?" Jim asked. "What's wrong? Your folks ok?"

Danny set the letter down once more. Perplexed, he turned his head toward Jim. His eyes were wide and the color had gone from his face.

"Yeah...yes, my folks are fine...it's just...they're coming here, to California!"

"To visit?" Jim asked.

Danny used his left arm to push his body up in the bed to be more comfortable. He exhaled sharply with the effort.

"Apparently, no!" Danny blurted. "Things are becoming politically divisive at home. Downright dangerous. They're selling the farm, packing up, and moving here. Ma, Pa, and Seth."

"Well, that sounds like great news!" Jim smiled at his words. "I cannot wait to meet them."

"They'll like you just fine. I'm just a little stressed over what I need to get done before they get out here. It's January...and they'll be leaving in just a few short months! If all goes well for them, they could be in California by summer."

"That's true, but it's a good five or six months away," Jim reasoned.

Danny motioned to his arm in the sling and frowned.

"This anchor ain't gonna help much. As it is, I'll be practically useless at work. I cannot even figure how I'll prepare for my family."

Jim grabbed hold of Danny's left arm and held it firmly.

"My Boy...one step at a time. One step."

Danny appreciated Jim's plain advice, and he embraced the fact that he was right. He'll get done what he can when he can. And truly, if he greeted his family in good health and with love, then all would be right.

***

Scotty and Will left the next day. After all, Scotty did have a business to run.

Jim, Francis, and Danny stayed on at the camp for two more days. It made no sense at all to have Danny travel until he was able to do so. He had to get used to his arm in a sling. And then there was the pain. There was hope that it would begin to subside and the swelling would decrease.

Over those two days, Jim and Francis rounded up the stray mules and horses and tended to them in the corral. The men decided that they'd see if any of the horses belonged to any men in the vicinity of Keyesville. If so, they'd be returned. If not, they'd leave them in the possession of Francis for a time and post notice at Scotty's where the stock could be found. The mules, branded with the mark of the J. Kinney Freighting Company, would naturally return to Sacramento with Jim.

Danny took it easy, adjusting to his new, hopefully short-lived, normal. He spent his time alternating between lying in the bed, sitting in a chair inside the cabin and then outside the cabin, and taking short walks.

His strength was returning, and he was adjusting to life in a sling. It would be several weeks, maybe even as many as six weeks, before he could release his right arm for good. There is no way it'd be healed by then, but it'd be stabilized to the point where he could start to rehabilitate. It was all a matter of time. And it was all about tolerating the nagging pain and stiffness daily until he was completely healed. Patience was key.

On the third day, the day they planned to depart and travel to Scotty's Saloon, a small group of men appeared outside the camp. They were unarmed and as non-confrontational as they could make themselves. The group of men announced their presence as Jim and Francis were preparing the mules and horses for the trip.

"Ho there!" the leader of the group shouted into the camp.

Wary of strangers, Jim placed his hand on the butt of his revolver. Francis dropped what he was doing and had a shotgun in his hands in what looked like a lightning-quick motion.

The group's leader raised his hands, palms toward the two armed men. It was a motion to indicate that they intended no harm, as much as it was to show that they had no weapons.

"Hey, mister...we mean you no harm. We come up from Scotty's. Word is that the Roberts Boys are no more."

Jim relaxed a bit, but his hand remained on the handle of his revolver.

"You heard right," he said and motioned to a flat knoll up behind the camp, "if you're looking for them, they're in the ground up there."

"I think you got us wrong," said the leader. "This here camp used to be ours. We built it and lived here while we worked our claims until the Roberts Boys came along. They took what they wanted, and done run us out of here."

Jim and Francis relaxed at hearing this. Jim walked over to the mounted leader and extended his rough, calloused hand in greeting.

"Well, welcome back. The place is yours. We were just getting ready to leave."

The men shook hands and exchanged introductions as Danny walked out of the cabin. He was dressed for travel wearing a heavy coat, thick wool trousers, felt slouch hat, knit scarf, and gloves. The sling, worn over the top of the coat, held his right arm in place.

"Say," Jim inquired, "any of them horses belong to your group?"

The leader looked over the animals strung together and identified two of the stock as belonging to his group. Francis removed them from the string and turned the animals over to the owners of the camp.

"I'm afraid some of your camp is in disarray, what with the gunfight and all," Jim spoke to the men. "The cook shack there is a mess!"

The men began to dismount.

"No worries, friend," the leader spoke, "we're just happy them Boys are gone and we get to move back home!"

"Glad to hear that," Jim stated with only a hint of concern in his voice. "I beg your pardon, but we've a ways to go, and it'll be a slow ride. Besides, I'm sure you folks are eager to get back to your camp."

It was an amicable parting. The men were looking forward to making the camp their home once again, and they realized that making small talk delayed all parties involved.

Danny approached the horse he was to ride and prepared to mount. In his present state, it'd be incredibly awkward for him to get into the saddle on his own. With his left foot in the stirrup, and with the strength from his left arm, he could push and pull and work his way into the saddle. It'd be a struggle. Difficult, but not impossible.

But there was no need for Danny to prove that he could do things on his own. That would come soon enough. Until then, he had the helpful hands and brawn of Jim and Francis. They were more than willing to help Danny into the saddle and make sure he was situated as comfortably as was feasible.

Both of the men steadied the horse and pushed Danny's body into position. The leather saddle creaked under his weight, and the horse gently whinnied. He sat in front of his tied-up bedroll and knapsack. Within the bundle was Danny's revolver and his broken shotgun. They'd be of no use to him until he was healed. Danny took the reins into his left hand and was ready to leave.

Jim and Francis, each with a string of either mules or horses, climbed up on their steeds and slowly rode out of camp.

When Danny rode up the north fork of the Kern River to find the Roberts Boys he was focused on the task at hand. Whether it was following Will or sneaking into the camp, Danny paid little attention to the beauty that surrounded him. But now that he wasn't stressed and trying to set up an ambush, Danny had the time to take in his surroundings.

The cold, gray granite precipices. The towering pine and fir trees dusted with snow. Small herds of deer off in the distance, grazing across draws and ravines. And the ambling Kern River, with its icy-cold water originating high up in the Sierras at Mt. Whitney, and added to by the ebb and flow of snow that accumulated and then melted throughout the winter. The flow of the water, rambling down rocks and waterfalls, created a frothy mass and then ran into stretches that were clear and calm in appearance. The romanticized river scene was repeated mile after mile until the north fork flowed out of its canyon and merged with the south fork to continue through the Kern River Valley.

The trip to Keyesville felt like a leisurely ride to all three men. There was no rush, no immediacy, no urgency. They wanted to reach Scotty's Saloon before nightfall, and even at that slow pace, they'd have no problem with that goal. They talked about the land and its potential all the way to the saloon. Their plans for the future were also talked about; trapping, hunting, freighting, traveling to Sacramento, and further exploring the Greenhorn Mountains.

They also stopped periodically when they encountered others on the trail or when the trail neared a camp. It allowed Danny time to rest. It was also pleasant to stop and talk with others about nothing in particular.

In the late afternoon, they reached Scotty's. It wasn't a rigorous ride, but it took a lot out of Danny. He was drained.

Scotty's Saloon was lively that evening, with drink, food, and gambling. Much to their appreciation, Scotty made arrangements for the trio to lodge overnight in the back room of the saloon that he called home. They all watched the night slip away while they enjoyed each other's company for what might be the last time. It felt bittersweet.

Chapter 13
Passing On

———•◆•———

"**T**his is gonna be tougher than I figured," Francis said to Jim and Danny as they ascended the Greenhorn Trail out of Keyseville.

After spending the night with Scotty and Will, the three men said their goodbyes and headed to Francis' cabin. They left three horses at Scotty's just in case the rightful owners came along.

So, the men headed up the mountain with three horses and two mules. It was a trip that normally took four or so hours on horseback. But, just like the trip from the camp on the north fork of the Kern to Scotty's, there was no telling how long the trip would take. Danny's condition dictated their progress.

On the gently sloping grades that made up portions of the Trail, remaining mounted wasn't a problem. It was when the grade became extreme and the Trail hit switchbacks that the men caught the most grief.

Normally, there'd be no problem handling the horses while negotiating the Trail. However, they weren't willing to chance Danny's horse becoming skittish and throwing the young man. With only one working arm, controlling his horse was an exercise in balance. If he happened to fall or was bucked off, Danny could be seriously injured or damaged even more than he already was. It could be even worse. Impacting the ground, especially if he hit his head, could be deadly.

Avoiding a catastrophe, the men thought it best to dismount the animals from time to time to reduce their fatigue and give Danny's core muscles a break. They also decided to walk, instead of ride, up the hairiest stretches of the Trail. It was a matter of common sense.

And just like along the Kern River, the men ran across Argonauts and merchants headed to the Kern River diggings. Even though the travelers heading downslope were eager to reach their destination and potential wealth, men still stopped to exchange gossip and old news.

Naturally, men asked the trio about conditions in the mines. They were disappointed with the limited amount of information they had to exchange, but appreciative nonetheless. They also brought news from back east, including news on the tension brewing in the Kansas Territory, as well as the political animosity that was simmering in the nation's capital. This heightened Danny's anxiety over his family's safety, but it also made him feel better about their decision to come to California.

They made it about halfway up the eastern slope of the Greenhorn Mountains when Jim and Francis decided that Danny looked frail. Whether it was the demand put on his core body muscles while trying to stay in the saddle, or the energy required to repeatedly climb up an incline, Danny was nearing collapse.

Just off the Trail on a low ridge, the men established camp for the night on a flat piece of land that was dotted by a healthy-looking stand of black oak. From their vantage point, they could look down into the Kern River Canyon.

As the late afternoon became early evening, the men made camp for the night. It was a basic setup. A place to rest. A place to eat. A place to sleep. Jim laid out bedrolls while Francis gathered kindling and large pieces of oak wood for a fire. Danny sat off to the side on his saddle and watched the goings on.

To prevent the horses and mules from straying, their front legs were hobbled. It didn't harm them at all. Their ability to run away was eliminated. The animals were happily grazing.

"I'm sure sorry about slowing us down," Danny commented to Jim and Francis.

Francis was breaking dry sticks and building a tipi with them to start a fire.

"You ain't doin' that at all," Francis said as he struck a locofoco. "The way I see it, it's just another day for me in the woods. I could be here, in Keyesville, at my cabin. It don't matter to me one bit, I'm just a happy old man."

Jim unpacked a coffee pot and a frying pan from their gear.

"It's kinda like a vacation for me," Jim volunteered. "I ain't been campin' for the sake of campin' in years. I'd rather the circumstances were a bit different, though."

Jim spent the next fifteen minutes recounting the last time he'd been camping in the Rocky Mountains. Danny listened to the details and was amused by the story. Francis continued with his task as he listened.

What started as a tiny flame from the match in Francis' hands grew bigger and stronger as he added first pieces of kindling, and then larger sticks of oak. It was a valuable skill. Building a crackling fire from scratch and growing it into a manageable tool that was useful to produce warmth and to cook on was indispensable.

Francis watched the fire and waited for the wood to produce glowing coals. To the side of the fire pit, he dug a key to cook on.

"How do you boys like your steak and eggs?"

Scotty was kind enough to send the men on their way with fresh venison backstrap and a half dozen eggs.

Danny licked his lips and was the first to chime in. His appetite was returning.

"Any way you want to cook 'em!"

"Sounds about right to me, too!" Jim added.

"Well," Francis said to the men with a big grin on his face, "you're in luck. That's the only way I cook."

The three chuckled at Francis' statement and passed around a bottle of whiskey for a little nip.

Francis scooped some coals out of the fire with a small shovel and placed them in the cooking key. The cast iron frying pan became hot over the bed of coals, and the water in the coffee pot started to warm.

Danny and Jim turned their attention to what Francis was doing and became captivated. He cooked a few pieces of bacon to generate a good base of grease to cook with. The smell wafted on the breeze and danced around their noses. The men chewed the finished product and relished the salty, chewy crunch.

And then Francis placed the three slices of venison backstrap, one at a time, into the pan. With each piece of meat, a sizzling chorus sang to the trio. There was no talking. They just listened to the song and enjoyed the smell of the cooking steaks. Backstrap is considered one of the most delicious, and tender cuts, off of a deer. Their anticipation continued to grow.

As the steaks neared completion, Francis moved the medium-sized medallions of meat closer together, and then cracked several eggs over the empty cast iron surface and cooked them over-easy, sunny-side up.

Sensing that the time was near, Jim poured coffee into three cups and then readied three tin plates to receive the eggs and meat. One at a time, the food was dished onto the plates. Jim passed a plate to Danny and then held a plate in each hand until Francis was ready to take his seat with his friends to dine.

They were three men. Friends and business partners. Sharing a common experience. Sharing a meal.

Not much was said between the men during the meal. It would ruin the experience. Only the sounds of chewing, forks moving across tin plates, and the hypnotic sound of wood burning were heard by the three.

With one arm supported by a sling, eating could be exasperating and problematic. But not this meal. Eggs were eggs. The backstrap, however, was so tender that Danny could bite small chunks of meat right off of the fork. Such a fine meal with such little effort needed to consume was a welcome respite from the pain in his shoulder. *It was almost worth being shot*, Danny thought. Almost.

Once finished, with grease around their lips and plates that were practically clean, the men were full and content. They sat around the warmth of the fire and enjoyed each other's company in the steadily depleting hours of the evening.

Underneath the canopy of the stars in that far western sky, the men bundled into their bedrolls and blankets, and nodded off to sleep.

***

Danny was the first to awaken in the middle of the night. It wasn't like he was getting any form of quality sleep anyway. The nagging throb of the injury in his shoulder prevented him from sleeping any significant stretch of time.

"Pssst! Hey! Francis...Jim! Wake up!" Danny forcefully whispered into the darkness that was barely illuminated by the low fire in the pit.

First Francis, and then Jim, woke from their deep slumber. They lifted their heads and looked at Danny.

"What is it? You ok?" Francis whispered back.

"Shhh!" Danny admonished.

They all listened and heard movement nearby in the darkness. A snort. Heavy steps. Ragged breathing. The men heard it all, and it was getting closer to their campsite.

"What is that?" Danny asked in a hushed voice.

Francis started to climb out of his bedding, grabbing his rifle as he rose to his feet. Jim did the same but armed himself with his revolver.

"Sounds like a bear," Francis answered. "Sounds like a big bear!"

And it was. Out of the darkness, on the periphery of the light from the fire emerged a bear. Not a run-of-the-mill black bear, but a California grizzly bear. *Ursus arctos californicus.* It was rather large, shaggy, and curious about the smells emanating from the campsite.

All grizzlies in North America are genetically related. However, there are differences between subspecies. It has been said that the California grizzly bear was very similar in size and color to grizzlies found on the southern coast of Alaska. Numbering as many as 10,000 in the early 1800s, these bears could reach a height of eight feet when standing on their hind legs, and weigh over 2,000 pounds. They possessed ferocity, muscle mass, powerful jaws, and protruding claws that made them an apex predator. Omnivorous, it didn't matter much to the bear what it ate, just as long as it ate. These beasts were feared. And most men preferred to avoid an encounter with one, especially in the dark.

"Damn! That's a monster!" Jim exclaimed.

Both he and Francis were on their feet ready to confront the bear if it came down to that. Danny felt helpless tucked into his bedroll and with his arm in a sling.

The bear, sniffing the air and slowly rocking back and forth on its front feet, remained on the perimeter of the campsite. The bear knew the men were there. It popped its jaws as a warning.

"It might smell the grease from dinner last night," Francis spoke to Jim and Danny.

"Maybe it just smells us!" Jim expressed, concern in his tone.

"Regardless," Francis plainly stated, "he's too close for comfort! I don't mind shooting one from a distance, with a rifle and in the daylight, but this is too risky right here!"

"Should we just try to scare it away?" asked Jim.

"I think that's our best option."

The bear growled and continued to move side to side like it was contemplating if this was worth its trouble. It even started to stand on its hind legs, but then returned to all fours and popped its jaws some more.

Francis was the first to act, hoping the bear would back down and move on.

"Yaw! Go on bear! Go on! Go away bear!"

"Hey, hey, hey! Whoop! Go away!" Jim added.

The bear seemed unfazed and hardly impressed with the yelling. It looked at the men and let out a half-hearted roar. They could vaguely see the bear's breath in the cold night air.

Francis picked up his revolver, cocked it, and aimed it into the sky. He fired a round.

"Yaw!"

He fired again, and Jim joined in on firing one shot of his own.

This was, however, a somewhat questionable tactic. The loud noises from their discharged weapons might do the trick in running the bear off. But what if it didn't? What if it chose to charge? Both Francis and Jim fired a few shots, leaving nine rounds; Francis had four and Jim had five. Rounds from a revolver might penetrate the thick coat and muscle mass of the bear, and it might slow it down or even kill it. But neither Jim nor Francis had the desire to test that theory out.

Francis did have one shot available in his heavy rifle. One shot. If it came down to firing the rifle at the bear, at this close of a distance, then one shot was all he'd get. It may be the last shot he'd ever fire.

But luck was on their side. Although interested in the food that could be had at the campsite, the bear was put off by the shouting men and gunshots. It assessed the situation once more, then turned and trotted out of sight. There was easier food to be had in quieter locales.

If they had the power to see into the future, they may have become saddened to know that the last California grizzly was spotted in 1924.

What was once wild and free, just like they were at that moment, would be hunted to extinction; a victim of "progress" and human predation.

Each man issued forth a sigh of relief, especially Danny. Lying on the ground, and with one bum arm, made him feel particularly vulnerable. At least Jim and Francis had firearms to defend themselves. All Danny had was the power of persuasion, and that was a less-than-stellar weapon when faced with a charging, enraged grizzly bear.

Relieved, but on edge, Francis and Jim thought it better to remain vigilant. The two men agreed to take turns staying awake and watching out for trouble throughout the rest of the night.

There were no further disruptions. However, the chance that the bear could wander back their way was unnerving, and sleep came sporadically.

***

The rest of the trip up the Greenhorn Trail to Francis' cabin was relatively uneventful. It was more of the same slow plodding toward their destination. They stopped occasionally to rest. They walked when the Trail was too steep or rough. They marched onward.

When they rode into Francis' yard Danny felt like he was returning home. Granted, he was extremely happy to reach a destination that offered a modicum of comfort.

Jim and Francis helped Danny down from his horse and into the cabin. While Jim cared for the stock, Francis tended to Danny. He demanded that Danny take the comfort of his own bed, leaving Francis with a place on the floor. Danny protested but relented.

The air inside the shelter was cold and damp, longing for heat and life. Francis set to remedy that by starting a fire in the hearth like he'd done a thousand times before. Francis tossed into the flames the letter that Danny wrote before he left to track down the Roberts Boys. They both watched it burn. Smoke curled upward from the wood and out through the stone chimney. In a short time, the glow of the fire slowly spread heat throughout the cabin.

The rest of the evening was spent telling stories, eating rabbit stew, and drinking elderberry wine. It was a bittersweet moment in time. Danny, with his family coming out to California, realized that he had to go back to Sacramento to meet them. He also had a partnership with Jim that required his attention. But a portion of his soul felt anchored to this mountain and to the friendship he'd developed with Francis.

Danny easily imagined life in these mountains, valleys, and along the Kern River, just as easily as he saw himself working away at the J. Kinney Freighting Company in Sacramento. He was young, and his sentiments for a home flitted about like a butterfly on the wind. Only time would tell where he'd eventually call home.

As the night wore on, and darkness enveloped the mountain, the men inside the cabin grew tired. It'd been a long day. The last week had been trying. Slumber was a welcome respite. Inevitably, and unfortunately, the morning would bring goodbyes.

***

"Francis...I...I want to thank you," Danny stammered, emotion in his voice. "You've shown me more care than I deserve."

Francis was a rough man with emotions buried deep within. But his eyes filled with tears, just like Danny's.

"Never you mind, Danny."

Danny interrupted Francis' words. He stuck out his left arm and the two men grasped hands in a firm handshake.

"No...you encountered me, we met as strangers. We now leave as family."

The tears now flowed down the cheeks of both men. It wasn't shameful. It was a reflection of their genuine care for each other.

"But...I'll be back. Don't know when, or for how long...but I'll be back, Francis."

Francis said nothing. He was too shocked by the reaction he had to the parting with Danny. Emotion got the better of him. He gave Danny a bear hug.

"Ow," Danny unexpectedly said as a dull pain shot from his shoulder.

"Uh...sorry...I kinda forgot," Francis said as he stepped back and wiped the tears and his runny nose on the sleeves of his shirt.

"My door is always open, Danny. Same to you Jim."

Jim raised his hand to his hat and tipped it forward as he thanked Francis.

"You ever find your way to Sacramento, you look me up, Francis," Jim offered. "We'll set you up just fine."

Jim helped Danny mount his horse and then climbed atop the horse he rented out of Visalia.

They had a long ride ahead of them, one that'd be slower than preferred and more uncomfortable than Danny would've liked. But it was the only way home.

They rode out of Francis' yard and toward the Greenhorn Trail. Danny, a weak smile on his face, looked back to Francis. Francis raised his hand in a motion to say goodbye. Danny returned the wave by slightly raising his good arm as he held the reigns.

I'll be back, Danny thought to himself.

Close to an hour later, Jim and Danny were on the Greenhorn Trail and near the spot where Danny was almost killed.

"See that branch there?" Danny motioned to Jim. "That's my lucky charm! Someday, I'll build myself a house and I'm gonna place that piece of wood over my fireplace as a mantle. Mark my word!"

"Oh, I believe you will," Jim said with a smile.

They rode on, passing the cluster of flat boulders with grooves etched onto the flat surface, a product of generations of Indians grinding acorns. The grinding holes would forever remain a testament to tribal life. They'd outlast their creators and all who'd eventually examine them in wonder. The number of future hands who, out of respect, scooped leaves and dirt out of the grinding holes would never be fully known.

Down the twisting, dropping, and climbing Trail they rode, taking great care to be mindful of their horses and Danny's situation. Surprisingly, they experienced no difficulties other than the discomfort Danny had in his shoulder. It was a bearable situation, made better by the crisp air and clear, blue sky. Days like that made a man truly appreciate God's creation, and revel in the fact that he was alive. That was the feeling both Danny and Jim had.

That afternoon they stopped alongside the Poso Creek and set up camp. There was no use in pushing Danny's endurance. The human body is an amazing mass of cells, muscles, tendons, and bones. An injured body is a fickle machine that needs to be worked slowly. Danny was figuring that out the hard way.

The next day they were in Linn's Valley, and then several days after that they rode into Visalia. It was a trip characterized by repetition: riding, resting, talking with passing strangers, making camp, sleeping, and starting over each day. An established routine that was neither unpleasant nor delightful. It just was.

Entering Visalia broke the routine. It was a proper little town, and Jim and Danny had a few things to do before continuing on home.

The first stop was the livery stable where Jim needed to return the rented horse and settle up with the owner. He also wanted to sell the horse Danny was on. The stretch from Visalia to Stockton, and then on to Sacramento would be by coach, so they wouldn't need their horses anymore. It'd be a more relaxing ride for both of the men and quicker, too.

The second stop was something that Jim insisted they make. It was a visit to a local doctor to check on Danny's wounds and change the bandages. Danny didn't think it was necessary, but he respected Jim's advice.

"Did a doctor do this for you, or was it a butcher?" Dr. Madsen asked in a heavy New England accent.

Danny was a little offended by the question.

"Come on doc, it ain't that bad!" Danny protested.

Dr. Madsen arched his eyebrows in response to Danny's contradiction, as well as his improper English.

"Well, it *isn't* that bad, as you say. But the incisions could have been cleaner, and this one here," Dr. Madsen gently poked at one of the wounds, "should be stitched up."

"I was lying on a table and my friend only had a knife, so, there's that."

"All things considered," Dr. Madsen relented, "the necessary steps were taken. The splinters and shrapnel were removed, the wounds cleaned and then cauterized. If you want, I could stitch that wound closed."

Danny pondered the offer.

"Will it heal correctly, otherwise?"

"It should, as long as you keep it clean and don't do any rigorous activity that may open the wound further."

Danny sighed, resigned to the fact that, once again, he should probably take the advice of someone who knew more than him.

"Better safe, than sorry. Doc...do what you need to do."

Dr. Madsen had Danny lie down on an elevated bed so he could get to work. The wounds were cleaned, dead tissue trimmed, the bigger incision site stitched, and then the whole mess was properly bandaged. The procedure took no more than ten minutes in the practiced hands of Dr. Madsen. Danny took the manipulation of the wounds in stride. The pain was no more than anticipated, and he did his best to ignore it.

"Please see another proper doctor in a few weeks to see if the stitches are ready to be removed," Dr. Madsen instructed. "Clean the wounds at least every other day and replace the bandages. If you follow that advice, all should heal well."

Danny thanked Dr. Madsen, and Jim paid and collected a supply of bandages the doctor provided. They left the doctor's office and headed to their last stop before catching the next stage north.

Jim wasn't pleased with what Danny wanted to do next. He didn't think it was necessary, and he surely didn't believe that it was in Danny's best interest.

But Danny was raised in a good home, and he had a moral upbringing. What happened between him and the Roberts Boys had been done. They were dead. He lives on. There were no regrets, however, one thing began to gnaw on his conscience over the last couple of days: was he legally justified in his actions? That's what worried him and prompted the last task in Visalia.

Just by chance, a circuit judge was in Visalia for a week to hear cases. It was a service provided to rural and outlying communities throughout the United States. Many communities didn't have populations large enough to necessitate law enforcement officers, courts, and judges. And the nearest legal services may be hundreds of miles away. So, the law periodically came to the communities to adjudicate cases and process records.

Judge Cooper was his name, and by all accounts, he was a fair and efficient man. Danny, ignoring Jim's protests, sought him out.

He wasn't hard to find. Judge Cooper held court in the back room of a saloon. It had a suitable amount of space for him to work, consult with complainants, hear testimony, and even seat a jury if necessary.

Danny waited thirty minutes in the short line to see Judge Cooper.

"Next!" Judge Cooper shouted from inside the room as a dejected man walked out, apparently unhappy with the disposition of his case.

Danny and Jim walked into the room to find the judge seated behind a table, sipping on a small glass of amber-colored whiskey.

"Name?" Judge Cooper demanded as he was poised to write the information down.

Taken aback by Judge Cooper's brusque nature, Danny stammered.

"Oh...um, Daniel Vance, sir."

Danny and Jim stood there silently. The scratching sound of Judge Cooper's writing was all that was heard.

"Mr. Vance, what is your current residence?"

Danny thought about the question for a moment, somewhat unsure of what to say.

"Well," Danny began, "I'm from Missouri, and have a place in Sacramento, but I've spent the last few months in the Greenhorn Mountains."

Judge Cooper let out a sigh and began to write.

"Sacramento it is."

Judge Cooper took a sip of the whiskey in his glass, relished the spicy rye taste in his mouth, and then swallowed it down. He breathed in sharply as a result of the burn in his throat from the liquid.

"So, Mr. Vance...what brings you to my court?" Judge Cooper inquired as he looked over the young man in a sling standing before him.

"It's a complicated matter, sir...but, essentially, I killed three men up in the mountains," Danny started.

"But he didn't murder those men...and I didn't murder the two men I shot, either," Jim interjected. "You can call it self-defense."

Judge Cooper looked back and forth between the two men in front of him as he leaned back in his chair.

"Why don't you men pull up a seat and start from the beginning."

And they did. They sat with Judge Cooper and told the story of the Roberts Boys and their toxic relationship with them over the last several years. From the harassment in Missouri, their preying on the innocent on the way to California, the fight in Sacramento, and then the ambush in the Greenhorn Mountains that resulted in the death of Sam and the near-death of Danny.

Judge Cooper listened closely and seemed enthralled with what they had to say. Surely, it was more interesting than the disputes over mining claims, land deeds, and sundry other commonplace legal proceedings that he heard day in and day out. He took notes as the tale unfolded.

"So," Danny was finishing his story, "that's when Jim here entered the cabin and saved me from being beaten to death."

"Yeah, it was an unfortunate...unavoidable situation," Jim said with believable regret in his voice.

Judge Cooper finished scribbling a sentence down on the paper in front of him. He took a minute to read over the notes, and then he set the paper down and exerted a puff of air that Danny took as a chuckle.

"Wooddale!" Judge Cooper shouted into the attached saloon. "Come on in here!"

Both Jim and Danny momentarily tensed up at the thought that they may be arrested for their actions, but that was only a fleeting fear.

"Sir?" Wooddale asked as he poked his head into the room.

"Sit down Wooddale...you gotta hear this!"

Wooddale sat down to the side of Judge Cooper. The star indicating he was a man of the law was pinned to the outside of the light jacket that he wore.

"Ok," Judge Cooper referred to his notes, "Daniel Vance...will you please repeat what happened."

And he did, only this time Judge Cooper and Wooddale periodically interrupted Danny and Jim as they recounted their story. The judge busily added information to his notes as Danny and Jim responded to their questions.

"Who were you packing supplies for as you headed into the Greenhorn Mountains?"

"Pleasant Parker out of Sacramento," Jim answered.

"Who was with you on that pack train?"

"Antonio Marquez Gonzales, Ah Joe, and Sam," Danny offered. "All three are employees of the J. Kinney Freighting Company."

"Ah Joe and Sam are celestials?" Wooddale asked.

"Yes, sir, they are originally from China," Danny added.

Judge Cooper continued jotting down details as the story continued.

"Who was present at the lynching of Sam and the attempt on your life?"

"A few of the Roberts Boys were there—Eli Roberts, and two men by the name of Harry and George."

Danny paused as he thought, and the realization spread across his face.

"I have no idea what their last names were."

"No worries," Judge Cooper reassured Danny, "please continue on."

"Ah Joe witnessed Sam's lynching...and the Roberts Boys told me themselves that they did it. And, of course, I witnessed everything they did to me."

"Of course," Wooddale agreed as Danny continued.

"And who is it that found you on the ground?"

"Francis...Francis Rutherford."

"What about the encounter in the saloon at Keyesville? Who witnessed that?"

"Well, there were half a dozen miners in the place, none of which I know personally," Danny responded. "But the saloon keep, Scotty, was there and saw it all. Francis came into the saloon shortly after."

"Good," Judge Cooper nodded and continued writing.

The story continued to unfold with no variation from the first account. the only thing different was the request for the verification of names by Judge Cooper and Wooddale.

"What's the boy's name that led you to the camp up on the Kern?"

"Will Watkins."

"And those Roberts Boys? What were their names, and who killed who?" Wooddale inquired.

"The man I killed with my knife, I'm told, was named Jacques," Danny said and then paused. "And I shot Harry with a shotgun. I grazed Eli Roberts with my shotgun, too, before his shot laid me out."

Jim interrupted Danny and finished the account.

"And I shot Eli as he tried to kill Danny. Me and my men also killed a man named Johnny who was fixin' to ambush Scotty, the saloon keeper."

"What men are you referring to?" Wooddale asked for clarification.

"There was me, Francis Rutherford, Will Watkins, and the saloonkeeper from Keyesville named Scotty."

They finished the story and waited for Judge Cooper to stop writing. Jim and Danny couldn't tell what his disposition was because the judge's facial expressions remained the same throughout the recounting of the events. Wooddale was just as unreadable. Perhaps it was the nature of their careers? Or maybe it was just the result of practice? Either way, Jim and Danny found it nearly impossible to truly know how they felt about what the two had told them.

Judge Cooper finished writing, picked up his glass of whiskey, and then relaxed in his chair. All three of the men opposite Judge Cooper watched as he took a drink and then crossed one leg over the other. He opened a box that sat on the corner of the table, pulled out a skinny cigar, and then tilted the box toward the other men as an offer. First Wooddale, and then Jim, selected a cigar. Danny passed but thanked Judge Cooper just the same. As the men bit the end off of their cigars and lit them, Judge Cooper thought a moment and then proffered one last question.

"That's one Hell of a story, boys...with names and details...pretty much everything I need to make a ruling."

He puffed on the cigar and his brow furrowed.

"But there's just one more thing I want to know. What happened to their bodies?"

Jim and Danny looked at each other and then back to the judge. Jim answered before Danny had a chance.

"After Francis mended Danny, and while Danny was laid up in a bed, me, Scotty, and Francis...and then just Scotty and Will...we dug graves at that camp and buried them. We didn't place any markers, but the mounded-up dirt is plain enough to indicate what's in the earth."

For the first time that hour, Judge Cooper dropped his guard to reveal his opinion. What began as a low chuckle turned into a laugh that revealed his amusement and disbelief.

"You two are something else," Judge Cooper said.

"What we said is the truth!" Danny exclaimed in their defense.

Judge Cooper raised a hand to silence Danny's protestation.

"Settle down, Mr. Vance. Now, I didn't say that I didn't believe you! But what is amazing to me is that you willingly, without any obligation whatsoever, sought me out, waited in line, and then told me how you and your partner here were party to the deaths of five men. Five men!"

His laughter and obvious amazement continued throughout his explanation.

"And then you tell me that after all of that...you buried the bastards? That is something else!"

"It just seemed appropriate," Jim muttered.

"Tell you what," Judge Cooper began, and then took another long draw on his cigar, "you two go get something to eat...give me a couple of hours to draw up the paperwork and make a copy for you...I'm ruling this an act of self-defense...justifiable homicide."

Jim and Danny sat there listening, somewhat confused. They didn't know what to expect, but it certainly wasn't this.

"We have standards in our society, even out here in the wilds of California, that dictate proper conduct. 'Thou shall not kill' is the forbearance of a polite, civilized people. But there are some sons of bitches that just ask for it! Hell...I'm surprised it took this long before someone put them in the ground."

"That's it?" Danny cautiously asked.

"That's it. Now, get out of here so I can get this done so you can go on with your lives."

Danny and Jim rose from their chairs. They expressed their gratitude and turned to leave. Before they left, Wooddale asked a question that stopped Danny in his tracks.

"You ever thought about becoming a lawman?"

Danny turned his body back toward Wooddale and placed his hat back on his head.

"It never crossed my mind."

He pulled on the corner of his hat as a parting salutation and then walked on with Jim to find a meal.

***

Danny and Jim checked on the availability of the next stage north before hunting down a meal. There was always the possibility that they may have to stay overnight, or perhaps even a day or two before the next stage with room for two more passengers was available. But luck was on their side, and another stage was scheduled for later that afternoon. They purchased two tickets.

It didn't take long to find a decent restaurant after asking a few locals. The business didn't look like much from the outside, however, the plate of pork chops, mashed potatoes and gravy, and freshly baked bread told the story of this hidden gem. Their bellies were full and their appetites satiated.

They kicked around town to encourage digestion and eat up the requisite amount of time before returning to Judge Cooper. He was just finishing up when Jim and Danny knocked on the outside of the door to what served as his makeshift office and courtroom. Judge Cooper looked up from his work and beckoned the men into the room.

"Come in, come in. I'm just putting the finishing touches up on your copy of the paperwork."

"Thank you, sir," Danny said with genuine appreciation in his voice and a twinkle of pride in his eyes. "That piece of paper gives me a measure of relief."

"I can understand your concern, and your precaution," Judge Copper continued. "It's doubtful anyone would've come after you for what was done, but I suppose it's better safe than sorry. That's still the damnedest turn of events I've heard in quite a while!"

Danny smiled wryly, as did Jim.

"Believe me...I'm every bit surprised at how it turned out, too."

Jim cleared his throat to politely get the attention of the men.

"I hate to interrupt, but we probably should get a move on to secure a decent spot on the coach."

Judge Cooper stood up as a sign of respect for the men.

"No worries..." Judge Cooper began and then looked at the paperwork to remind himself of the man's name, "Mr. Kinney...the stage waits for no man."

Judge Cooper signed his name to the documents to make them official, blew on the ink to help it dry, and then handed a copy to Danny.

"I wish you luck, Mr. Vance. Hope you heal up quickly, and you're able to avoid any and all trouble that you cannot handle."

He reached into his jacket pocket and drew out a small card with his contact information on it. He tucked the card into Danny's coat pocket.

"If you ever think about going into the law, you make sure you look me up. There's a good chance I can find you some work."

"Much appreciated," Danny warmly said.

Jim and Danny exchanged pleasantries with Judge Cooper and left the saloon to walk the relatively short distance to the stage office.

It wasn't long after they arrived that the stage pulled into the station and prepared for the next leg of its journey. The tired horses were unhitched and exchanged for fresh ones. Passengers disembarked, arriving at their destination, and those continuing on the trip north exited the stage to stretch their legs. It was business as usual.

Thirty minutes later, and all was prepared to venture on. The stage crew loaded luggage and the personal belongings of the passengers into storage compartments, including the bedrolls and weapons Danny and Jim toted with them down from the Greenhorns.

Seeing Danny's condition, the other passengers on the stage were kind enough to allow him his choice of spots. Wisely, he chose a seat that allowed him to lean the left side of his body against the frame of the stage. It offered him a modicum of comfort while shielding his injured shoulder from the jostling of the coach. Jim sat to his right.

And in this way, they traveled the rest of the way home. From Visalia, up through the numerous little hamlets and stage stations that dotted the land. Across the many streams and rivers, forded and crossed by ferries. An evolution of passengers came and went, arriving at their stops or beginning their journeys. The days passed as the miles traveled ticked away. And it wasn't long until they pulled into Stockton, repeated the same process that they did with every stop, and then moved on towards Sacramento.

A few days after leaving Visalia the stage pulled into the stop in Sacramento; home. They gathered their possessions and left the station, walking amid the hustle and bustle of the busy streets.

To Danny, it was familiar and strange in the same instant, a stark contrast to the tranquility and refuge of the cabin on Greenhorn Mountain that Francis welcomed him into.

Sacramento was a home and place of comfort, in a different way. Mrs. Kinney welcomed them both back to town, and she spent a great deal of time fussing over Danny. Her care for, and worry over, Danny was appreciated. She cried softly, a result of relief and sympathy for him. It was like his own mother was there. He could have drank in that love for hours, but exhaustion started to get the better of him.

At that moment in time, in the early evening, all that Danny was looking forward to was a stiff drink and the comfort of his bed. He'd find both within the hour.

Chapter 14
The Letter

————◆————

D awn brought a new day and a slew of errands that Danny needed to address. As instructed, he called on a doctor to look over his wounds and change the bandages. He was told that the healing process was progressing as expected and that he could probably ditch the sling in another week or two.

After that, he met Gonzales for breakfast at a restaurant near the freighting office. Danny told him what happened in the time since they parted at Francis' cabin. It was an hour-long conversation, full of questions and answers, intrigue and disbelief. There was also a hint of envy and regret. Gonzales wished he could've been there to bring the Roberts Boys to justice.

They also talked about the journey north that Gonzales and Ah Joe took with Sam's body. How it was a lonely trip that seemed much longer than it was, largely due to the silent miles that passed between Gonzales and Ah Joe, interrupted only by the inquiries of people they met on the road and in towns. Strangers wanted to know the story of the man wrapped in the blanket, lying dead on the flat of the buckboard. They wanted to know Sam's story. It was more interest than most people had ever paid to the quiet man named Sam. Morbid curiosity brought more interest in his death than his life ever did.

With breakfast consumed and paid for, and with Sam fresh on their minds, Gonzales took Danny to the Chinese cemetery just outside of town.

They wandered amid the grave markers written in a language they couldn't read or understand until they reached a tidy little plot. It was Sam's resting place. Danny paid his respects and promised himself that he'd make sure Sam's family in California was taken care of. It was the least he could do.

By the time they returned to town, it was late morning. Gonzales needed to prepare for a run to the gold fields far up in the mountains to the northeast.

Technically, Danny had work to do, too. Surely, he wasn't any use loading or unloading wagons. And he was unable to rig or care for any of the stock they kept. He could, at a bare minimum, look at paperwork and meet with customers. That didn't require much of a man with a bum arm.

However, Danny realized that the most taxing thing he might have to deal with was explaining over and over again how he was injured. He decided that unless it was a person who worked for the company or was a personal friend, then he'd just deflect questions by stating that he was injured while freighting. It was all anyone needed to know.

When Danny entered the shop of the J. Kinney Freighting Company a chorus of salutations greeted him.

"There he is!"

"Welcome back!"

"Great to have you back home!"

They were genuine in their words and were polite enough to give him space to acclimate to being back in the office.

Danny made his way into the office where he found Jim perched at a desk looking over bills and orders. He looked up as Danny approached.

"Mornin' Danny," Jim greeted. "Funny thing...I'm gone for a few weeks and the paperwork just piles up!"

Jim was disgusted. He pushed aside what he was looking over and rubbed his eyes.

"I think I'd rather be on the trail!"

Danny laughed and pulled up a chair.

"Well, now that I'm here, at least I can help with the paperwork," Danny commented.

"True...misery loves company. Coffee?" Jim asked as he stood up to refill his cup.

"Please, if you don't mind," Danny answered.

Jim poured the rich-smelling concoction into two cups and returned to the desk. He set down his cup and then cleared a small space on the cluttered desk for Danny's mug.

"You know," Jim started, "you don't have to come back to work so soon. Granted, I'm willing to share this paper burden...but you can take some time."

Danny sipped hot coffee from his cup and chimed in.

"Oh, I know...and I'll do what I can. Believe me, I ain't gonna try to do more than I can. And, I may take you up on that offer to take some time. But it'll take time to figure it out."

Danny sighed and thought over his situation. He had lots of options to consider.

"Heck," Danny added, "maybe I'll try to track down Stephen and see how he's doin'. Or maybe I'll accompany a run up to the American River region...look in on my old cabin and see how the Banks family is doing."

Jim's eyebrows slightly arched at Danny's words. He picked up a shipping log and looked it over, shifting his focus back to the job at hand.

"Understood...you, uh, looked in your mail cubby?" Jim said as his voice trailed away and the numbers on the document were looked over.

"Not yet," Danny said with inquisitiveness in his voice. It was almost as if Jim was prompting him to do so.

Danny set his cup down and meandered over to the wood shelving unit that was attached to a nearby wall. It had dividers evenly spaced along the shelves, creating slots or cubbies for all types of paperwork. Invoices, bills, logs. Incoming and outgoing. And there was a section for each employee. A place where mail and other personal documents could be stored. Many of the men employed by the J. Kinney Freighting Company received their mail at the office. They were on the road a lot, so it made sense to have correspondence delivered to their place of employment. That was Danny's sentiment, as well.

Jim watched Danny out of the corner of his eye, half minding the tallies on the page, half interested in what Danny would find.

It didn't take long for Danny to look through the items in his mailbox. There was a stack of old newspapers from back east. Danny liked to read of news from back home. It made him feel connected to what he left behind, even if the stories were months old. Whatever happened back east often had a ripple effect on the Far West. At the very least, reading passed the time.

Nestled amidst the stack of newspapers was a single letter. By its location, it must have been placed in the cubby several weeks before. He finished shuffling through the newspapers, gathered them together, and placed them back into the cubby.

Danny examined the letter as he slowly walked back to his chair. He read the writing on the envelope. *Danny Vance*. Written in a delicate cursive, the curves and lines of the words hinted that it was from a woman. The faint hint of perfume emanating from the envelope was also strong evidence that it was from a person of the female persuasion.

Jim did his best to pretend that he was occupied with work. He wasn't very good at hiding his interest.

"Whatcha got there?" Jim asked, betraying his disinterest.

Danny sat down and fumbled with the envelope. He was getting better at using his right hand, even if his arm was tied up in a sling.

"Well, Jim, it looks like a letter. My guess is you already knew that, though."

"Humph!" Jim retorted and tried to refocus on his work.

Danny slid the letter open and laid it flat on the table, pinning it down with his left hand to prevent it from folding up. He leaned forward, looking at the lettering that matched what was written on the envelope, and then he began to read.

Dear Danny,

I was hoping that you'd be in town when I stopped by, but I'm told that you are on a delivery far to the south and won't be back for some time. It is my hope that this letter finds you well, and that you receive it sooner, rather than later. I would have preferred to talk with you in person, but I suppose this will suffice.

The last time we talked was heartbreaking to me. It wasn't your fault. You were concerned about how I was being treated, and about how Carl had laid hands upon me when he was drunk. Yours was the voice of a man who cared and showed a true fondness for me. I knew it, and I could see it. But, being a married woman, I was duty bound to ignore it. That wasn't an easy thing to do, for I felt the same way about you. I remember the first day I saw you, when you appeared at our camp on the river, and how we must have seemed like a band of tramps, our condition being so rough and desperate at that time. And you went out of your way to help us get on our feet. And then you helped me start a business. A very successful business, at that! We entered into a partnership that was, from my perspective, fair. And then you went out of your way to make sure that it was an agreement between equals. You didn't have to do that. It was the action of a man who cared. And, I suspect, it was the action of a man who was smitten and in love with what he couldn't have.

Danny, I want you to know that I felt the same way...I feel the same way. That's what I wanted to talk with you about in person. Maybe it's easier to write than say in person. Either way, it needs to be said and I need for you to know it. You, Danny, hold a place in my heart. A place that threatens to expand and overcome my senses. I needed to say that, and I want you to know that if there is a chance for us to foster that love and tenderness, then it must be so.

When you saw me on that day with the side of my face bruised by Carl, I saw the anger welled up inside you. I saw the potential for murder in your eyes. That scared me, Danny. But it also made me realize the truth about your feelings. A love that was pure and expected nothing in return. It was an unfair position for you to be in. And when you left...when it was evident to me that you couldn't bear to see me like that and that I may never see you again, I knew right then that it wasn't what I wanted. I hoped that our paths would cross. I yearned for it to happen.

God has a way of working in mysterious ways, Danny. When you left, I was an unhappy, married woman. Carl took his frustrations out on me. He had difficulty accepting that my business—our business—was flourishing and his efforts at mining were floundering. When his brother abandoned Cal-

ifornia and went home, and when Carl began to realize that none of what we had was due to his own efforts, that's when his sickness began to consume his being. He began to hit the bottle with more consistency, and with that, he began to abuse me even more. I bore the abuse the best I could, all in the hope that it'd stop. Maybe there was part of me that believed that the man he once was could be found, somewhere, buried deep inside. But I was just fooling myself, denying my heart what it truly deserved. I plotted my escape, dreaming of how I could run away into the night, or even just wait until he was passed out from drink and just walk away from it all.

In the end, I didn't have to do any of the such. A man with his particular illness has a tendency to be his own worst enemy. I suspected that he might eventually meet his end through over-consumption, or maybe even delirium tremens. That wasn't the case, though. Carl went on a bender down at a saloon not far from my kitchen. He hit the bottle hard that night. And then he got into an argument with another man. He picked a fight with someone who wasn't me. Carl drew a gun on the man, but he was so drunk and slow that it was no contest. The man drew a knife and stabbed Carl. He was dead before he hit the ground.

Surely, I was aggrieved...at least on the surface. A dutiful wife would be deemed heartless if she didn't at least put an appearance of sorrow. But I got over it. Those who know me at the kitchen, my employees and the regulars, they were all supportive and understanding. However, that was a sign that it was time for me to move on. A clean break, so to speak. A newly widowed woman desiring to make a change. Who could question that or blame me? Luckily, my business has continued to grow and prosper. You'll see that when you check the amount of money that is in your account. And its prosperity hasn't escaped the eyes of some of the men. In fact, I was able to sell the kitchen and all of my holdings to them for a handsome sum. That, too, should be evident by the amount of money I deposited into your account to make up for the demise of our partnership.

It isn't the business partnership I'm really concerned about, though. It is the future. I'm not concerned with money. I have money. Plenty of money! What I'm unsure of, though, are my options. I don't know if I'm too late to have your love. Perhaps you've moved on, or you've grown bitter? I'll have no idea until I speak with you. It is my hope that you'll be open to kindle the flames of what could be.

When you get this letter, I should be in San Francisco. I hear that it has developed into quite a proper city. With nowhere to be, and with nobody to be with...for the moment...San Francisco might be the diversion I need. At least for a while. I'm open to being distracted otherwise. Come find me, Danny.

Affectionately yours,

Julia

Danny read the last paragraph of the letter again, his lips uncharacteristically moving with each word.

He smelled the paper the letter was written on, and inhaled the light smell of lavender. It smelled like Julia's skin.

Jim watched Danny. He'd never seen him act this way. Danny was a man captivated by words. When Jim saw him smell the letter, he knew it could only mean one thing.

"Danny?" Jim asked, prompting Danny to come back from the cloud he was riding.

Danny lowered the letter and looked at Jim. He had a serious expression on his face and a look of victory in his eyes. A smile, small at first, burst into a broad grin across his face.

In the few short minutes it took to read the letter, the dull, throbbing pain in Danny's shoulder subsided and he forgot about any difficulties he currently had. Life had the potential to change, just like that.

"What?" Jim inquired.

The smile dissipated from Danny's face and he spoke with a sense of grave urgency.

"Jim...I have to go to San Francisco!"

✲✲✲

To be continued...

Book 3: Preview

————————◆————————

The Following Is A Preview of Book 3 in the Golden
Empire Series:

Love & Loss on the Razor's Edge

Available Now!

The Bay City

————•··•◆•··•————

T here they stood. Hundreds of wooden shells and a forest of masts bobbing up and down and side to side by the wind-driven waves that rolled into the San Francisco Bay and finished its kinetic energy at Yerba Buena Cove. The creaking and popping of their wooden planks, as well as the occasional dull thumping sound of hulls bumping and scraping against one another, could be heard in moments of stillness.

It was a menagerie of ships. A cluster of different types of vessels and timber was a reflection of the people and places where the ships were constructed. Oak, pine, walnut, and teak. Brigs of various sizes, as well as schooners, New Bedford Whalers, and clippers built in shipyards across the world. They were vessels originally constructed for fishing, fitted for trade, or solely for the transport of people. All of them began their journeys in relatively far-off locations, but destiny and the lust of men for opportunity drew them to San Francisco Bay. Whatever their original use, they were now individually and collectively clogging up the Cove.

How the ships wound up here, abandoned, is a story intricately tied to the history of California. When word that gold had been discovered by James Marshall at Sutter's Mill it quickly spread to the sleepy little hamlet of San Francisco, slowly at first and then by design. Sam Brannan, a business-savvy merchant who operated a store at Sutter's Fort, accumulated all of the mining supplies and foodstuffs he could, filled a small glass vial with gold flakes, and then rode to San Francisco to spread the word. It helped kick off the rush for gold, as well as make Sam Brannan one of the first millionaires west of the Mississippi River.

Since the Spanish era, what would be San Francisco was central to the Pacific Basin. Ships participating in the Manila Galleon Trade, fur hunters from the Russian-American Company, American merchants sailing up and down the coast of California during the hide and tallow trade, and whalers all periodically sailed into the Bay. Each ship was a beacon of news from other parts of the world, and the flow of rumors and events from California worked in reverse. News of gold sailed out with every ship leaving the port. It wasn't long before a frenzied rush to the goldfields was on.

Beginning in 1849, over 42,000 Americans headed to California over-land in wagons, on horses and mules, or foot. But over 25,000 American gold-seekers boarded ships on the East Coast and in the Gulf of Mexico to make the quicker, but more expensive, journey down around Cape Horn, the southern tip of South America, and then up the Pacific coast of the Americas to California, or to the isthmus of Panama, across the mountains to the Pacific coast, and then up to San Francisco.

And it wasn't just Americans who flocked to California. Argonauts from Europe, Mexico, Chile, Australia, India, the Hawaiian Islands, China, and other far-flung corners of the world rushed to California with dreams of striking it rich. It was a menagerie of humanity.

Being that San Francisco was the closest town to the Sacramento Valley with a Pacific port, it became the natural jumping-off point for those arriving by sea. By December 1849, the small village of about 1,000 people ballooned to over 25,000. As the days rolled into weeks, and the weeks piled into years, ships continued to arrive. Passengers disembarked, the cargo was offloaded, and crews readily abandoned ships in favor of their desire to seek out fortunes in the dirt and gravel of California. The harbormaster estimated that 62,000 people had entered California through the port by April of 1850 alone. Most headed to the creeks and river drainages surrounding Sacramento, but a growing number of disgruntled miners and entrepreneurs ended up back in San Francisco. The town's population was close to 35,000 by 1852, and it continued to grow as time progressed.

The byproduct, of course, was the growing number of crewless and ownerless ships in the Cove...as many as five hundred at one time. The *Envoy, Garnet, Edwin, Louisa,* and *Francis Ann.* The *Ricardo, Othello, Apollo, Fortuna,* and *Noble.* Just a few names of the hundreds of ships anchored in the Cove. They were floating reminders of the lust for gold; evidence that men will alter their course in life for a chance at "easy" wealth. The abandoned ships were an eyesore and were problematic in the growing need for space in the Cove. But they were also a potential solution.

As the population of San Francisco grew, and the fact that it emerged as a major staging point for individuals and groups heading for the Sacramento Valley, new opportunities arose. There was a growing need—an opportunity—to provide goods and services to people settling down and passing through. It was a chance for those choosing not to seek gold to still make a living, and even strike it rich, by supplying what was in demand. Lodging, food, goods and supplies, fanciful and exotic items, and entertainment. Everything imaginable that was in demand could be provided by opportunistic businessmen and women, in a similar manner that Sam Brannan had. And with a port with access to the world abroad, procuring items in demand was a relatively easy task.

The issue, however, was the immediate availability of building materials. Surely, the coastal forests and Sierra Nevada Mountains could provide ample amounts of lumber, but that takes time. Lumbermen needed to fell trees, mill the lumber, and transport it to customers. That would be done in due time, and the growing population of California would fuel the growing lumber industry, eventually producing fortunes for those entrepreneurs as well.

No, those wanting to construct their storefronts, hotels and restaurants, saloons and gambling halls, as well as the great variety of other businesses that were in demand right away looked not to the great forests of California, but to the clogged Cove. There, gently floating in the water, was the immediate solution.

Resourceful individuals utilized the abandoned ships. Docked at wharves, some watercraft became temporary floating storehouses and hotels. Other ships were stripped of their timbers to be used in the initial construction of buildings. Quite a few ships were sunk near the shoreline and filled with debris and dirt to expand wharves and the amount of land available to build upon, entombed as part of the earth only to be periodically revealed many years later. The San Francisco Maritime National Historical Park has documented over three dozen vessels that were sunk, filled with debris and dirt, and then incorporated into the landscape. Every day modern-world San Franciscans walk over and carry on their daily lives amongst the repurposed reminders of a time gone by.

And so was the situation in the spring of 1853. The center of culture in California; San Francisco was the place to be. It was, perhaps, the most American of all the cities in the United States. Multiple cultures and ethnicities—a cross-section of the world at large—made up the people of this soon-to-be metropolis.

It was this hub of commerce, this town on the Bay full of prosperity and ruin, failure and success, and divinity and sin that drew Danny Vance on a mission. His wasn't a quest for wealth or opportunity. He had his share of that already. No, Danny was heading to San Francisco to pursue a gnawing desire within. It wasn't lust. It wasn't revenge. It wasn't hunger. It was something deeper and harder to extinguish. His new purpose was to find Julia Banks in this town on the Pacific. The gnawing in the pit of his stomach, tugging on his very soul, was love.

About The Author

Richard Roux was born in Bakersfield, California, and has resided there his whole life. By profession, he is a social studies teacher at Centennial High School and an adjunct history professor at Bakersfield Community College. With an interest in a wide variety of topics and activities, Richard brings to his writing a mixture of history, anecdotes, and humor. When not spending time with his family, teaching, playing hockey, and enjoying the outdoors, he continues to research and write a mixture of nonfiction and fiction works.

Dear Reader

R esearching and writing is something I do for fun. This isn't my career. I enjoy the challenge. In a sense, it is personally and professionally satisfying to me. As I like to joke, it's my side hustle. I also enjoy talking with people who have read my books and hearing praise and ideas on how my writing and storylines could be improved. That's all part of the process for me. Sadly, though, my readers typically don't leave many reviews of my books on marketplaces like Amazon. Because of a very competitive market, many readers won't give my books a chance because they depend on the reviews of others to guide their choices. And the lack of reviews means that my books get less notice because of the algorithms on Amazon.

So, even if you don't have the time or desire to write a complete review (which is understandable) if you can please at least give it a rating that would be both pleasing to me and helpful. My sincere thanks!

www.ingramcontent.com/pod-product-compliance
Lightning Source LLC
Chambersburg PA
CBHW020109180626
46812CB00006B/2531